COACH'S CORNER

ALSO BY J. LEE

The Hubley Case

The Silent Cardinal

The Deadly Deal

The Reluctant Reckoner

Praise for *Coach's Corner*

"*Coach's Corner* is a mystery that adds elements of suspense and thriller writing into its plot, grounding action, characters, and outcomes in a maze of thought-provoking events to draw readers into a whirlwind of intrigue. Finding the killer becomes half the battle, under Lee's hand. The rest of the mystery is a powerful focus on a summer of simmering deception that proves nearly impossible to put down. Small-town crime…and flawed justice systems are just a few of the many themes that flow seamlessly through this gripping story. Replete with satisfying twists based on powerful character-building and clashes readers won't see coming, *Coach's Corner* is very highly recommended for mystery fans who look for broader perspectives, social inspections, and thought-provoking moments from their reading." — *Midwest Books Review*

"With *Coach's Corner*, J. Lee crafts a detailed and engaging murder mystery set in a rural town—where everyone knows everything about everyone else. Lee's keen attention to detail and dedicated storytelling gives readers a gripping story that has them wondering not only who the killer is, but if the victim had it coming." —*Citywide Blackout co-host Max Bowen, published audiobook voice actor and journalist*

"J. Lee is especially adept at framing lives and events in the context of bigger-picture thinking and decision-making impacts…libraries seeking a murder mystery which reaches well beyond the whodunit audience to consider "*why* do it?" will especially appreciate the broader implications and themes in *Coach's Corner*, which will also lend to book club recommendation." — *Donovan's Bookshelf Recommended Reading*

Praise for *The Reluctant Reckoner*
"Best Thriller of The Year" Finalist by BestThrillers.com

"J. Lee has created the perfect everyman. It's so easy to imagine a Chris Pratt or a young Jimmy Stewart as Mark, well-meaning and sincere in every respect, yet rendered utterly helpless by forces he cannot even begin to understand. *The Reluctant Reckoner* simmers throughout as the three-dimensional chess match between the terrorists, the FBI and Mark reaches new levels of intensity. Fans of thrillers will relish the numerous schemes that come to light along the way, and Lee demonstrates his gift for action scenes. Another white-knuckled gem from J. Lee. Move *The Reluctant Reckoner* to the top of your list." — *BestThrillers.com*

"I have rarely read a fiction like J. Lee's The Reluctant Reckoner. I couldn't put it down and loved it!" — *Litpit Book Review*

"A cryptic e-mail leads accountant Mark Richter on a journey of discovery when his abilities are called into question and a mystery arises that seems to point to him as incompetent at best, or an embezzler at worst. Readers will become thoroughly engrossed in a plot that shimmers with tension, revelation, unexpected twists and turns, and a foray into questions, dubious answers, and tests of trust." — *Midwest Books Review*

"J. Lee evolves a diabolical plot…resulting in a rollicking ride through business pursuits both legal and illegal, underworlds and everyday life, a relatable protagonist caught in the middle of it all just trying to protect his family, and revised perspectives on purpose and reality. All will delight: the classic beach reader looking to be entertained with a great mystery/suspense novel to try to figure out, libraries seeking multifaceted stories of intrigue, and readers who look for more than intrigue alone when making their reading choices." — *Donovan's Bookshelf Recommended Reading*

"As we've come to expect from J. Lee, be looking for clever harbingers, red herrings, multiple points-of-view, and very unexpected plot twists. The books keep getting better with this guy and despite having thoroughly enjoyed J. Lee's first three, this one is at the top." — ***The Two River Times***

"The Reluctant Reckoner by J. Lee is a wonderful book that is full of plot twists. It is action-packed and full of mystery with masterfully crafted reveals." — ***Litpick Book Review***

Praise for *The Deadly Deal*
"Medical Thriller of The Year" by BestThrillers.com
And Chanticleer Int'l Book Awards (CIBAs) Finalist

"The Bottom Line: A perfectly crafted conspiracy thriller with a truly noble hero at its core, *The Deadly Deal* is the twisty tale we've been waiting for. Highly Recommended." — ***BestThrillers***

"The Deadly Deal is a fast-moving, page-turning thriller propelled by rapid scene changes, frequent plot twists, and an enemy that grows more powerful and menacing as the full extent of the conspiracy. Fans of plot-driven thrillers will find plenty to like…" — ***Windy City Book Review***

"The Deadly Deal evolves superb characterization, satisfying twists of plot, and a focus that will keep even seasoned thriller readers guessing about its outcome." — ***Midwest Books Review***

"J. Lee does it again with *The Deadly Deal.* Fans of mysteries and thrillers will love this new cliffhanger. I was immediately hooked as the story began to unfold and this fast-paced and intriguing mystery kept me guessing until the very last page. Impossible to put down, I finished the book in days and loved every minute of this captivating read!" — ***Nicky Steinberg, Publisher of Downers Grove Living Magazine***

"J. Lee is a must-read new talent." — ***Mike Lawson, Edgar Award Nominated author of the Joe DeMarco series.***

"I have to say, I was very impressed. THE DEADLY DEAL is the real deal! Great characters, both protagonist and antagonist. A plot and subplots that keep you guessing. A scenario that is both absurd and realistic, reaching to surprising levels. J. Lee is a first-rate storyteller." — ***Goodreads Review***

"Action packed and sharply written. Grabbed me from the start and wouldn't let go. I've already made room on my nightstand for the next J. Lee thriller." — ***Davin Goodwin, author of PARADISE COVE and the Roscoe Conklin Mystery Series***.

"*The Deadly Deal* is my kind of thriller. Clever premise, complex characters, a pulsating plot and a satisfying, but in no way predictable, ending. Easily J. Lee's best work, and that alone is saying something." — ***Drew Yanno, author of In the Matter of Michael Vogel and The Smart One***.

"A terrific follow-up to *The Hubley Case* and *The Silent Cardinal*. J. Lee lays out an explosive tale of political intrigue, government conspiracy, and murder. If you haven't yet read Lee's thrillers, it's time to jump aboard the bandwagon." — ***Alfred C. Martino, author of Pinned, Over The End Line, and Perfected By Girls***

"Regardless of how you feel about the pharmaceutical industry, this book is a must read. J. Lee pulls you into a fast-paced thriller of good vs. evil that never ever lets up. Extremely tight writing, intricate plot, very believable characters, and a sharp, fast-moving dialogue that gels it all together. Put this one on your reading list!" — ***Jesus Leal, author of True Diversity***

"Set yourself some time to read *The Deadly Deal*, because once you start, you will NOT want to stop turning the pages. J. Lee's third book is not only as good as his first two suspense novels, it's the best one yet! The twists and turns are unexpected to the very end." — ***Pamela S. Wight, author of Twin Desires, The Right Wrong Man, Flashes of Life, Birds of Paradise, Molly Finds Her Purr***

Praise for *The Silent Cardinal*

"A twisty, fast-paced novel-intrigue of the highest order. Highly recommended!" — ***Ward Larsen, USA Today bestselling author of Assassin's Strike***

"THE SILENT CARDINAL is a taut, complex thriller that grabs the reader on the opening page and refuses to let go until the last." — ***James L. Thane, Author of A Shot to the Hear, Fatal Blow, South of the Deuce, Crossroads, Tyndall, and Picture Me Gone***

"*The Silent Cardinal* packs a powerful punch with a looming terrorist threat, multiple kidnappings, unexpected killings and some high level political infighting. Lee keeps the reader guessing right along with the hero, struggling to determine who to trust, the payoff coming at the very end with a twist I never saw coming. You won't be disappointed." — ***Drew Yanno, bestselling author of In the Matter of Michael Vogel and The Smart One***.

"Millions of lives hang in the balance in this fast-paced nail-biter. J. Lee delivers a thriller with constant twists and turns, taking readers on a thrill ride that is hard to put down." — ***Steve Brigman, bestselling author of The Orphan Train***

"*The Silent Cardinal* is a standout. A crew of people need Ben to solve this race-against-time case: the FBI, CIA, military, and terrorists all stake a claim on the skills of Siebert. But his family, friends, and ultimately, his country are at risk as Seibert fights a lethal enemy to unravel a d eadly mystery." — ***Pamela Wight, author of The Right Wrong Man and Twin Desires***

"Fans will not be disappointed with his follow up t hriller, *The Silent Cardinal*. Readers will surely cheer the return of former marine Ben Seibert, while enjoying the wild ride of espionage and murder in this taunt page-tuner." — ***Alfred C. Martino, author of Pinned, Over The End Line, and Perfected By Girls***

COACH'S CORNER

J. Lee

Moonshine Cove Publishing, LLC

Bowling Green, Virginia U.S.A.

First Moonshine Cove Edition October 2025

ISBN: 9781952439988

Library of Congress LCCN: 2025911133

© Copyright 2025 by J. Lee

Cover provided by the author; interior design by Moonshine Cove staff.

For Brad, who changed my life 28 years ago and remains my best friend today. Thanks for everything, hermano.

Acknowledgments

I wanted to especially thank—for reasons beyond writing—my four wonderful parents. Two raised me so well, made me who I am, and I'm so grateful are still a big part of my life; two welcomed me into their family with undying love and show it every day; all encourage and support me. I'm so lucky to have you.

Coach's Corner

1

The game was five-card draw. Ante five cents, with Jacks or better to open and trips to win, meaning three-of-a-kind or better was needed to rake in the pot. It was the go-to poker game in Southern Illinois in 1997, usually nickel-dime-quarter, over cold beer, fresh deer sausage, tobacco dip, and a bucket of sunflower seeds. Every now and then the dealer would switch to seven-card stud, low spade in the hole splits the pot, but never wild cards. Barry Ray felt wild cards dirtied an otherwise pristine game.

Dressed in a plain white T-shirt and dirt-stained blue jeans, Barry Ray never looked into the eye of his opponents. A Styrofoam cup half full of wintergreen-flavored dip juice sat next to an impressive stack of blue chips, the highly regarded quarter-value token. Instead of watching them, he focused on the five cards in his hand with unflappable concentration. His lower lip bulging from the tobacco wedged within, he stroked his rugged goatee and then took another drag from the Winston that lay in the ashtray beside his chips. Charlie watched from the other end of the table, not nearly as confident in his own hand.

"Give me two," Barry Ray instructed Brad, the dealer and Charlie's best friend. It was barely above a whisper, yet everyone took notice. Barry Ray was the group's leader, and when he spoke, the others listened. At almost twenty-one years old, at least two years older than everyone else at the table, he'd introduced them to many things over the years, including the specifics of a woman's anatomy and a number of experimental vices. Yet despite the pedagogical, almost mentor-like relationship he offered, Barry Ray had no trouble taking their money.

The cards were old, bent, ripped, and impossible to confuse with a new deck. The color stains wouldn't allow such a mix-up. They all had a black scribble in the upper right corner because a few years earlier Barry Ray became convinced someone had marked the ace of diamonds with a black marker. No one else could see it, but that didn't stop Barry Ray from marking each of the other fifty-one cards in the same fashion.

Huddled around a small table in his garage in front of two small house fans, Charlie wiped his forehead and pulled out another beer from the ice-filled cooler. After he folded his long shot chance for a small straight, he felt relieved, more than happy to watch the action unfold from the sidelines. It was his fourth beer of the game and he was only a month over eighteen years old, but such was the norm in Germantown. With a population of under 1,000 and no restaurants or stoplights in town, underage drinking was the norm and nobody made much of a fuss about it. Brad's father was the town sheriff, and even Sheriff Thrower had seen the four of them drinking in Brad's basement without objection.

Brad, whom he'd known since kindergarten, dealt the cards and asked the opener to start the betting. Mack, as predicted, checked to his older brother. Barry Ray shuffled his cards slowly, intently eyeballing the other two players still in the game. It was habitual and predictable, yet still intimidating. Though all three of them tried to play it off, Barry Ray shuffling his cards felt like a lion staring down its prey.

Charlie took a long swig of cold beer and instantly relished the refreshing result that combated the sticky June humidity. Half the can was gone in one gulp, and it went down like water. Mack and Brad remained focused on their hands, each obviously trying to read Barry Ray's reaction to his two new cards.

Barry Ray kept the cards flat on the table and then ever so slightly peeled up the corners, showing no emotion whatsoever. Then he threw in the maximum bet: fifty cents. Brad folded immediately, wanting no part of it. The dealer's stack was higher than when the game started, and he had no intention of jeopardizing that.

Thus, only the Olson brothers remained.

2

"Almost time. You ready for this, bro?" Barry Ray asked Mack with a smirk. It struck Charlie as odd. Barry Ray rarely chitchatted, and the sort of pseudo motivational way he said it, while staring Mack straight in the eye, briefly made Charlie wonder if Barry Ray was referring to something else. But another long swig of beer seconds later helped him move past it.

Mack put his cards down and faced his older brother eye-to-eye. He stroked his chin as if he had stubble to stroke, but his fifteen-year-old baby face hadn't yet met a razor and everyone knew it. In many ways, Mack was the opposite of Barry Ray. Five years younger and even smaller, weaker, and clumsier. He had short, light brown hair in contrast to Barry Ray's thick, curly dark hair that hung down to his shoulders. Mack had innocent, almost sad blue eyes in comparison Barry Ray's dark laser beam projectors. Mack struggled with the girls; Barry Ray was the stud of his high school class a few years back and had kept the title. Mack was also at least five inches shorter, stuttered when he got nervous, and idolized his older brother. There were times Charlie thought it seemed they weren't brothers at all because they were so different, yet their love for each other was undeniable.

Mack held his ground and called Barry Ray's bet. Charlie thought to himself that Mack's cards must've been better than they showed, and glanced over at Barry Ray, nibbling on his cuticle.

He never did find out who had the better hand.

The pounding on the garage door startled all four of them. It was a loud, aggressive series of thumps that almost caused him to drop his beer. When Charlie answered it, Sheriff Marcus Thrower was on the other side, a stern expression on his face. The group didn't scramble to hide the beers, and Sheriff Thrower didn't ask. The pointed look in Brad's father's eyes told Charlie this was far more serious than beer and poker. Sheriff Thrower walked right past him without even saying hello.

"Barry Ray," he said softly. Barry Ray looked back curiously more than anything. Charlie and Brad stared, motionless. It looked like Mack was going to say something, but didn't.

"Yes, sir?" Barry Ray responded.

"Come with me, son."

"What—"

"Now."

Without another word, Barry Ray got up and walked away with Sheriff Thrower, his cards and blue chip stack still on the table, the Winston still burning, tobacco still tucked under his lip.

Charlie would find out soon enough that Barry Ray was taken into custody for questioning related to the murder of Jimmy Patino.

2

Within an hour, Charlie and Brad were on Brad's four-wheeler, testing the limits of its engine and maximum speed. Mack stayed behind in the garage at the poker table, weak and unwilling to move or even speak, so they gave him a fist bump and got moving. First they went to Barry Ray's house where his father, Kurt Olson, seemed to be waiting for them, based on the fact that he didn't so much as shift his weight in his recliner after they barged through the door. After a long swig of orange juice from a plastic glass, Kurt wiped his forehead and nodded at them both. He didn't say much, but told them he knew what'd happened and needed a favor.

Apparently, Sheriff Thrower had stopped by Kurt's before he picked up Barry Ray. That was probably a no-no as far as proper police procedure was concerned, but such was often the case in Germantown. It certainly wasn't the first time professionalism had suffered at the hands of friendship in the small town.

Even so, Kurt's lack of reaction felt surprising. In fact, the only thing he said was equally short and stoic. "Guys, I've got to get to the police station. Do me a favor and head out to Grandpa Joe's. He hasn't been answering his phone, which is hardly unusual, but I want to make sure he knows what's going on."

* * *

The dark-green ATV topped out at forty miles per hour, making Charlie wish even more that they had a car. A lot of his buddies had them, and experience behind the wheel certainly wasn't the issue— every male in Germantown had been driving ATVs, cars, or farm equipment since he was ten. It was typical for a male to be behind the wheel before puberty. The problem was money. Brad's family didn't have enough to buy him a car and Charlie's simply didn't think it was a necessary expense.

It took twenty minutes at full throttle, the wind blowing in his face as he clung to Brad's waist. Brad took the standard shortcuts through the cornfields, met up with abandoned country roads that cars had long since stopped driving on, and went through ditches and mud puddles at an alarming rate in the name of speed.

When they finally arrived at Joe's, nothing seemed out of the ordinary. It was a little after 12:30 in the afternoon, which meant even when they scurried into the red brick ranch through its large, screened-in breezeway nearly out of breath, Joe didn't so much as stir from his seat. Two screen doors at the front and back of the room offered a crosswind for the breezeway, but inside the house it was stuffy.

Joe kept his head down and studied the seven rows of playing cards laid neatly on the dining room table, playing solitaire the exact same way he had every day for years. Grandpa Joe Olson was Mack and Barry Ray's paternal grandfather, Kurt's father. Though he'd earned the title honestly, Joe was a young grandparent at only fifty-six and younger than several of Charlie's friends' parents. He'd had a hard road, too. Joe never talked about it, but his wife passed away when Kurt was only ten, so he'd been a single parent for the past twenty-seven years. Charlie wondered every now and then how hard that had to be, but if there was anyone who could do it, it was Joe.

He treated Joe like he would his own grandpa. Joe let them play Wiffle Ball out in his large double lot using two trashcans, an old car floor mat, and tires for the bases. The mound was a piece of plywood that rested twenty feet from home plate and hadn't ever moved so far as he knew. Both of his grandpas died before he was born—as had Brad's—so Joe had filled that role in all their lives.

"Joe—" Brad started to say before Joe lifted his hand with the index finger extended.

He watched Joe analyze the cards intently, wearing the same John Deere hat he wore every day, complemented by a rust-colored flannel shirt that he wore every day regardless of the temperature. His thick, black-rimmed glasses were for two things: reading and solitaire. A pack of Marlboros created a rectangular bulge in his left shirt pocket.

Solitaire was a religion for Joe, one that he perfected through relentless repetition. His wrinkled yet strong hands flipped the cards over three at a time with slow intentionality, void of emotion. Aces, twos, sevens, it didn't matter. He acted like it was five-card draw and refused to show his poker face. When he finished lining up the final pile of seven rows, he always surveyed the hand he'd been dealt and took a sip of Ginger Ale from the same faded green plastic cup. Warm, no ice. He didn't like the condensation ice created, even though he used a coaster.

Joe's philosophy hadn't changed in thirty years. Practice makes perfect, and repetition makes practice. He always finished dealing before making a play and never jumped the gun when an ace popped up. But that was common enough. Most people did the same thing. His methods went much deeper.

Always flip three cards at a time and never allow yourself to see the two cards underneath the top one. Press the edges together before turning them over and place them in the output stack so all the cards line up perfectly. When you see a play, pick up the cards with your right hand and use your left to prop up the card it's going on top. That kept the columns clean and crisp. If there are multiple columns you can play on, always pick the one with the most hidden cards beneath it. If it's a tie, work from left to right.

Joe played every hand he dealt no matter what. He followed the rules and adhered to the system without exception. "You're only cheating yourself if you cheat at solitaire," he said.

There were three clocks in Joe's living room that each chimed every fifteen minutes. But since their times were slightly offset from one another and Joe refused to synchronize them, loud banging emanated from one every couple of minutes. Charlie had heard so

7

many dings and dongs over the years that it felt like nails on the chalkboard waiting for Joe to get through his stack of cards.

"It's 12:38, guys. I got seven minutes until I need to start putting my shoes on."

"But, Joe..."

"Only twelve minutes until I need to get back to the barn."

Joe could've stopped working years ago, but for him, farming was a way to hold onto routine. It seemed like an odd hobby to Charlie, and he could never understand why a man would *choose* to do something he'd been forced to do for forty years. But Joe couldn't be convinced to stop by anyone, family or otherwise.

And summer was a busy time for a farmer, especially one who didn't believe in combines. There was watering, picking, and tending to be done. He preferred to work it by hand and hire young summer help as needed, believing that an honest day's dollar could only come from an honest day's work.

"Can this wait? I'll be done at a quarter 'til five."

"Barry Ray's been arrested, Joe." Charlie mustered it out as directly as he could, but his voice still cracked towards the end.

Joe's typical deadpan expression shifted as he folded his hands behind his head and sat back in silence. The reaction wasn't as pronounced as Charlie'd guessed it would be, and Joe replied in a near whisper.

"When?"

"Um, about an hour ago. We were playing cards and...and Sheriff Thrower came over and told Barry Ray he had to go with him." He hurried the words out in direct contrast to Joe's calmness.

"What on earth for?"

Charlie looked at Brad, trying to siphon some courage. He finally drew in a breath and prepared to spit the answer out quick. As anal as Joe was, he was still a sweet old man who loved his family more than anything. This was going to crush him.

"Jimmy Patino...he's dead."

8

"I heard about that on the radio. So Sheriff Thrower thinks *Barry Ray* had something to do with it?"

"I don't know, Joe. He just took him away."

Joe's breathing got louder. He took off his thick glasses and aggressively rubbed his eyes, as if trying to massage this unsettling information into his stiff old brain.

"Did you tell Kurt?" Joe asked. Contrary to traditional suburban and urban upbringing, Southern Illinois small-town children were expected to call adults by their first names, except when referring to law enforcement or doctors. It was considered insolent not to. Adults preferred to think of themselves as young teenagers with the rest of their lives ahead of them, and hearing Mr. and Mrs. made that hard to do.

"Kurt's the one who told us to come find you," Brad answered.

Joe walked towards the living room, pacing the orange carpet floor with his bare, veiny feet. He mumbled something to himself as he worked his lower lip with his yellow teeth, but Charlie couldn't make it out.

Finally, Joe turned around defiantly, as if he had made a decision of some sort. He yanked upward on his belt before he spoke.

"Come with me, gents," was all he said, heading to the garage through the kitchen door and out the breezeway. The car keys were in the ignition. Joe didn't lock the doors, shut the windows, or even close the garage when he pulled out. It was country living, peaceful and quiet without a neighbor for miles. People in Germantown didn't have to worry about burglary or destruction. Their families and possessions were safe, and they trusted their homes would be the same when they got back.

But Charlie could feel that changing. Jimmy Patino, the prick from Germantown High just a few years earlier, class bully turned local plumber's apprentice, was dead. Apparently, *murdered*. And his good friend was in custody. A mountain of trepidation surrounding him, he went with Joe to find out why.

9

3

Jimmy Patino was pronounced dead at 10:32 a.m. The cause of death was multiple gunshot wounds to the chest with a Remington Model 760 rifle, a model that had ceased production sixteen years earlier but was still quite prevalent with hunters in Southern Illinois. His body was dumped in a cornfield three miles from town on Highline Road, a mile away from the nearest residence. It had been stuffed in a black plastic bag held together by a slip knot. A father and son found it on their weekly bike ride through the countryside.

Charlie stood next to Brad with Mack, whom they'd met up with at the station, listening quietly to Sheriff Thrower describe the details of the case to Joe, again not necessarily proper procedure.

Joe was *that* guy. The person everyone in town respected and never questioned, even though he lived like a recluse. He didn't associate with anyone outside of family and Charlie, and seemed to purposely avoid doing so, yet every Germantown resident knew who he was. That popularity carried with it special privileges.

Kurt stood next to Mack, his usually sturdy 6'3" frame hunched over as if a stiff wind would knock him over. His swollen eyes told a sad story, and immediately Charlie could tell he'd been crying. Those usually full-of-life blue eyes were rimmed with red and Kurt held a handkerchief to constantly wipe them. It seemed to Charlie that even breathing was painful for Kurt. His breaths were quick and sporadic, like a father coming to terms with the fact that his son had just been taken into custody for murder.

Kurt's life story was a rough one. His two sons—Barry Ray and Mack—were his whole world. Joe, his father, had helped Kurt raise them over the years because Kurt's wife left the family years ago. Charlie had never heard Kurt discuss it, but it wasn't a secret. Barry Ray and Mack never talked about her, or why she went to bed as

10

usual one night and left town the next morning. He assumed they didn't even know.

Yet, Kurt got through it all and still managed to be a great father to his sons. He worked hard at the GM factory in St. Louis during the day, did various jobs around town at night to put potatoes on the table, and never drank at the bars the way most dads did. The way Charlie's did. Kurt got to all the summer baseball games he possibly could, made dinner every night, and opened his home to Brad and Charlie. It was inspiring and sad all at the same time. He'd grown to admire Kurt even more as an adult, realizing everything the man had done for his sons.

But in a small town where the rumor mill is the only form of entertainment and everyone knows everything about everyone, the fact that no one seemed to know why Kurt's wife left made for ample conversation. Theory after theory had been discussed and passed along amongst the gossipers many times over. People acted kind to his face, but he often wouldn't have it because he knew what they said behind his back. Charlie was sure Kurt didn't want their pity. He wanted to be left alone to raise his family.

To make matters worse, Barry Ray and Mack weren't exactly model sons to the conservative-minded residents of Germantown. From Charlie's perspective, they were swell guys to hang out with, but the small town had its own perceptions. Barry Ray was a long-haired punk who didn't respect his elders, and Mack was a pushover who didn't stand up for himself. They were viewed as opposites, even by Brad and Charlie, with only one commonality: neither was good enough for the Germantown community.

And as Sheriff Thrower discussed Barry Ray's situation, Charlie realized that from that point on Kurt would never get his wish to just be left alone.

"No fingerprints as of yet," said Sheriff Thrower. "Hopefully, some will turn up." Fingerprinting was the primary source of identification; and it took some criminals longer than others to learn to wear gloves.

Joe, his arm on Kurt's shoulder, asked the sheriff patiently, "Have you found the weapon?" Kurt just stared ahead blankly.

"Not yet. We'll keep looking, but it doesn't seem to be there."

He went on to explain about the stretch of road the body was dumped on.

"For that quarter mile, it's that hard white rock, which means there ain't no tire tracks. Aside from that small stretch, the whole road is loose gravel and dirt. That explains why he dumped it there," Sheriff Thrower said defiantly in a self-congratulatory manner, as if he'd cracked the case. Even Charlie had thought of that. Kurt's face changed expressions and suddenly they all realized he was angry.

"When you say *he*, whom are you referring to, Sheriff Thrower?"

"Oh, I was just—"

"Because I *know* you wouldn't presume someone guilty in this great nation, and I *know* you wouldn't be accusing my son of murder in front of his dad and grandfather without the evidence to back it up."

Sheriff Thrower froze, caught like a rat in a trap. He apologized and said he didn't mean to implicate anyone, but everyone knew his only regret was the stupid comment that awoke the sleeping giant. Brad and Charlie looked at each other and shook their heads, knowing Kurt wasn't going to take that from anyone.

"Why have you arrested him?" continued Joe. "Looks to me like you don't have much evidence. No fingerprints, no tire tracks, no witnesses, no traceable weapon. What makes you think Barry Ray played a part in this at all?"

Charlie waited impatiently for Sheriff Thrower to respond, as he'd had a similar thought. Though not in production anymore, the Remington Model 760 was a common weapon that had been around since the early fifties and that many people used for deer hunting. He'd shot one before, with the spitzer bullets from a box magazine, just as every other male in his class had.

"Hold on now...wait just a minute," the sheriff said diplomatically, holding his hands up in defense. "First of all, he ain't under arrest.

Let me make that clear. He *ain't* under arrest at this time. We just have some questions for him. We wanted to talk to him because he's the only person we know of who had a motive."

"You took a twenty-year-old into custody because of a supposed motive?" Joe asked.

"You bet we did. Someone was going to make him a suspect. It was either us or the state police or the feds, someone else who don't know his background or that he's a good man. C'mon now, ya'll know what happened a few weeks ago. I figured it'd be better to nip it in the bud than to let the state police do it."

A few months earlier, Jimmy Patino had made a pass at Barry Ray's girlfriend, Denise Owens. When she blew him off, he followed her to her car and grabbed her. According to Barry Ray, Patino pushed her up against the fender and whispered all sorts of things into her ear that a lady should never hear, rubbing her ass as he did.

When Denise, who was a few years older than Charlie and one of the most attractive women around, told Barry Ray what happened, there was no stopping him. He unloaded on Patino like Sonny on Carl in *The Godfather*. Right outside the school, during a track meet, no less, he jumped on top of Jimmy Patino and beat him to a bloody pulp with a gym shoe, holding Patino's hands to the floor and whaling on him with the Nike. Broke his nose, mangled his face, cracked two ribs and would've done far worse if folks hadn't broken it up. By the time they pulled Barry Ray off him, Jimmy was dripping with blood and wheezing for air.

As he was being pulled away, Barry Ray yelled in plain sight of everyone what would happen if Jimmy ever touched Denise again.

"I won't waste time busting your face again, I'll just pump your sorry ass full of lead. You hear me, Patino? I swear I'll kill you!"

Despite giving Jimmy what almost everyone in town felt he deserved, Barry Ray was reprimanded and a restraining order was taken out against him. For that reason he couldn't attend graduation ceremonies, which people in Germantown as a general rule attended for at least three years after their own. He was lucky he didn't get

13

charged with assault and battery, and in a larger suburb such as O'Fallon, he would have. Charlie remembered thinking that as much of a prick as Jimmy was, Barry Ray's response still seemed like an overreaction. Now it had come back to haunt him.

Everyone reacted in his or her own way. Mack stood motionless, close behind his father. Kurt had calmed down and was tending to Mack, patting him on the back and assuring him it would be okay. Joe told Sheriff Thrower to keep him posted, and Brad and Charlie just looked at each other, still in shock.

After a few minutes of silence, Brad and Charlie were trying to cheer Mack up, telling him it was okay, that his brother didn't do it, and that they didn't have any proof he did, that Sheriff Thrower was actually trying to spare Barry Ray from other cops that wouldn't be as friendly towards him. Joe and Kurt had pulled Sheriff Thrower aside because a small crowd had congregated around the police station. The news was getting out. It would be all over town by the end of the day.

Joe then came back and pulled Brad and Charlie aside.

"Can you two get home by yourselves? I'm going to stay here with Kurt and Mack for a while."

They nodded.

"What's going to happen to Barry Ray?" Charlie asked.

"It's tough to tell. They have a motive but nothing else. Sheriff Thrower's right though: it's enough to justify bringing him in." He paused, staring into the distance, as if in deep thought. "You two head home. There's nothing more you can do. I'll let you know what I find out." His voice was calm and subtle. "Pray for Barry Ray tonight."

4

As they paced down the shaded sidewalks and blue star homes, Brad was the first to venture into the horrible subject of whether or not Barry Ray had killed Jimmy Patino. The conversation didn't feel right to Charlie—discussing the likelihood of Barry Ray's involvement as he sat in the police station, unable to defend himself—but it didn't stop them from speculating.

"Jimmy did give Denise a hard time, you know?" Brad said while biting his lip, unwillingly admitting that Barry Ray had a motive.

"And Barry Ray can get really pissed really fast," Charlie responded, immediately regretting it, knowing he was feeding the fire that Barry Ray was guilty. He told himself not to judge and reminded himself of that unfairness.

"They don't have any fingerprints..."

"Or a weapon," he quickly added.

Charlie looked down Main Street, a mixture of antique shops and uneven red brick roads that formed huge bumps in an already rundown road. Out-of-towners were always surprised by how slowly they had to drive over the built-in speed bumps that paved the entire two-mile strip. There had been talk of fixing it, but the town preferred to spend that money on the summer carnival.

Parallel to the east-west main drag were side streets lined with modest but clean-looking houses, white concrete sidewalks usually adorned with children riding their bikes, and maple trees that covered the yards along the way. And as they crossed over en route to Brad's house, Charlie ran through the possibilities. His mind didn't have his permission, but it didn't ask.

Jimmy Patino was pretty worthless and pathetic from his perspective, and he wasn't the only one who thought so. Despite being 24 years old, the previous year Jimmy had a restraining order

15

taken out against him for stealing from a high school freshman. Shaw Littleton was on his way to school when, according to the report, Jimmy jumped him from behind and took his lunch money. What kind of 24-year-old man gets his jollies by taking a couple of bucks from a high school kid?

And in Germantown, where family dominated a largely traditional lifestyle, such acts felt even more despicable. Most adults were already married with kids, dads went to work, moms brought up the children. Dinner out on Friday, barbeque on Saturday, Little League on Sunday. Tradition prevailed, and life was slow. In the summer, there was a lemonade stand every few blocks; in the fall, kids raked leaves into monstrous piles for proper jumping; in the winter, there were snowmen and Christmas lights as far as the eye could see. It made a scumbag like Jimmy feel even scummier.

A few years earlier, Jimmy was caught smashing mailboxes and vandalizing properties. Before that, he was accused of arson when an old, dilapidated house in the country was suddenly engulfed in flames started by a gallon of gasoline that matched what was in his garage a few weeks before. And before that, he was pulled over for reckless driving, alcohol obviously involved. Though, that wasn't saying much. The whole town and area was saturated with underage drinking. Clinton County had the third-highest underage drinking percentage in the nation.

It was clear Jimmy was on a bad track and had made plenty of enemies, but it was equally clear how untouchable he seemed. Jimmy had been arrested three times that Charlie knew of and never served a day behind bars. He'd beaten up children ten years younger and half his height, but never faced any penalties beyond community service.

His aggression towards women was even more disturbing. A few years ago, a girl from Breese, about five miles south, accused him of groping her and trying to force himself on her at a party. She was sixteen; he was eighteen. So maybe, when Patino picked on Denise,

Barry Ray saw a familiar pattern emerging, which was why he decided to nip it in the bud with a gym shoe.

Even the way Patino spoke to women could be categorized as harassment. They were very regular parts of his vocabulary that any woman could hear at any time: locals, out-of-towners, older women, young kids, whatever. It didn't matter. They were all targets. Jimmy crossed the line far too often, and everyone knew it.

And yet, no one ever wondered why the scumbag never got punished for what he did. The answer was simple.

"I wonder what Mr. Patino's going to do," Brad asked.

Mr. Douglas Patino was a man of great power in Germantown. A huge fish in the smallest of ponds, he owned everyone who walked the streets and plenty of people who didn't. He was the king of favors, dirt no one wanted outed, and the ability to use both. Even Sheriff Thrower abided by what Douglas Patino wanted most of the time. He had enough money, contacts, and influence to whittle his son's record down to a few minor infractions. Jimmy's permanent police record was squeaky clean, and his actions had resulted in no meaningful punishment.

Jimmy was ordered not to get within 300 yards of Shaw Littleton. Germantown was only one square mile. The judge, police, Patino, and Littleton knew there wasn't any chance of that being honored or enforced, but it didn't matter. So instead, the Littleton family moved to Centralia, twenty miles east. Good for them, but not much help. A few weeks later Jimmy knocked on their door just to say hi—a slap in the face and proof that he was untouchable as Douglas Patino's son.

The Breese girl who accused him of sexual harassment abruptly stopped complaining a few weeks after the alleged incident, and her father was seen driving a brand new Camaro the following month. The arson case also didn't go anywhere. The police rationalized that it was a dilapidated building full of dry wood that was bound to burn down naturally. Never mind the fact it managed to stay upright for over thirty years before someone threw a torched gas can into it.

All complaints against Jimmy either disappeared or were thrown out, and he had a license to do whatever he wanted. He had amnesty to live as a narcissist, and used it every chance he got. A part of Charlie couldn't help but feel that Jimmy Patino got exactly what he deserved.

"You think he did it?" he blurted out the question they were both thinking.

Brad stopped walking and stared, his eyes gazing in the distance, as if he was surprised he asked.

"Well, I—"

"Brad!"

They looked up to see Brad's sister, Sarah, walking towards them.

Changes were occurring in Sarah Thrower's body. The annoying little girl he'd known his entire life was suddenly becoming a woman, and it felt both awkward and exhilarating to witness the transformation. He'd grown up tolerating her presence as he and Brad hung out, rode bikes, played at the pool, and stayed up late around a bonfire. She was his best friend's sister, two years younger and more of a tagalong.

But one day, without warning, that changed.

Her shoulder-length brown hair curled near the edges and looked smoother than Brad's dishwater blonde rag. A "pretty" brown, he'd caught himself thinking once. Her big brown eyes seemed to jump out. She had a dimple on the right side of her cheek and had gotten into smiley face stickers and mood rings.

She wore a long denim skirt with a matching blue jean purse around her left shoulder. Despite the heat, an angel-sleeved cotton blouse hung off the edges of her arms like bell-bottom sleeves. It was clearly too large, but the combination served her well. He couldn't deny that she looked good. And that was a strange feeling.

"I can't believe what's happening!"

"How'd you hear?" Brad asked.

"It was on the radio at the bowling alley. I left as soon as I heard. Did you talk to Dad? Is Jimmy Patino really dead?"

"Yeah..." Brad exhaled deeply.

"Well, he got what was coming to him."

That took him by surprise. Yes, Jimmy Patino was a dirt bag and yes, he'd had a similar thought. But saying it out loud felt different. Jimmy was dead, shot in the chest. The finality of it all made spoken words feel inappropriate.

But it was also attractive. A girl who wasn't afraid to come right out and speak her mind. A lot of girls were shy in Germantown— modest, reserved and, in general, pretty quiet. Too quiet. Sarah, on the other hand, was a fireball who spoke her mind.

"Do you think Barry Ray did it?" she asked.

After a few seconds of staring at her, he sighed deeply. He couldn't deny it to her any more than he could to his own brain. He did think Barry Ray murdered Jimmy Patino.

5

The next day, the newspapers were flooded with articles describing the homicide and subsequent events with few facts and plenty of opinion. Barry Ray had been taken into custody but details were provided, and reporters happily replaced data with opinion.

For as long as Charlie could remember, *The Germantown Sun* newspaper only came out on Thursdays. Yet here it was a Tuesday, and there was a special edition.

Also, Sheriff Thrower was on the local news. That didn't happen often. It was a big deal, and he guessed Brad's family was huddled around the television at six-thirty to watch. He gave a prepared statement that referenced seeking justice and presuming innocence, but it felt like lip service, nothing more than a well-rehearsed speech.

In Germantown, enforcement of the law was subject to whom you knew. Teenagers drove around the country roads drunk as skunks and were given a slap on the wrist. Boys drove ATVs and cars through town long before they were sixteen and weren't questioned. High school baseball players chewed tobacco, often in plain sight of policemen who, all on duty, were in the stands to see it.

It's just the way it was. And if your dad's brother knew Sheriff Thrower from high school, you'd get a break. If you were a star athlete, you got more than one get-out-of-jail-free card. You learned at a young age it's not what you know, it's who you know. Plus, the cops weren't exactly world class, nor did they care to be. They liked the free cars and gas, the power to hold a gun and sound a siren, and the fact little kids treated them like a god. Put all that together and the idea of justice being served in the name of law didn't feel very genuine.

But maybe this was different. Jimmy Patino was dead, and though everyone knew Sheriff Thrower's face, watching him discuss a *murder* investigation was new territory. Especially when the victim was Douglas Patino's son.

Charlie's parents reacted the way he expected: concerned, and insistent that he keep his distance from the Olson family. His mother especially struggled with any connection whatsoever between him and murder, and an argument or two ensued. He knew her concern came from the heart, but as was happening more frequently, he had a different opinion.

Turning his back on the entire Olson family, including his good friend Mack, who was just as innocent as he was, didn't seem like the right thing to do.

The day after Barry Ray was arrested, Charlie's truck driver father, asked him if he wanted to join him on a long haul to Georgia. It would last over two weeks, on the road in the eighteen-wheeler cab the whole time, just the two of them. Interstates and truck stops, motels, diners, windshield time and man-to-man conversation for seventeen days.

Charlie knew his mom wanted him out of Germantown, and the disingenuous invitation infuriated him. He asked his father why he'd never offered before and a huge argument followed. One that included loud shouting from both sides and a sobbing mother at the end of it. He swore that he'd never go anywhere with his father and bolted out the door to baseball practice.

If he'd only known what was about to happen, he would have jogged behind his dad's truck all the way to Georgia.

6

Charlie was excited for practice, grateful to be away from his father and near his friends. But it was strange. Coach Burdi, whom everyone called Skip, treated it like any other day and got to business as usual. But even so, several of the guys were badmouthing Barry Ray behind his back. He heard a few of them pestering Mack about his murderer brother. Brad told them to back off, which they did for a few minutes, but it was ephemeral. Mack knew he had similar pestering to look forward to for a long time, and the fact he was younger than everyone else made him an even easier target. Skip told Mack to focus on shagging balls, but it didn't take, and Charlie wasn't surprised.

The sad part was Mack never stood up for himself in the first place. He'd never seen him get into a fight, argue firmly, or even stare someone down. If he got picked on, he froze and then gave in. Barry Ray tried to tell him that was a mistake, that people would only come back for more, but he never could convince him.

Charlie and Brad had played some version of summer baseball every year since they were six, beginning with park district little league as youngsters and graduating to legion ball a few years ago. When he was a kid, the prospect of playing in the majors drove his engine. Travelling teams, Saturday double headers, baseball seven days a week, no time for anything else. But now, that dream was dead. He didn't have what it took and knew it, a harsh realization that virtually every athlete encounters at some point in his or her career. But after twelve years, he just couldn't quit. He talked Brad into one more summer with the game before they had to figure out what came next in life. Mack was allowed to play despite being a few years younger, only because there weren't enough guys otherwise to field a team. Beggars can't be choosers.

Germantown Field was clean and simple, not littered with advertisements. It was always lined with chalk, the grass was green, the infield usually dragged. The dugouts had a clean concrete floor and brick enclosure with buckets of sunflower seeds conveniently positioned at both sides to go with a freshly painted, splinter-free wood bench. It was 400 feet to center and 333 down the lines, and Mack stood in front of the right field sign with a posture that grew more sluggish by the minute. Slumped over with his hands on his knees, looking down at the ground, his eyes were shielded by a hat pulled too far down over his head. He didn't say a word.

Even Skip stopped trying to encourage or inspire him. He also didn't stop Jason Hand and the others from making fun of him. After a half hour of ridiculing, poor Mack bolted from the outfield and ran to the parking lot, hopping on his bike and pedaling away with a cloud of heckling behind. Charlie watched it all unfold with one overarching thought.

Why didn't I go after him?

* * *

Instead of going after him, he made his way over to Brad, who was tuning out the others and focusing on shagging flies. Grass stains covered his sweatpants and his hat was brown with dirt, shirt tucked in, cleats crusty and worn from overuse. Charlie looked at his almost shiny cleats and shook his head.

"How's it going, man?" Charlie asked.

"Good. Wish I could say the same for Mack."

"Yeah, I feel bad for him."

"Me too." Brad stopped, fielded a grounder, and then continued, "But he can't just sit there and take it. Jason won't stop."

Charlie nodded. "Did your dad tell you anything else about Barry Ray?"

"Not much. They figured out that Jimmy got killed between eight and nine yesterday. Barry Ray swears up and down he was playing

23

Wiffle Ball with Mack in the woods. Said they played the whole morning, from like seven 'til eleven. Then they headed to the garage and met us for cards."

Behind Mack and Barry Ray's house were two acres of woods and a small creek. It was a great place to have as a teenager. They took the ATV down there all the time and built forts, dug trenches, and played sniper. Years ago, Kurt had cut down some trees and planted a grass field. It was small, but big enough for some great Wiffle Ball games. The brothers often played in it.

"Did your dad talk to Mack?"

"Yeah, he backed up Barry Ray's story. They always play Wiffle Ball out there."

"Anyone else play?"

"Nah, and that's the problem. Mack's too scared and messed up right now to do a lot of talking, and they can't really take Barry Ray's word for it."

"What about Kurt?"

"Had the first shift at the factory. Seven-thirty start. Told my dad that when he left the house, they were out in the woods."

He tried to put himself in Sheriff Thrower's shoes. The pickle was obvious. The only person who could vouch for Barry Ray's whereabouts was Mack, who was in emotional shambles. Even so, Barry Ray's brother was a biased alibi. Not much to go on, though Charlie couldn't imagine Mack lying, even to save his own brother. It just wasn't in him. Kurt said he saw them, but he also left long before the time of the crime. They could've played Wiffle Ball until eight, and then Barry Ray could've left and gone to see Jimmy. Not to mention the obvious conflict of interest with Kurt, too.

He couldn't stop wondering if Mack would be okay. Mack was fragile. He didn't do well with conflict, and emotionally would be even worse. Barry Ray was his big brother. A brother who beat him up all the time, but a brother nonetheless. Despite their differences, there was no doubt they had a bond Brad and he could never experience. And deep down, he was jealous of it. Perhaps Brad was too, though they never talked about it.

But now Mack was alone. He had his dad and Joe, but he'd lost his best friend. People were mocking his brother and either did the same to him or ignored him. He was alone, ridiculed, and confused. Brad's question was a fair one, and he didn't know the answer.

"I hope he's going to be okay," Brad finally replied.

"Me too."

"Hey, stop the yapping and shag some balls!" Skip yelled from the mound. He hated it when players talked during batting practice. That ended the talk and Charlie was fine with that. The rest of practice he did his best not to think about Mack, but it was to no avail; he kept picturing him running away while the others laughed.

Why didn't I go after him?

When practice ended, Jason Hand approached as they started to hop on their bikes.

"You guys gonna go see the killer's brother now? Tell him I said hello," he said smugly. Jason wasn't intimidating. Standing a few inches under six feet tall with a round pair of brown glasses to match his long, curly hair and an acne-covered face, he wasn't the stereotypical bully. That's why he only picked on weaklings like Mack. He had virtually no muscle and wasn't much of an athlete, which meant he usually sat next to Charlie on those freshly painted benches.

"You'd better back off before I beat your ass," Brad hissed.

The look in his eyes was belligerent. He'd never seen Brad so fierce. Jason's mouth fell open and his nervousness was exposed in an instant. Suddenly, he wasn't so tough. Even though he'd already lost, he tried to save face by playing it off.

"Chill, man. What's it matter to you anyway, Brad?"

"He's my friend, and I think he's got enough going on without your mouth on top of it."

Then Jason quieted down and they started to pedal away on their bikes. Just as they'd gotten far enough away for him to think he was

25

safe, Jason shouted out, "That's okay, your sister can't have enough of my mouth."

Brad slammed on the brakes and pulled a one-eighty like the roadrunner on the slingshot. Within seconds, he was gaining speed on a now-running Jason Hand, hunting him down like a predator attacking its prey. Charlie didn't even know what was happening until Brad was already halfway to the field where Jason was running.

Jason ran towards the field to negate Brad's bike advantage, but that didn't help because Brad was faster than him on foot. Jason was screwed, and the rest of the team watched in anticipation. Brad was off his bike in a flash, and Jason panicked as he ran as fast as he could. He made it halfway between the dugout and the mound before a fuming Brad Thrower jumped him from behind and started punching his face while straddling his body.

"Fight! Fight!" the others shouted, alerting Skip. That meant Brad only had a few seconds, so he made them count. Jason's glasses shattered on the dirt next to him, Brad continued to swing his fists into his nose from both sides. Not a direct hit every time, but about every third punch landed solid.

"What'd you say about my sister?" Brad screamed as he landed another punch.

"You two, break it up. Break it up!" Skip yelled as he pulled Brad off his victim with both arms. "Break it up" was the phrase that all fight onlookers hated the most. Even those partial to Jason didn't want the beatdown to stop. "Brad, cool down, son! Cool down!"

Skip had a big plug in his mouth that he didn't bother taking out. It was condoned, if not downright encouraged, for baseball coaches to chew tobacco. He spit and then stared down the pugilists without an ounce of forgiveness.

"*Brad*, head on home. I know he might've deserved it, but get out of here. *Hand!* Next time you piss off one of your teammates, don't you dare go running on my field for cover. Get up! *All of you*, get on home! Show's over."

They didn't say a single word the whole way back. He didn't compliment Brad on the fight, Brad didn't stop fuming. They split at the corner of Birch and First to head to their respective houses and planned to meet later that the evening.

But it never happened.

As Charlie approached his house, down the street he saw red lights flashing, a rare sight in Germantown, and one that evoked attention. A crowd hovered around the area and he squinted his eyes to get a better look.

The lights were from police cars and ambulances, and they were at Kurt Olson's house.

He kicked it into gear and pedaled as fast as he could towards the lights. He flew down the sidewalk and veered into the street, hitting every seam in the concrete road along the way. He didn't check for cars when he crossed County Line Road and he jumped the curb to steer the bike in between people to get a better look.

He made his way to the front of the crowd and saw Sheriff Thrower by the front door getting ready to make a statement. His heart sank when he noticed a small patch of what had to be blood on his light brown uniform.

Sheriff Thrower raised his hand to quiet the crowd and prepared to start speaking, and Charlie squirmed internally.

"Ladies and gentlemen, there's nothing to see. Please go home," the sheriff said before people barked back demanding to know what happened. Was it connected to Barry Ray? Was Kurt Olson okay? Why were there police cars and an ambulance at his house?

Whether it was professional inexperience or knowing that it was going to get out eventually anyway, the sheriff finally decided to speak again after a moment of silence. It seemed to Charlie he was trying to figure out whether it made sense to tell everyone or not, and that he'd decided it did.

"About an hour ago we received a phone call informing us that Mack Olson was attacked. The paramedics are tending to him, but I can confirm that he was assaulted. That's all I can say for right now."

It was Mack's blood. He suddenly couldn't move.

"Will he be okay?" The question jumped out of his mouth almost involuntarily, summoning everyone else's silence.

"I think so. But prayers can't hurt."

Then Sheriff Thrower disappeared into the house, leaving people shouting out additional questions.

Charlie thought about the murder, the name-calling at baseball, the empty look in Mack's face, and the sight of him running away. All of the sudden, of all the questions he had asked himself that morning, there was only one that mattered.

Why didn't I go after him?

7

Charlie flicked the paper aside and stared out the window, a potent combination of disbelief and fear coursing through his veins. News of Mack's assault made the front page of yet another special edition of *The Germantown Sun*. Nervous parents imposed seven o'clock curfews on children. Folks were scared, confused, and angry. A few days later Germantown, one of the first German settlements of Illinois, was distraught. Even the devastating tornado that ripped through three years earlier in 1994 paled in comparison. And no one thought it would get better soon.

The newspaper argued that the community and world were going downhill and had been for some time, dating back to the birth of Rock n' Roll forty years earlier. Atheism and godlessness were blamed, as well as anything that pulled young people away from traditional lifestyles. The only tidbit of useful information in the entire four-page feature article was a comment from Sheriff Thrower verifying Jimmy Patino had been murdered between nine and ten the morning his body was found. An official autopsy had been performed by the county coroner in Breese and confirmed the cause of death. The investigation was ongoing.

Murder and things like that just didn't happen in Germantown. Felonies were for the big cities of the world, like St. Louis, 40 miles west of Chicago, 300 miles north—cities with gangs and drug dealers and the mafia. Not for lemonade stands, summer baseball, and the good families of Germantown. How could this be happening?

Church attendance rose even higher than it was before. Over ninety percent of the town was Catholic, and the faithful doubled their efforts in St. Boniface on Munster Street and St. Bernard's in Albers to seek guidance from a higher power. Bars, the only type of business that outnumbered churches in attendance and locations, closed early and hung signs in their windows in support of poor Jimmy Patino. The irony wasn't lost on Charlie that in the same day he'd seen two signs: one in a watering hole's window that said, "WE'RE PRAYING FOR YOU" and the other on a printed flyer announcing "CHURCH PICNIC—FREE BEER."

He'd spent the last few days blaming himself for not following Mack and felt like a coward for not defending his bud the way Brad defended Sarah. He hadn't been Mack's friend when he really needed one, and he vowed that if the chance emerged again, he wouldn't show cowardice twice. The story of Peter promising Jesus he wouldn't betray him flashed into his mind.

He had a dream that night that Mack died and he was asked to give the eulogy. In it, he lost control when one of the onlookers called him out on all the things he could've done for Mack but didn't. The heckler ridiculed him while all others in attendance, including Kurt and Barry Ray, watched him with scornful and disillusioned eyes. He softly wept and kept repeating the words "I'm sorry," only to watch Kurt put his head down in shame. Then he woke up drenched in sweat.

Why didn't I go after him?

When he called to check in on Mack, Kurt laid no guilt on him whatsoever and said it'd be best to give Mack time to recover. A day later Charlie walked over to the house with a few packs of new baseball cards to cheer him up, and Sheriff Thrower met him at the door. He said Mack needed rest and no visitors would be permitted.

Sheriff Thrower questioned Jason Hand and the rest of the legion team about what'd happened just before Mack's attack, but that's where it ended. Jason was confirmed to be with his mother in the grocery store at the time of Jimmy's murder, and was quite shaken up by the coincidence of events. The conclusion was that Jason was a punk, who got what he deserved, but had no involvement in Mack's assault.

The following day, Friday, Brad called at around one o'clock and asked to meet. Charlie was happy for the invitation, so he hugged his mom goodbye and hopped on his bike, headed for the car wash parking lot. There, Brad gave him the whole scoop on what Sheriff Thrower had revealed to his son about the investigation.

"Mack's pretty banged up. Three cracked ribs, broken arm, busted nose...someone really did a number on the guy."

"Who does your dad think did it?" Charlie asked as they started walking down First Street in the evidently not-so-safe neighborhood. The heat was already making them both sweat.

"You mean who attacked Mack?" Brad asked as he kicked a pebble on the sidewalk while wiping the sweat off the bridge of his nose beneath his sunglasses. The clouds blocked the sun every few minutes, but when they didn't, it beat down on them both.

"What else would I be talking about?"

"Chill out, man. I didn't know if you meant Mack or Jimmy," Brad replied. It made Charlie frown. Brad was right. There had been two crimes committed, both against people his age, give or take, that had resulted in a severe beating or death. At that moment the enormity of it all hit him like a freight train.

"I'm sorry. I didn't mean to snap."

"No problem man. Tough times."

He nodded and Brad went on.

"Dad really doesn't know. Mack told him he got back from baseball practice and cried on his bed for a while."

"How long?"

"Maybe ten minutes. Then he heard a noise near the front door and got up to check it out. Before he even got there a guy grabbed him from behind and started beating on him."

"An adult? Did Mack give a description? Did he see his face?"

"He didn't see much. Said the guy was in all black, and had on a black mask over his face. Wasn't a lot of time to look for more details."

"A black sweatshirt, T-shirt, or what? Did he have anything on his skin? Did Mack say anything about how tall he was? Didn't he see anything?"

31

"You remember this is Mack we're talking about, right? He doesn't exactly handle pressure well to begin with. And the poor guy got jumped from behind. He didn't have the time or thought to look for that sort of thing before the guy pulled a cloth over his head and started beating him to a bloody pulp. Hell, I don't think *I'd* be able to remember much."

Right again, Charlie thought. "Is he...okay? I haven't gotten to see him. The newspapers don't say."

"I haven't seen him either. I think my dad and Kurt are the only ones who have. They wouldn't let the stupid reporters in. What do you think *The Germantown Sun* would do if it got a picture? Dad put a guard by his house to make sure we don't find out."

"Good move." Charlie had observed the sheriff's deputies sitting in a car ten hours a day, eating a few boxes of doughnuts while supposedly protecting Mack.

"As for Mack, if you mean will he survive, yeah. It's not life threatening. But will he ever be the same again, your guess is as good as mine."

"How long was the guy there?"

"I'm not sure how much Mack remembered, or if what he thought he remembered was true, but he told my dad it seemed like a minute or two. Who knows though? A few seconds of that would feel like an hour."

"No doubt. I bet Jason felt like the whipping you gave him lasted an hour."

Brad smiled. Charlie laughed in return and the two shared the kind of levity-filled moment that their summers had been full of until that dreadful day Barry Ray was taken into custody. It was the first time they'd laughed since that happened six days ago. Charlie ripped a leaf off a low-hanging branch of an oak tree, crushing it into his palm.

"They find any fingerprints?"

"No, and they dusted. Said the guy must've used gloves. They would've found something by now if he hadn't."

The moment of escaping into laughter was over; it was back to the harsh reality. The clouds shifted and again offered temporary asylum from the summer blaze, so Brad took off his sunglasses. After he cleaned them thoroughly and wiped the beads from his forehead, Charlie returned to questioning.

"Any news from Barry Ray?"

"Nada. Keeps saying he was playing Wiffle Ball with Mack, and there's nothing that proves that wrong. My dad talked to Douglas Patino, and he said he didn't know what Jimmy was up to that day. He was at work, his wife was shopping, and when they both left Jimmy was still sleeping. No idea what he had planned."

"They were pretty torn up I bet."

"How could you not be? Even though...well, you know the Patinos. They didn't like him as much as they like Scotty. Everyone knows that. But even so, how could you not be sad. Still their son, even if he was a jerk."

"Yeah...anything else?"

Brad stopped walking and looked up at the sky before turning back.

"There's one more thing, Charlie. Look man, you know that when I tell you this stuff, about what's going on with the case and all...you know that's big-time Coach's Corner, right?"

"Coach's Corner" was a phrase Brad's dad had coined almost five years ago. He'd take Brad to various high school sporting events—baseball in the spring, basketball in the winter, soccer in the fall—and make comments about the players and coaches that weren't usually flattering. He'd say things like "that kid isn't worth two cents," or "they need a coach who knows his ass from a hole in the ground." The blunt opinions were never politically correct, and Sheriff Thrower was an elected official. The small town gossip factory would eat him up if it got out. He'd never work again.

But for some reason, rather than simply not make the comments to his son at all, Sheriff Thrower stressed the importance of keeping it between them. Whenever he prefaced a conversation with

"Coach's Corner" Brad knew what it meant. He was sworn to secrecy that he'd never repeat it. Brad shared the phrase with him, and it stuck into their adulthood.

"You don't even need to say it. Of course it's Coach's Corner."

He looked him in the eye when he said it, and Brad returned the stare. They never joked about Coach's Corner. It was a sign of respect to be included in conversations that required it, and both knew if they were ever kicked out of Coach's Corner, they wouldn't get back in.

"Just wanted to make sure." Brad put his arm around him. "I gotta get home for a few chores. You up for something tonight? Maybe the bowling alley?"

"Sure," he replied, welcoming the idea of spending some time out and trying to stay distracted from Barry Ray and Mack.

Then, Charlie was alone again. He felt empty and lonely. But as bad as he felt, it wouldn't compare to what was coming.

8

Charlie trudged down the side streets, looking at the ground and letting his mind feel overwhelmed. So much was happening in such little time: Mack's injuries and the mysterious attacker in black, his inability to see him, Barry Ray sitting in jail, Kurt dealing with it all, the tension with his dad, and the fear of the unknown. Suddenly, baseball and what he would do with his life after it were of little importance.

He walked past the bowling alley, one of the few social settings in town, and thought about going in. Maybe if he bowled a frame or two, or talked to some folks who might be inside, he'd feel better. Maybe he wouldn't blame himself for Mack, Jimmy Patino would suddenly come back to life, and all of this would go away. Maybe it was just all a bad dream and he'd wake up in a puddle of his own drool at the card table, and Barry Ray would give him a noogie for drifting off.

It was just as he decided not to go in that he heard the whisper.

"Charlie?"

He turned his head slightly, convinced he'd heard his name, but not able to verify it. He suddenly felt frightened in the oversized gravel parking lot, the sun beating down on his neck. No one was there as he scanned the empty lot, so he made his way around to the side of the bowling alley. Nothing. Then he checked around back. Nothing. *Hearing things already*, he thought to himself before turning back to walk home.

Then again.

"*Charlie.*"

He walked to the other side of the red-brick building desperately searching for the source of the whisper. Someone was messing with him, and his primal instinct was to lash out aggressively, the way Brad did at Jason Hand. He gritted his teeth and clenched his fists, ready for a fight.

"*What?* Here I am. Show yourself, you coward!" he yelled. He couldn't care less what anyone watching might think as he kicked the rocks and screamed into the air.

"Shh. Keep it down. I'm over here," a soft, almost muted voice said from near a tree twenty feet away by the edge of the fence. He followed the voice until he spotted Shane Littleton standing next to the large maple, staring at him through thick glasses.

"Come with me, okay Charlie?" Shane said.

He followed Shane towards the back entrance of the American Legion, connected to, but isolated from, the boisterous bowling alley filled with rowdy teens. There was a quiet bar with a small kitchen, inhabited only by the manager, waitress, and two locals who spent way too much time there. While the bowling alley was layered with fluorescent lights providing an optimal competitive environment, the legion was so dim that he felt his eyes dilate when he walked inside.

Shane walked to the table farthest from the bar, by itself in the corner against the wall beneath a window. The legion hall was in the basement, so you had to walk up the stairs to get to the bowling alley and main entrance. The concrete floor was hard and sticky in contrast to the carpeted bowling alley, and as they sat down at the four-person high top, he couldn't help but wonder what Shane was going to say.

Shane was the younger brother of Shaw Littleton, the freshman whose milk money Jimmy Patino had taken the previous year. Much like Shaw, and Mack for that matter, Shane didn't project a lot of self-confidence. At twelve years old and heading into seventh grade, he was so scrawny, so rail-thin that he looked emaciated.

Shane's long hair didn't curl the way he wanted it to. Instead it just hung down near his shoulders like an unwashed mop head. He got picked on for that. He didn't play sports, but word on the street was that he was a genius. Blew his peers away in math and science. Got picked on for that too.

Shane was wearing baggy blue jeans and a blue-and-yellow striped T-shirt. It seemed much too hot for long pants, but Charlie had never seen Shane wear shorts.

Shane looked at him through those thick black glasses before taking them off and rubbing his eyes. He was nervous, like he was trying to muster up the courage to say something. Charlie didn't say anything, trying to figure out what they were doing in the basement legion hall, while at the same time trying to conceal his own fear. Finally, Shane broke the awkward silence.

"I just didn't know who else to talk to. I have to talk to someone. And I saw you...and I...I need to talk to someone."

His breathing was shallow and quick, and he wrung his hands nervously as his knees bounced up and down.

"No problem, bud. Sorry I yelled in the parking lot. I didn't mean to. What's up?"

Shane looked at him and took another long, deep breath.

"There's no way Barry Ray killed Jimmy Patino."

9

"How do you know that?"

Shane Littleton didn't respond, other than to stare back with petrified, moist brown eyes. He jerked his head around as if on a swivel when he heard a sound from behind. His breathing hadn't slowed down, and he wiped his drenched face with his hand before dragging it against his jeans to dry off the sweat.

"I know you're smart, Shane. Maybe too smart. But you're not the police. I know you want to help, but making stuff up isn't—"

"I saw Barry Ray the morning Jimmy died. He didn't kill anyone. I watched him the whole time they said Jimmy was being murdered."

Charlie's mind was already racing, but now his poor heart was thumping so loud he could swear he heard it. Squinting his eyes in an untrusting, skeptical way, he considered the possibility. Barry Ray was innocent? And Shane could set him free? Could everything go back to normal after all?

"How do you know when Jimmy was killed?"

"The paper said between nine and ten. That Jimmy Patino was killed between nine and ten. I was watching Barry Ray that whole time."

"You watched him for an hour? What were you doing?"

"I was in the cornfields, doing my bug collection for this book I'm reading. It's called *Common Insects*. I'm trying to learn more about a few bugs' anatomies."

Shane got made fun of for that, too.

"What the hell kind of bug were you looking for in a cornfield?"

"There are lot of bugs that like sweet corn, like stink bugs and corn rootworm beetles."

He didn't doubt Shane was doing a bug collection in the middle of summer, sadly enough. Twelve years old and the kid was reading

38

a book about insects for fun, trying to study their anatomy, but the shoe fit pretty well.

"What happened, Shane?"

"I was out in the cornfield collecting, and I saw Barry Ray pull up in his truck. He was smoking weed. I didn't want him to see me watching him—"

"Spying on him, you mean?"

"I...I guess. I didn't want him to know I saw him smoking. He'd beat me to a pulp."

Charlie nodded at the salient point. Barry Ray wouldn't do time, not in Germantown, but he wouldn't want Shane to see him breaking the law, either.

"I didn't know what to do, so I hid. Now I wish I hadn't, but I did. Stayed low in the corn and watched him. And I'm telling you, Barry Ray was there the whole time. I know because he got there at 8:33 and didn't leave until 10:12. I saw the numbers on my watch." Shane held up his right arm and pointed to the Casio digital watch with his left.

"Why were you checking your watch?"

"My mother was picking me up at ten, and I had no idea how late I would be. I'm telling you, Barry Ray was there until 10:12, just smoking his joint."

"What cornfield?"

"On Herman Church Road out past Rose Hurtle, towards Albers," he said.

Charlie knew that cornfield well, having worked there a few summers earlier. The 500-acre farm had been in Farmer Kuhn's family for years and was a few miles east of town, the opposite direction of where Jimmy Patino's body was found. Halfway to harvest time, there were rows and rows of tall, light brown cornfields; plenty of opportunity for Shane to remain concealed. It was ten minutes away as the crow flies, another five or ten to get there by car.

"How far from Barry Ray were you?"

"Maybe fifteen feet," Shane answered, followed by a long sigh. "Close enough to get a real good look."

He considered each of the possibilities he could imagine one by one. Could the autopsy be incorrect, and Jimmy's time of death actually be either before nine or after ten? That was the most unlikely scenario. Aside from the fact it required the coroner to have made a huge mistake, it didn't make sense. The body was found just after ten-thirty by a father and son riding bikes, so if Barry Ray had pulled the trigger, he would've had to do so as early as eight o'clock to be in the cornfield smoking by 8:33.

Perhaps Shane didn't really see Barry Ray. Maybe it was someone who looked like him. The problem with that theory was that Barry Ray had a very distinct presentation, and it would be hard for Shane to mistake someone else for him. The bushy goatee, the long dark hair, the busting torso. Charlie couldn't think of anyone who looked even remotely like Barry Ray. And, Shane knew Barry Ray. At only fifteen feet away, it didn't seem likely to be a case of mistaken identity.

It was possible Shane was lying to him, but why? Maybe he was mad about Jimmy taking his brother's lunch money and wanted Barry Ray to go free? Maybe he thought Jimmy deserved it? Maybe he just wanted to spare Barry Ray spending time behind bars. All of that seemed like a stretch, but if true, why tell him instead of the police? Was it because the police would be more likely to spot the lie? Was Shane assuming it would get to Sheriff Thrower anyway because he and Brad were best friends?

It was also way out of character for Shane to lie. Despite having been made fun of for doing so in some instances, the kid always told the truth. And if it was all a lie, if Shane was making it up, the kid was going to be the next Tom Hanks because he came across as genuinely frightened and nervous as anyone Charlie had ever seen. Bottom line: Shane lying just didn't pass the sniff test.

However, if Shane was telling the truth, then the police had made a terrible mistake and there was a major mess to straighten out. It also meant Barry Ray, as well as Mack, had lied to the police about where he was. But why would Barry Ray lie about his whereabouts if they could actually prove his innocence? He was breaking the law by smoking pot, but that wasn't even in the same ballpark. From that perspective, Shane telling the truth didn't pass the sniff test either.

"Why are you telling me all of this? Why didn't you tell Sheriff Thrower? Why didn't you tell anyone?"

Shane paused and then looked down at the floor, squinting as if searching for something. For a moment, the long pause made Charlie think the truth was finally about to come out.

"I did. I told Mack as soon as I saw him. And I was going to tell Sheriff Thrower, but..."

"But what?" Charlie replied, rotating his wrist to elicit a quicker response.

"Right after I told Mack, I was walking back to my house and this guy pulled up beside me. He jumped out of his truck and pushed me into the alley behind the IGA. Then he pushed me against the wall and told me that if I told anyone about seeing Barry Ray, he'd beat my brother and me to death. Then he...he pulled out a knife and held it to my throat. He said he'd be watching, then walked back to the truck and drove away."

The look in Shane's eyes implored that this was no lie. Charlie noticed his lips were trembling, and his hands were shaking like a whole body spasm.

The IGA was the lone grocery store in town, right on Main Street with only 6,000 square feet and one checkout lane. It was impressive how much food Mr. and Mrs. Greeson had piled into five small aisles, but it was still only a fraction of the supply compared to the Target or Walmart thirty minutes away in O'Fallon.

Charlie used to play hide-and-seek near the IGA's loading bay in the back with Mack, Brad, and Barry Ray, and knew it well. He pictured Shane standing there when a knife was being held to his throat, and he no longer doubted his story. Fear spoke truth, even if he was too naïve to believe it at first.

"Was the guy wearing a mask?" he asked.

"No."

"So you saw his face?"

"Yeah, pretty well. I think I've seen him before but I don't know his name."

"What's he look like?"

"Dark hair, short. Clean-shaven. Kind of normal weight and height, maybe six feet tall and 200 pounds."

"How old?"

"About Barry Ray's age. Maybe a little older."

That surprised him and was encouraging. If it was someone about Barry Ray's age and someone Shane had seen before, there were a finite number of possibilities.

"Did you get a good enough look that you'd recognize him if you saw him again?"

"I'll never forget his face."

He started thinking about how he could get his hands on a bunch of yearbooks, from both their school and nearby schools, over the past few years. It felt too simple: have Shane flip through all the pages, recognize the perp, call the cops, pick him up.

Everyone knew everyone in Germantown, and half the people were related to each other throughout Clinton County. Between the churches and bars, most folks saw each other in at least one of the two, and the majority were at both at least once a week. High schoolers and those who'd graduated in the last three years had three major hangouts: the roller rink a half hour away, the movie theater fifteen minutes away, and the car wash right in town. The bowling alley closed too early and there was nothing else.

The car wash was the highest probability. It was at the corner of the only four-way intersection in town. A candy machine and soda machine sat next to three open car bays with adjoining hoses and vacuums. Teenagers parked their cars, congregated, and pretended to be drinking soda from the machine. Of course, the coolers full of beer in the trunks were the beverage of choice.

All three places were highly popular with kids too, including Shane's class, but the car wash was that much closer. Once they had the perp's picture, he was confident they'd get a name. At that point it would be time to get Sheriff Thrower involved.

It was unfortunate that Shane didn't know the guy's name. However, if he didn't go to the same school, it also made sense. That's where Charlie hoped the limited hangout spots would come in handy—maybe Shane would recognize his face and be able to point him out.

As he contemplated everything in the quiet, almost mobster-style setting of the American Legion, with its dim lighting and 1970s décor, he noticed Shane looking around incessantly. He turned his head to sway his neck from side to side, and even looked up and down as though expecting someone to jump out from the ceiling. He was still sweating, though he'd refused the cold Pepsi Charlie offered to buy him.

"Are you okay, bud?"

Shane looked back after replacing the glasses over his nose and sniffing to clear it out. He coughed, and took a few deep breaths. "Yeah, I'm just...look, I'm...I'm s-sorry I g-got you involved. I just didn't know what to d-do...He said he'd kill Shaw, and I...I don't know."

"You've got to lay low, Shane. Keep to yourself and let me see what I can do. Let's get out of here. I'll get in touch with you soon."

"That knife. It was so big."

"Stop talking! It's not doing you or me any good. Try to relax. Head home and try to relax. I'll find you when I've got something."

"Okay."

They got up and headed for the same back door they'd entered. Charlie didn't want folks in the bowling alley to see Shane and start asking what was wrong, or for anyone to see them together at all for that matter. When they reached the door, he put up his hand to suggest that he go out first.

Before he did, Shane grabbed his arm.

"Charlie. Please don't tell anyone what I said." He looked so young and weak, his bony arms visibly shaking and eyes wide.

"I won't...for now. I promise. We'll figure what happens later, later."

When he opened the door and stepped outside into the light, the bright sun blinded him and he had to hold his arm up to block it as he slowly ascended the stairs.

His first thought as his vision returned was to tell himself that this mysterious perp was just trying to scare Shane as opposed to actually hurting him. Shane was clearly terrified, which meant the perp had accomplished his goal.

Then he remembered Barry Ray, accused of a crime he apparently didn't commit. But *someone* had killed Jimmy Patino, and someone had threatened Shane for exposing evidence that would prove Barry Ray innocent. Could it be the same person? Maybe even be the same person who attacked Mack as well?

The lives of a twelve-year-old and his brother had suddenly been jettisoned into Charlie's hands, or so it felt. And he'd allowed it, without a clue of what to do next.

10

Three days after Shane spilled his secret, Charlie was no further along on figuring out who was involved or what to do. Mack had gotten marginally better physically, but out of an abundance of caution, visitors were still not allowed, Kurt turned reclusive and disconnected, and Barry Ray had spent 72 hours locked up awaiting the legal proceedings. Formal charges were forthcoming.

Charlie had visited the Clinton County Jail in Carlyle two years ago with a service project for church. He remembered the brown rust on the bars and diffuse stains on the mattress. The space smelled like urine, and then there was the dirty water that dripped into a small puddle in the far corner of the cell. It originated from a leaky roof authorities appeared to be in no rush to repair. He remembered how much that reoccurring splash had pierced the awkward silence.

He'd gotten copies of three different high school yearbooks from local libraries, spanning a total of seven years' worth of graduating classes, using Barry Ray's as the midpoint. Germantown had no high school, so he started with Central and Mater Dei Catholic high schools, both in Breese, as well as Carlyle High School some fifteen miles northeast.

Unfortunately, after looking at every single male picture carefully, Shane was adamant that he didn't see the person who threatened him. It was possible the guy went to a different high school further away, was older than Shane had guessed, or had a habit of missing picture day. Perhaps he was homeschooled or lived in another state, and Shane took him for someone else he knew.

Regardless, it turned out to be a dead end. He was no further along than he was before they started. The Sherlock Homes detective squad wouldn't be calling anytime soon.

45

According to both the papers and Brad, the police hadn't made much progress in the Jimmy Patino murder investigation or anything else. Barry Ray had been offered a court-appointed attorney and was in custody for a crime he didn't commit, there was no mention of Mack's assault in the news or paper, and in general the small town rumor mill was outdueling the discussion of facts. Several folks had already accepted Barry Ray's guilt, and the longer he spent behind bars the easier that conclusion was to believe.

Mack remained secluded in his house with no visitors welcome. Brad and Charlie tried to act normal but didn't know what that looked like anymore. Two of their four friends were either locked up or recovering from a beating.

His mom had insisted he distance himself from Brad, and a heated argument or two had taken place. Charlie knew she was caring for her son the best way she knew how, which translated to stressing that he stay away from Mack and remain in the house, but he felt the urge to fight for his freedom. Barry Ray was actually in jail; he sure as hell wasn't going to act like he was too. Faced with his passion, his mother backed off and they hugged, then the cycle repeated itself in the next couple days. At least his father was still out of town.

He thought about quitting baseball. He was having a hard time having fun on the field, and really the only reason he hadn't quit already was because of Brad. But he could sense Brad felt the same way. Everything had changed.

While sipping a Ski, a caffeine-charged citrus soda bottled in Tennessee and among the most popular drinks in Clinton County, he realized the time had come. He could no longer keep the information Shane had shared to himself. The decision seemed to land on him unexpectedly and with a great deal of unwelcome weight. But the truth was, it wasn't helping to keep it a secret. Barry Ray was no closer to freedom, and Charlie knew it was time to stop playing junior detective. If he waited any longer, it might be too late.

He slipped on his shoes and walked over to Brad's house to find Sheriff Thrower.

The place could've been a study of opposites. He walked up the settled stairs to the modest white home with olive green trim. The shutters were old and full of cracks, yet the grass was magnificently mowed and edged—as were a majority of the lawns in Germantown—something residents took very seriously.

The metal knocker was freshly polished, but the welcome mat on the floor had the same rugged "THROWER" he'd seen all his life. He'd been in this house so many times it felt like a second home, but this visit was different. It felt like venturing into the unknown.

He knew Brad was working at the bakery and knocked on the recently replaced front door hoping Sarah would answer in one of her short sizzler skirts. He briefly pictured her infectious smile before yanking himself back to reality, and realized when Sheriff Thrower opened the door that his palms were sweating.

Despite Sheriff Thrower's warm hello and invitation to come inside, when he told him about Shane, the sheriff seemed almost apathetic. He didn't try to conceal his frustration as Sheriff Thrower continued to quietly listen and nod his head, but his response felt like lip service. At one point Charlie saw him roll his eyes, prompting Charlie to squirm in the uncomfortable wooden chair at the kitchen table.

"Charlie," Sheriff Thrower said softly, "I know you care about Barry Ray, but this isn't the way to help him."

"Sir, I'm telling you the truth. Shane said the guy had him up against the wall—"

"I know you're upset, son. Barry Ray and Mack are your friends. Brad's my son, and we've talked about how hard this is for you guys. But that doesn't make Shane Littleton's story true."

"I didn't believe him at first. But sir...the way he said it, the way his face looked. He was telling the truth."

"Charlie, is this the same Shane who's looked up to you for years? Who wants you to like him? Wants to impress you?"

47

He nodded his head in frustration, knowing where the Sheriff was going and deciding to head it off.

"Sheriff Thrower, this kid doesn't lie. All I'm asking you to do is check into it. What if he's telling the truth? What if Barry Ray—"

"Charlie, I appreciate you sharing and your willingness to help. Have you spoken to your mom and dad about this as well?"

Sheriff Thrower's freshly cut hair was amongst the shortest in town, yet he ran his hand through it as though it were thick and lustrous. The sheriff offered a willing expression, a compassionate glance that was supposed to convey empathy. Instead, it just pissed him off.

"Look, Sheriff Thrower, I'm telling you something really important. All you have to do is look into it. Barry Ray didn't do this! Talk to Mack and see if Shane—"

"Of course I will, Charlie," Sheriff Thrower replied, holding up his hand.

Stopped mid-sentence, Charlie snorted and shifted his weight. "You will?"

"Of course, Charlie. That's my job, as you've pointed out. You've brought a serious allegation to me. I'll investigate it right away. And I hope it's true. I was just trying to prepare you for the fact that my experience tells me it's probably not. It's so easy for a young man like Shane Littleton to tell you, a person he idolizes, something he knows will give you hope."

He didn't respond, suddenly deflated.

"But rest assured, I'll speak with young Shane and get his statement, then I'll see if I can find someone who matches that description. We will look into it right away, son."

He nodded slowly, still looking into the sheriff's compassionate eyes.

"Now, can you do something for me?" Sheriff Thrower asked.

He nodded.

"Let me do the police work here. I appreciate that you tried to get some old yearbooks and handle this yourself. It's commendable, but this is my job. You have to understand that even if you had found something, there are very specific rules that define how we are allowed to gather evidence. Rules that I had to go to school for a long time to learn. If you break them, any evidence you gather could be inadmissible in a court of law. So please, Charlie, leave the investigating to me."

"Yes, sir." He was quite relieved to be given the order from law enforcement. He knew he was out of his league, which was the reason he went to Sheriff Thrower in the first place.

"Good, son. Run on home and focus on your summer. I know it's hard, but try to enjoy it. You guys won't be eighteen forever, and I don't want you to miss out on more than you already have."

"Yes, sir."

"And Charlie?" he asked, as he opened the door.

"Yes?"

"Please let me know if I can help you. I know your father is out of town a lot, and sometimes man-to-man conversation is what a guy needs. Coach's Corner."

11

Charlie watched Brad walk out of the barbershop forty-five long minutes after he'd arrived. Jerry, The Barber Czar, had the gift of gab, and preferred his conversations with customers to drag on until quite literally both parties had nothing else to say. There were any number of ways to accomplish such a feat, but it always involved a never-ending supply of questions, recycled jokes, and obligatory laughs. Depending on the year and how good the team was, Central or Mater Dei basketball got woven in as well. Brad looked loose, much to his envy. His best friend could've even been whistling.

Charlie cracked his knuckles, fidgeting as he pressed his back against the jagged bark of a tree in front of a Jim's Formal Wear across the street. The sky was overcast, so he removed his sunglasses and clipped them on his T-shirt. When Brad picked up the pace walking down the sidewalk, he cut diagonally across Main Street to catch him.

"Hey man," he said innocently as their eyes met.

"Hey, Charlie! How's it hanging? Haven't seen you in a few days. What've you been up to?" Brad asked like he didn't have a care in the world.

"Been lying low. My mom needed some help around the house." It was a lie and he was near certain Brad knew it.

"That's cool. What's up?"

"Can we talk for a minute?"

"Sure."

"It might not be something you want to hear."

Brad shook his head and rolled his eyes. "Brothers forever, remember? C'mon, spit it out," he replied. Then Brad popped open a can of Skoal Long Cut Cherry chewing tobacco and put a plug into his mouth, signifying he was ready to listen. Baseball had him hooked on the stuff and he always chewed it whenever he wanted to concentrate.

He laid it all on Brad, everything from Shane's story to the yearbooks, to his visiting Brad's dad, to his theory that Jimmy's killer might be the guy who beat up Mack and threatened Shane. It felt good to get it off his chest. And who better to dump it on.

Brothers forever.

Brad listened with seemingly deep concentration. He wasn't an academic all-star, but he had an astuteness that always seemed to show up at the right time, an impressive level of common sense. It didn't translate to Math and English, but Brad had more street smarts than he did. His best friend looked him right in the eye the whole time, even when he turned his neck to spit on the ground.

Brad kept quiet and remained stoic the whole time. Charlie couldn't get a read on what he was thinking. Part of him thought he might end up like Jason Hand when he told Brad about visiting his father when he wasn't there. Brad's exploding attack on Jason still mystified him. He'd never seen such aggression out of Brad. But even when he talked about visiting Sheriff Thrower, Brad remained emotionless.

When he finished, Brad looked back at him with his new haircut, the brown hair neatly trimmed around the ears. It wasn't nearly as short as Sheriff Thrower's, but shorter than most their age. He also had visible, dark stubble along his chin and neck.

"Sorry I didn't tell you sooner, man."

"Why not just let my dad and the cops take care of it now?" Brad asked. Reasonable question, as its answer hadn't been covered in his recap. He'd omitted that one little part. He didn't think it was realistic, and he trusted Brad through and through, but he decided to err on the side of caution.

"He's so busy that I—"

"Cut the crap, Charlie. That's his job. I know law enforcement ain't exactly Dragnet in Germantown, but sell that story to someone who's buying. What's the real reason?"

"Okay..." He paused. "It just seemed like..."

"Like what, dude?"

"Like right off the bat, he didn't think Shane was telling the truth. He jumped right to it. So I'm worried he won't really do much with it."

Brad studied him closely. The slight nod of his head indicated he was more satisfied with that answer, but his squinty eyebrows sure revealed skepticism.

"All I'm asking is we do a little checking on the side. Your dad's got all these rules he has to follow because he's a cop. All we'd be doing is walking around—"

"Spying on people."

"I just want to check out Shane's story. These are our buddies, you know? Barry Ray and Mack. And I really don't think Shane was lying. I understand why your dad does, but he doesn't know Shane. This is *Shane Littleton* we're talking about! You really think he made it up? If your dad thinks Shane's full of it and doesn't really check it out, then Barry Ray pays the price. And if he does check it out, then great. We back off right then and there."

"So basically, you don't think my dad will do his job and you want me to help you do it?"

Brad was testing him. They both new the hard answer was yes, but Brad wanted to hear him say it. He sensed that Brad would go along, their friendship would make it tough to say no, but he wasn't going to make it easy.

Brad stared back, shaking his head and tsking.

"Brother...if what Shane is saying is true, Barry Ray didn't kill anyone. But he's locked up right now. I know us checking into things might be wrong, but not that wrong."

"Okay. I'll go along...for now. I don't know what you think we'll find, but you're my brother from another mother. We better keep this one Coach's Corner. My dad finds out and you'll be looking at two homicides."

Under normal circumstances they both would've chuckled, but it didn't feel quite right. He nodded slightly, while closing his eyes. Brad continued.

"One other thing...if we find something...*anything*...that the professionals could actually use, we get it to him right away."

"Without him knowing it came from us."

Brad returned the eyes-closed nod.

Part of him felt like a hypocrite. He'd told Sheriff Thrower a few days earlier he'd leave the investigating to the law. But after Barry Ray was brought before a judge following the 72-hour holding period, he'd been formally charged and was now awaiting a trial. It wouldn't likely happen anytime soon, but the idea of Barry Ray rotting in a cell because Shane's story got dismissed too soon wasn't right. Guilt trumped hypocrisy like a right bower in euchre, and they shook hands to seal the deal. There was no turning back now.

12

Two minds were supposedly better than one, but Charlie and Brad hadn't proved that saying true.

Their goal was simple, yet elusive: figure out what the hell to do next. They had decided to join forces in breaking the law to play detective behind Brad's father's back—an idea that grew increasingly unappealing as time passed—but they didn't know where to start.

They sat in the bowling alley booth eating nachos and sipping Ski for an hour, and then bowled a few frames in between "thinking sessions." It was a lot of talking, but they learned they didn't have much to say on the subject of what to do. It was early enough in the morning that aside from Terry, an over-aged, grouchy clerk who sat at the desk with a newspaper and never spoke unless spoken to, there was no one else there. At least they had privacy.

"Look, we just don't have that many options," Brad summarized. "We don't need to follow Shane, Barry Ray's locked up, Mack's at his house recovering, my dad's at the police station like every other day, and we don't know who threatened Shane. If it even happened at all, which we still don't know for sure."

He nodded his head. "So what does that mean?"

"Well, who's left?" he asked. Charlie then gave the only answer he could think of.

And that led them to the Pine Springs Golf Course.

* * *

Pine Springs was an eighteen-hole public golf course that tried desperately to act like a private a country club. Streets such as Country Club Drive and Golfer's Paradise Lane lined the perimeter, and the main entrance featured a large, hand-carved wooden sign claiming it was "Clinton County's Premier Golf Course." A white fence, dotted with whimsical zinnias, and perfectly manicured grass surrounding well-watered putting greens suggested it was in a class all its own.

It was only a few miles from Germantown and there weren't any other courses within thirty minutes by car. Charlie and Brad had snuck onto it through a patch of trees next to a house on the par-three third hole and played through the ninth more times than either could count on two hands. But this time they left their clubs and brought binoculars. They had no intention of staying long, just long enough to confirm that Douglas Patino and his wife were there. They trudged through the woods that wove into and out of the community-centric golf course until they finally saw Douglas standing on the green in khaki slacks and a polo covered in tiny lobsters. The ensemble screamed "18 holes on Nantucket!"

He was with three other golfers and their caddies. Charlie marveled at how pretty the course was every time he saw it, and today it seemed especially surreal. The foursome was on the fifth hole, a long par four, and the slight breeze gave a cooling sensation that Saturday morning. Caddies weren't mandatory, but Douglas always used one and encouraged everyone he played with to use them as well. With caddies came image, and with image came status.

Douglas owned several businesses around town that Charlie was aware of, including the car wash, a landscaping company, a car repair shop, and the pizza market restaurant, but the good people of Germantown didn't hesitate to speculate that his business interests didn't end there. The gossip factory suggested he was also involved in various industries that ranged from the shadier side to the outright illegal. It was common knowledge that he was by far the richest man in Germantown, and that he owned roughly 25 percent of the town's real estate.

Douglas was also on the Germantown Board of Trustees, a distinguished member of the American Legion, some sort of elected official on the town's council, and a healthy and revered donor to several charities across the state.

He didn't hide his affluence, either. He ate at the fanciest restaurants on The Hill in St. Louis, tipped the gas station workers with twenty-dollar bills, and paid good money to have his lawn professionally cut, which bothered the Germantown residents more than his presumed crookedness. He also played golf. Lots and lots of golf.

Charlie had caddied for Douglas a few times. Douglas didn't pick up balls that went in the sand, teed off each hole with a brand new ball, had the most expensive clubs Charlie had ever seen, and made a conscious effort to out-dress everyone. Today, Douglas was the only one in the foursome not wearing shorts.

All that and he still couldn't shoot ninety to save his life.

Douglas's short, blondish hair was immaculately combed and his green eyes matched the collar on his seafood-emblazoned shirt. His face was clean shaven and tanned. He didn't look strong, but he did look fit. The kind of six-foot body one got by playing golf and tennis all one's life, rather than football and wrestling. His teeth were bright white, almost unnaturally so, and his smile was wide and contagious. When Douglas Patino smiled, other folks did too. And not always because they wanted to.

Charlie and Brad were lying flat on their stomachs under a tall tree that overlooked the fairway. It was a roughly twenty-foot descent with a significant slope, and it was out of bounds on the course. Twigs and bugs fell on their bare necks from the trees above, but the shade protected them from the hot sun, and the branches provided cover. Their bikes rested up against other trees, and they both were lying down on their elbows looking through binoculars at the foursome that walked from the green to the sixth hole's tee box.

"See him out there?" he asked softly as he passed the binoculars.

"Of course I see him. It's a league and they play every week. Of course he's there. What are we still doing here?"

"See how happy he seems?"

56

Douglas was telling jokes, drinking a beer, and laughing with the other players. He looked carefree and euphoric.

"So he's having some laughs. It is a golf course, man."

"His son was just killed, Brad. Would your dad—or even *my* dad—be at the golf course if that happened to us?"

"So because he's playing golf he must've killed his own son?"

"I didn't say that. But don't you think it's weird that the guy's acting like nothing happened. It hasn't been that long."

"Maybe he's just trying to move on."

Charlie took the binoculars back. Something didn't sit well. When not hitting, Douglas looked too relaxed, too comfortable. He was yapping and telling jokes and smiling the entire time, making big waving arm gestures with a shit-eating grin on his face, evoking what looked to Charlie like not-so-genuine laughter from the other golfers and caddies. Brad finally admitted he thought it was odd too, but that it wasn't enough for him to suspect Jimmy's dad of anything. He thought of what he'd once heard: *People grieve in different ways.*

They walked through the woods around the perimeter of the golf course towards the restaurant made to look like a Five-Star establishment. No casual clothes were allowed. Each table had a fine white tablecloth with a candle at the center and elegant dinnerware. Servers were dressed in vests and ties, and the menus were adorned with fancy cursive script that made them harder to read. The food wasn't all that good, but that was hardly a prerequisite of appearing like a country club dining room.

And there she sat. Mrs. JoAnn Patino, the blonde-haired trophy wife with a sassy attitude and a body that more than made up for it. Brad, Mack, Barry Ray, and Charlie had all made comments about her around the poker table that they'd be embarrassed to have their mothers hear, but her beauty was impossible to ignore: 5'8" or so, thin at the waist. Big round breasts. Long, tan, smooth legs. And a mouth with a set of lips to die for. She looked in a lot of ways like the woman from *Caddyshack* and flaunted what she had.

She was considerably younger than Douglas, and of course the talk around town was that she was a gold digger. Charlie didn't care, nor would he blame Douglas if it were true. JoAnn was that attractive.

She too was smiling, smiling like there was nothing to frown about. Smiling like her son wasn't dead and a teenager hadn't been arrested for his murder. Smiling like the whole town wasn't in chaos because of it.

She was with three other women—likely the wives of the men her husband was golfing with—sipping coffee from a fancy cup with an even fancier saucer. They sat like proper ladies, legs crossed and conservatively dressed with expensive clothes. Next to their drinks were small, overpriced pastries.

"Something isn't right, Brad," he said softly while passing the binoculars.

"I know...it's so hard to believe that *she* is Jimmy's mom. Talk about beauty and the beast."

Brad looked up from the binoculars and shrugged, looking down at the dirt and shaking his head.

"Okay, what? What do you want to do now?"

"He's on the sixth hole right now, right?"

"Yeah."

"It's an eighteen-hole golf course."

"So?"

"And JoAnn's drinking coffee and talking."

"Charlie, I told you to drop it."

"We've got at least a few hours, and that's if they don't have lunch."

"No!" Brad shouted, prompting them both to simultaneously hunch down and check around to make sure they hadn't been heard.

"We came here to make sure they weren't home. And they're not."

"We're not going to his house, Charlie! That's over the line! What we're doing now, we're just walking through the woods. We get caught, no big deal. We can explain it. *That's* breaking and entering, some serious shit. And if we get caught, we're neck deep in it."

"What about Barry Ray? We can't just do nothing."

Silently, Charlie wondered how many times he'd be able to play that card. Once more was all he was hoping for; the logic was starting to fade even for him.

It took a few more minutes of debate, but more out of weariness than anything else, Brad submitted. The punishment in a small town for breaking and entering wasn't likely to be significant, but it was still wrong, and if they got caught it would certainly embarrass Sheriff Thrower.

Brad kept mumbling about crossing the line as they hopped on their bikes and started pedaling down the steep slope towards Country Club Drive, heading back to Germantown and a line both knew they shouldn't cross.

13

Despite owning the biggest house in the entire county, Douglas and JoAnn Patino didn't lock their doors. Nobody did. There weren't break-ins or shootings or robberies or crime—Germantown was a minuscule community that was barely on the state map. Neighbors watched out for each other. People trusted that their possessions were safe, and reciprocated generosity was an unspoken edict.

Fortunately, the Patino residence also had only one neighbor. Next to it on the east was an empty lot, which they owned as well. They lived at the end of a winding road lined with trees that led to a cul-de-sac.

As they approached the sprawling, 10,000 square foot, three-story home that sat on a small hill and overlooked farmland in the backyard, Charlie wondered if the murder of their son had prompted the Patinos to lock their door.

It was a red-brick house with professional white-stone landscaping all around the front, meeting up with knockout rosebushes that varied from pink to red to white and lined the entire 20-foot walkway like beautiful soldiers. They left their bikes behind two large maple trees that shaded half of the acre-sized lawn and walked along a tall brown fence that served as a divider between the Patinos' property and their neighbors'.

The front door was indeed unlocked, and as Charlie walked into the spacious two-story foyer with marble floors and Patino's sprawling staircases, he immediately thought about how different this house was from his own.

The hallway to the left of the foyer led to a massive kitchen decorated with copper pots hanging from hooks above the center island stove. As Charlie made his way thorough the kitchen full of granite countertops and stainless-steel appliances, a beam of reflected light pierced his vision, forcing him to squint.

Turning the corner, he saw that the living room had brown leather furniture and a big screen television. The rug was olive green and had fresh vacuum lines; the walls were lined with large framed pictures of the Patinos in front of breathtaking backgrounds. One was of the entire family with skis in front of snowy mountains, another posing in hiking gear surrounded by magnificent red-rock hoodoos, and one was of the parents next to the Leaning Tower of Pisa, pretending to hold it up with their hands.

"Where to?" Brad asked. He was sweating profusely, something he hardly ever did, even on the baseball field. Charlie knew it was a bigger risk for Brad than for him because of his father, and as he looked around and out the window onto the surrounding farmland, it occurred to him that they were looking for a needle in a haystack. Why did he think Douglas would hurt his own son? What was he hoping to find? What were they doing here?

The more Charlie thought about it, the more convincing Brad became without even saying a word. Charlie finally saw just how dumb this idea was.

The more he looked around, the more questions filled his mind, including the one about Mack that still haunted him.

Why didn't I go after him?

Finally, he threw his hands up and admitted to Brad, "You're right, man. This is useless. I don't even know what we're looking for. Let's check one thing upstairs and we'll get out of here."

Brad nodded aggressively, clearly pleased with the promise they'd leave soon. They headed back to the foyer toward the staircase. When they got there, Charlie took a quick note of the hallway to the right of the winding stairs. It led to a formal family room with furniture that looked like it had never been used, a black baby grand piano that glistened in the window's sun, and some area rugs that appeared to have Japanese figures knitted into them.

Brad had joined him and they were both hit with reality as they made their way up the staircase. Pictures of Jimmy from a young age up until the present lined the wall leading all the way up. The photos reminded them both that he was dead. A jerk, a bully who hurt people for fun, but still someone's son. His childhood was hanging on the walls, evidence that someone had loved him and raised him. And that now he was gone and never coming back.

Brad broke Charlie's train of thought with a welcome interruption.

"Have you seen Scotty lately?"

Next to Jimmy in some of those pictures was his brother, Scotty Patino—a well-groomed, short-haired, good-looking guy who was thirty years old and working in Chicago. It was five hours away and many folks in town missed him, but he always seemed destined to fly the Germantown coop and soar in a bigger city. Adored and respected, he had a beautiful wife about the same age and worked as an engineer. Quiet, humble, and amiable. The exact opposite of Jimmy.

"Not since last year," he answered.

It was no secret that Scotty and Jimmy didn't get along. Many folks in town has witnessed at least one of their arguments and their huge personality differences were impossible not to see. Charlie wondered at times if those differences had contributed more to Scotty leaving than the allure of Chicago. Brothers do fight, but those two seemed to truly abhor one another. Scotty was as likeable and easygoing as anyone he knew, so it was pretty obvious from where the tension stemmed. Even still, Charlie wondered if there was something else that drove the wedge between the brothers. Something deeper than Jimmy's character that no one else knew about.

Regardless, one thing he had to give Jimmy credit for was that Jimmy was smart enough to know not to mess with his older brother. If Jimmy tried the tough-guy approach with Scotty, Scotty would have walked all over him. Scotty also didn't see eye to eye with Douglas

Patino, his father, but it wasn't to the point of hatred. Charlie believed Scotty just knew—like the rest of town—that his dad was crooked. That he loved his father but didn't respect him.

"Where are we going?" Brad asked when they reached the top of the staircase.

"I just want to check the bedroom for something."

They walked down a long hallway to a large room with double doors and hand-carved wooden handles, pushing them open and exposing a room of sheer opulence. If the rest of the house was an ornate hotel, this was the penthouse. An authentic vase with gold bands here, an elaborate Van Gogh painting there, designer sheets and bedspreads, perfectly placed pillows, an ostentatious dresser and nightstand furniture, an expensive rug, an exquisite master bath, and another television against the wall.

He went to the bed and got on his knees.

"What are you doing?" Brad finally asked with wide eyes.

"Looking for a safe box."

"This whole house needs a safe box!"

"Good point," Charlie nodded.

It was a long shot, but most of their friends' parents kept important stuff in what they called a "safe box," which could actually be anything from a shoebox to a small metal enclosure. Having a lock or a combination was not required and most safe boxes had neither. It was just a place to put important documents and spare cash. His parents had one and he thought maybe the Patinos did, too. Though, it was odd because everyone knew about them. It was like having a secret hiding place that everyone had a map for.

But a lot of things people did in Germantown didn't make any sense. He knew people who had indoor plumbing and still went outside to pee in the winter because they wanted to "feel the freedom." Just because things didn't make any sense didn't mean they didn't happen. Maybe the Patinos followed the trend.

Brad laughed nervously.

"What?"

"People like the Patinos don't use safe boxes. They're for poor folks like us. People like the Patinos pay the bank to hold their things. Safe deposit boxes."

He agreed with Brad, but much to their surprise, there was indeed a small wooden box sitting neatly up against the wall under the bed. He pulled it out with excitement and set it on the bed. It was about two feet by one foot and six inches deep. It wasn't varnished or smooth; instead, it had a rough texture about it. Brad looked around the room, as though he was afraid someone had been watching them.

They looked at each other, then at the box on the bed. Waiting.

An unspoken nod and reciprocated gesture later, and Charlie opened it up. There were only a few items, many of which were useless. Douglas Patino's business license, proof of insurance for a few of his companies, documentation from City Hall, a marriage license and proof of JoAnn Patino's legal name change, some identification documents for both of them including a Social Security Card and passport. Just when he thought they were finished, they got to the bottom.

When he first removed and studied it, he didn't believe his eyes. Even after reading it for a second time, he didn't trust it, so he gave it to Brad. When Brad's reaction indicated he'd read the same thing, Charlie frantically searched for Scotty's birth certificate. It was there as well, and when he read it, it proved that his eyes were telling the truth. He passed Scotty's to Brad, and then Brad received the same confirmation. Then they put them both down on the bed and stared intently at the pages in front of them.

First was the official birth certificate for Cory Phillip McDougal. Place of birth: Columbus, OH. It was dated September 1, 1973.

The next pages consisted of two forms that were held together by paperclip, beginning with an official name change petition certifying that Cory Phillip McDougal had legally become Jimmy Thomas Patino. Following that was a set of original adoption papers that had been issued to both Douglas and JoAnn Patino, each of whom had signed at the bottom. Both documents were notarized with an official state seal, along with the government's assurance that all the adoption records would remain confidential.

14

Things suddenly felt even more complicated than they already were. Charlie had written down the name Cory Phillip McDougal and Columbus, OH on a piece of paper, put the forms neatly back in the box and under the bed, then the two of them jetted out of Douglas and JoAnn Patino's house, planning never to return. He didn't see any security cameras and could only hope he hadn't just missed them.

They pedaled their bikes furiously without looking back, unsure of where they were going, but getting there fast. The wind felt good on Charlie's sweaty, sticky face, and his legs burned after the long ride up the steep street leading away from the cul-de-sac they both vowed never to return to. In total they'd spent a half hour in the house, which gave plenty of time before the Patinos got back. But a new fear drove their pedaling.

The next day Charlie didn't so much as speak to Brad. Seeking an invisible cover of safety, he retreated to the damp, cool basement bedroom that technically couldn't be considered as such because it didn't have any windows. He plopped down on the bed and hardly moved, eyes closed, holding a baseball glove tightly, "Bitter Sweet Symphony" playing softly on repeat, accompanying his repeated deep breaths. After at least two hours, he counted the tiles until he fell asleep.

The next day they sat outside the bowling alley, each holding a bottle of Ski. Charlie took a long swig, as if trying to swallow the fear.

"What do you think?"

Brad waited a few seconds to respond. "I don't know, man. I'm just so surprised. And I don't know why, but I'm scared. I mean, it's not like it's a bad thing. It's just..."

"Why doesn't anyone know?"

"Exactly," Brad replied nodding his head. "Why keep it a big secret?"

Charlie didn't really believe they'd find anything in the Patinos' house. Regardless of what he'd told Brad beforehand, deep down he was just as pessimistic. And while they didn't discover anything connected to Jimmy Patino's death, what they did find felt shocking. He stared with befuddled eyes at the piece of paper with the name and town.

"You think it's true?" he asked.

"Hard to say. Jimmy has never been called Cory as long as I've known him. Not by his parents, brother, friends, whatever. We saw all those pictures ever since he was a baby and just would never think. But hey, great parents adopt kids all the time. It doesn't mean anything, even if it's true."

"McDougal isn't a popular name," he replied. "I don't know any."

"Me neither."

They both let the non sequitur sit for a moment before Charlie returned to the real question.

"Yeah, kids get adopted every day. And it's almost always for the better, for the kids and adults. But did Jimmy even know that wasn't his real name? Does Scotty know? Did Scotty know, and that was why they fought so much? Why didn't they tell anyone?"

"Are you sure we should be trying to figure that out?"

"What do you mean?" he replied defensively.

"What do you mean, 'What do you mean?' It's none of our business if he was adopted. That's for the family, and we broke into their house to find it out. They gave him a place to live, food to eat, and clothes to wear. And they loved him. Why should they have to tell anyone? You're always complaining about how much you hate it that everyone knows everything about everyone in this town. But here you are questioning the Patinos because they didn't tell the whole town their son was adopted."

He looked at Brad with a slight smile and confirming nod. Preoccupied with trying to figure out if they *could* learn why, he'd never considered if they *should*. He admired Brad for seeing it that way.

The fact was, Brad had a point. What business was it of theirs, and why was he being such a hypocrite? Or so the angel on one side of his brain told him. The devil on the other knew he wouldn't be able to let it go.

"You're right. It's not for us to decide, but hear me out."

Brad shrugged his shoulders and let out a huge, overdramatic sigh. The message was clear: make it quick.

"Think about everything that's happened. Jimmy got murdered and Barry Ray was arrested for it. He swears he wasn't anywhere near Jimmy and there's still no proof that he was. In fact, with Shane there's evidence that he wasn't. Then Mack gets beaten up while his brother is behind bars. That means there's at least one more violent person out there, if not the murderer himself, with reason to attack Mack. Then we spot the Patinos having a grand old time at the golf course and restaurant, acting like nothing's wrong. And we learn that Jimmy wasn't really Jimmy and the Patinos aren't really his biological parents, which goes against everything they've told people all his life. Something doesn't add up."

"So you're saying because they adopted him you think they killed him?"

"No, I'm saying for them not to tell even your dad about it feels like they're hiding something. And could be hiding more."

"For all I know, they did tell him. It's not like my dad gives me a copy of the case file every day, Charlie. I get that it was weird they were out golfing and having a good time, but they raised Jimmy like their own his whole life and didn't have any more reason to kill him than Barry Ray did."

"At least not any that we can see..."

* * *

The morning breeze died down and the lunch hour was upon them. The sun was relentless and Charlie could feel his shoulders burning. They'd just finished their second bottles of Ski and mounted their bikes to give the wind a shot at combating the heat when Sarah and her friends turned the corner from behind the building and made their way up the sidewalk. She waved as they walked by.

Charlie smiled at her, and she smiled right back. Her smooth brown hair glistened in the sun and the smile showed itself in full frame. He tried to conceal the blushing he felt. She didn't have the full-woman look of JoAnn Patino, but she was good looking, and there was something alluring about her. Plus, he couldn't deny that the tabooness of her being Brad's sister only made him want her even more.

"It's weird how old she's getting," Brad said.

Now it was his turn to shrug his shoulders, preferring that the subject be dropped and never brought up again. The perfect segue.

"Don't you think all that about Jimmy is a little strange though? I mean, why wouldn't they at least tell people about the adoption after he died? It might help solve the case. I wonder if your dad does know. They should've told him."

"They probably didn't tell anyone because they knew if they did there'd be people like you questioning why they didn't tell sooner. It's none of our business!" Brad was adamant.

Adamant, and once again, correct.

"I still think we gotta look into it. I get that it's none of our business, you're right about that, but I'm really not talking about broadcasting their personal news to the whole town. Just trying to figure out if it actually means something."

"That's a pretty thin line, man."

"I know. But we went to the house because our pal is in jail for a crime I don't think he committed. Giving up on him isn't right, either."

"What do you want to do? I'm not going back there, that's for sure!" Brad almost yelled as he slammed on the brakes and came to an abrupt halt, his tires spitting gravel into the middle of the street.

Charlie stopped just as quickly and they were under a shady oak tree, the sweat dripping off Brad's forehead from underneath his St. Louis Blues hat.

"Let's just look into the name Cory McDougal. We've got enough info to do some more research, that's all. I'd like to check on some things."

Brad's forehead wrinkled and he nibbled his index finger, but he said nothing.

"All I'm talking about is going to the library to get some articles. No breaking into houses, no breaking the law. If there's anything worth reading, we read it. If not, we go home."

Brad continued to stare for almost a minute, then gave Charlie a deep blink before finally responding. "Fine. I can't stop you from going to a library anyway, and I guess I can get on board with that. But there's one condition."

"Name it."

"If you don't find anything—and I say *you* because I'm not helping, I'm just tagging along—you stop this detective crap and buy me a Ski?"

"A whole six-pack, buddy."

15

Germantown's library consisted of a few piles of used books with bent or ripped off covers, an empty magazine rack, and a funky odor that permeated the building. It smelled like a combination of sawdust and sewage. Something told Charlie that they wouldn't get what they needed there, so they rode east on country roads running parallel to Route 161 and made their way into the town of Bartelso. It was only five miles away and had a much bigger library. More importantly, it had access to resources that Germantown did not.

It was a smooth ride with the wind at their backs, and they tried to talk about movies, sports, beer and bonfires—the stuff they both knew they were missing out on when they were looking for evidence behind Jimmy Patino's murder.

When they arrived, they rested their bikes against the front of the entryway and headed inside. It was the first time he'd ever been excited about going into a library during the summer.

At the main desk near the entrance, there were a few newspaper racks and a couple of small aisles with current publications and recently released books, but Charlie quickly walked past them both. For what they needed, dating back over twenty years ago, the main source of information would be the endless rows of vertical files, archived microfiche magazines and newspaper prints. The 105 x 148 mm flat film spanned over a hundred years and was easy to store, and Bartelso had feeder libraries from numerous nearby counties as well as state libraries further north. If what they were looking for was out there, this is where it would be.

Along the window near the back also sat two IBM computers connected to the Internet via dial-up connection running on 30 Kbps of speed. With the World Wide Web having been released two years earlier in 1995, he'd used Yahoo! and AltaVista search engines to look things up before, and he even had a Hotmail e-mail address that had been released last year by Microsoft.

The problem was, search engines were very limited if you didn't have the specific information you needed and source where it could be found. Everyone knew the Internet was the future, and it was rapidly expanding every day, but with only 100,000 websites overall, the web simply didn't often get you what you really needed. And it took way too long through the dial up to sort through all the miss-hits it would return along the way. It seemed inevitable to Charlie that one day, someone in a garage would change that with a more powerful search engine, but at present the best source of data was the microfiche.

The name Cory McDougal was far too vague, even for the microfiche. But on the birth certificate there was also the name of the town: Columbus, OH. It was a bigger city with almost 700,000 residents, but it was the only place they had to start. As he walked up to the conservatively dressed librarian—roughly sixty, thick, light brown glasses, gray hair pulled back in a ponytail, nametag that said Emily—he wondered what he really hoped to find.

Did he truly expect something out of the ordinary? The odds weren't in favor of it, but a lack of options prevented them from trying anything else. They were trying to figure out a mystery and didn't have much choice but to play the only card they had. He'd originally planned to wear shorts, but Brad thought they might look more passable as library dwellers in pants and might've been right. But his legs—covered with sweat and dripping like a faucet—didn't care for the decision.

And Brad hung back, making it clear who would be doing the talking.

"Excuse me, ma'am?"

"Yes?"

"My name's Charlie. I've been assigned a summer research project for high school, and I'm supposed to learn everything I can about Cory McDougal. My teacher told me he was born on September 1, 1973 in Columbus, Ohio."

He silently prayed that his baby face would work to his advantage for once, and Emily wouldn't ask for an ID.

"What kind of research project is it?" Emily asked with more interest than he expected. She adjusted her glasses and offered her undivided attention.

"It's a personal narrative research paper. My teacher told us he wanted us to learn how to research and write a biography, and that we had to gather the information. I've tried, but I really need some help."

It felt corny, and he again worried Emily might not buy it, but instead it played right into her hand as a librarian and appeared to win her over.

"Okay, Charlie. Give me just a moment." She smiled before turning around and heading to the back. Her cheerful response had surprised him. He'd pinned her as a grouchy old woman, but instead she was eager to lend a helping hand.

Emily brought back some paperwork for him to fill out. Contact info including address, phone number, the usual stuff. She'd have to request the files from the Columbus library directly and that could take a few days. With any luck, Emily said, the Columbus library, or one of its affiliates, would have some materials. She'd let him know when they came in.

"Thanks a lot, ma'am."

"And thank *you*, young man," Emily replied in a sweet voice.

She actually bought it. She was really going to put the request in.

Brad made the puke sign with his finger pointed towards an open mouth when Emily turned her back, but Charlie was encouraged. He wasn't sure why he was so surprised—a student working on a summer research project would be grounds for a librarian's help if anything was—but after almost a week of nothing going their way, it felt good to get a win. Now they just had to hope it turned up something tangible.

Three minutes after Charlie and Brad left the library, a man in his mid-fifties walked in the door. The goal was to be both charming and forgettable; to get in and get out, leaving no lasting impression whatsoever. To change his appearance and appear younger, he wore khaki pants that concealed wrinkled, veiny legs, and a modern purple button down, sleeves rolled up. Untucked.

Hours earlier, he'd colored what was left of his thinning salt-and-pepper hair dark brown, shaved his face against the grain, and put on a brand new pair of trendy boat shoes. He left his black-rimmed glasses in the car. After shoving the pack of cigarettes from his shirt pocket into his pants, he peppily approached the desk.

"Good afternoon ma'am. I was wondering if by chance you knew what those two young men were looking for?"

"Um...if you don't mind my asking, who are you sir?" the librarian replied.

"Oh, goodness, where are my manners?" The man smiled, his teeth as bright as Chiclet gum thanks to his contact at Procter & Gamble, who gave him a prototype of the new and yet-to-be commercially available technology. "I'm so sorry. You must think I'm incredibly rude."

"Well, I didn't—"

"I teach high school English over at Central; have for almost twenty years. Gosh...time sure does fly." The man paused, smiling, looking up at nothing in particular. "I was having lunch across the street and noticed two of my former students walk in. So many of my students, especially the boys, wouldn't be caught dead in a library in the summer. And I guess curiosity just got the best of me. I didn't mean to—"

"Oh, heavens! Why didn't you say so at first?" the librarian exclaimed. "They were here for a research project they'd been assigned over the summer. They asked me to pull some information

74

from Columbus, Ohio. Would you like me to get the request form so you can take a look? It could be from one of your colleagues."

"Well, I'd hate to put you out..."

"It's no problem."

After another long pause, the man inhaled deeply, then smiled. "If it's really not asking too much, I'd sure appreciate it."

16

Not much happened over the next few days. Charlie and Brad were with each other most days, attending some baseball practices and in general keeping away from others. In Charlie's mind, that was the price to be paid for knowing Jimmy Patino was really Cory McDougal and the Patinos were not his biological parents. And for breaking the law to find out. No one had said anything to either of them, including Sheriff Thrower, so it seemed their breaking and entering crime had gone unnoticed, but that didn't stop both of them from looking over their shoulders.

There was the occasional glare from Jason Hand and his still-bandaged nose, an every-so-often coy smile from Sarah, and the constant anticipation, but that was all manageable. He did speak with Shane Littleton, who told him there had been no real follow up from Sheriff Thrower following an introductory conversation.

But five days later, Charlie was shivering with anticipation in spite of the heat as they walked into the Bartelso library. Brad, who'd spent the better part of the bike ride trying to convince him to turn around, chose again to hang in the background.

He thought of Barry Ray sitting in that jail cell and used it as motivation to approach Emily with the very best smile he could manufacture. Barry Ray didn't know it, but he was counting on them.

"Well, hello young man," Emily said when he got to the front of the short line at the reference desk. She wore the same light brown glasses with another sweater, but her face seemed a little perkier and her hair was up. Still wearing the smile of a sweet old grandmother, she again showered him with kindness.

"Hi ma'am. How are you today?"

"I'm doing just fine. Thank you for asking, Charlie. It's great to see you again. I don't see many students in the summer. I'll bet you're here for those articles for your research project," she said in more of a questioning tone than a statement.

He nodded his head. "Yes, ma'am."

She retrieved a brown folder from beneath her desk and handed it to him. It felt about twenty pages thick and had a rubber band around the middle to contain them all. Emily's face lost its smile and was immediately replaced with a wrinkled forehead and saucer-like, wide eyes.

"I have to tell you, I don't think much of public education these days."

He shot her a very curious glance. "I'm sorry ma'am. Did I say something?"

"Oh, heavens no," Emily exclaimed, shouting louder than you'd think a librarian would. But the near empty set of tables and lack of people in the aisles indicated it didn't much matter.

"No, what I mean is this research project of yours. Oh, Lord. It's just frightening what schools are having students research these days. Whatever happened to the basics? Diagramming a sentence, doing your times tables, things like that? But no, instead they're having you look up things like this. It just feels so discouraging to me; so unnecessary."

His heart beating like a jackhammer, he tried not to expose how confused he was. Emily was watching, and he was almost there. Still, the endless parade of questions flooded his mind. *Things like this? Discouraging? What is that supposed to mean? Why would she be concerned?* The answers were all in the pages he was holding, but he couldn't appear overeager.

Emily shook her head and spoke with genuine, heartfelt concern. Brad, having suddenly taken an interest, was staring at them both. He needed to end the awkwardness and end it fast.

"Well, ma'am, I guess they just wanted us to learn the research process."

"I suppose, but Heavens to Betsy," Emily said with a trailing voice. "I know you're just doing your assignment, so here it is. There are three clippings. I've labeled them and made some notes so you can follow along. Please let me know if you have any other questions."

"Thank you, ma'am. I really appreciate it."

She smiled and turned away, back to other business.

They walked very slowly towards the back of the library, in part not to call attention to themselves and in part because neither was sure he really wanted to know what they were about to find out. The urge to toss the brown folder in the trash receptacle, hop on their bikes, pedal home without looking back and never speak of it again crossed Charlie's mind, though neither one of them uttered a word aloud.

17

They sat in silence at a six-person table in the far corner of a private study room. Charlie lifted the window shade that blocked the bright sun from coming in and looked out at the town of Bartelso. It seemed so peaceful, full of relaxed people going about their days. He saw a couple kids going into McDonald's, a mother pushing a stroller down the sidewalk, several cars at the four-way stoplight that Germantown did not have. Brad kept his unblinking eyes aimed at the brown folder sitting on the wood table. After a few minutes of silence, they both knew it was time.

"Might as well," Brad said nonchalantly. He could tell that Brad's tone was meant to convey Brad didn't care and wasn't scared, but he knew it was an act.

He opened the crisp-edged folder and pulled out three separate newspaper reprints, separated by Emily's paper clips and handwritten notes. He held his breath and started with the one on top.

"Woman Abandons Child in Park," was the title of the article, from *The Columbus Dispatch.* Dated September 22, 1982, the worn yellow pages looked like they'd been stored in an attic for the past fifteen years. The typewriter print had started to fade and the pages looked crumbled, like someone had bunched it into a ball and then unrolled it. Its wrinkles remained intact.

It stated that a young mother named Shannon McDougal had abandoned her nine-year-old son at a playground in Columbus. An older couple were on their daily walk through the park on a perfect fall day when they spotted the boy sitting in a swing all alone and asked him where his parents were. When he shook his head and offered no answer, they grew concerned. The couple stayed with the child for over an hour before calling the police.

There was no mention of what happened next. The article merely said that an investigation would be conducted to find the mother, and that the boy, allegedly named Cory but unconfirmed due to him being a minor, was in the hands of the state and would likely enter foster care. Additional information would be provided at a later time.

In the final paragraph, the boy's father was identified as Nelson Towns, 35, also of Columbus. Towns and McDougal were not in a relationship and had in fact only shared one night together that drew vastly different accounts of what had happened. According to McDougal, after a few hours of drinking and increasingly flirtatious touching at Herman's Food Bar, on High Street, Towns cornered her outside the bathroom and forced her inside. Towns didn't deny that intercourse occurred in the lavatory, but claimed it was entirely consensual. After a three-week trial with no witnesses or physical evidence, Towns was acquitted and reportedly left Columbus.

The backstory was pertinent because approximately one month before the nine-year-old boy was abandoned, Towns was arrested for a similar allegation, this time of an unidentified minor from the town of Butler, OH. Towns was already behind bars as of the date of the article awaiting trial and would be arraigned in the coming weeks. The evidence against Towns warranted no bail be set.

It was no wonder that Emily, the sweet librarian, didn't approve of the supposed research project.

"Man," Brad whispered. "This is some bad stuff. Why did she give us this?"

He was equally stunned, but more focused, and scared, about what was coming. There were still two more articles in the brown folder.

The second article was dated September 4, 1982, roughly three weeks before the first. The connection between the two stories was obvious from the title. "Accused Man Behind Bars Nine Years Later," another story from *The Columbus Dispatch*.

Its copy was much cleaner. Whiter pages, fewer wrinkles, clearer print, a neater overall look and feel. It began by stating that Nelson Towns, 35, had been charged with first degree sexual assault of a minor in Butler, Ohio, a small town in Richland County an hour north of Columbus. It offered no information about the minor other than she was thirteen years old.

Thirteen.

As in the first article, there was no picture. Instead, the image of an innocent thirteen-year-old girl played in his mind. He wondered what she looked like. Was she petite? Did she have brown hair? Blonde? Did she have any lucky charms she carried with her? Did she read a book before she went to sleep? Was she close with her parents? What a sad story. *Thirteen years old.*

The article said the girl's father was at work around two o'clock on a Saturday afternoon when Towns reportedly gained access to the home by posing as a UPS delivery man. There was no mention of her mother. During the confrontation, the victim was able to alert a neighbor by shouting through a closed bedroom window. The neighbor raced over with a baseball bat, broke through the locked door, and hit the aggressor in the chest before the man scurried out of the house, leaving a switchblade behind on a table next to the bed.

They were both speechless by the time they finished reading. It was so quiet he could hear the shade tapping back and forth against the glass window because of the draft coming from the A/C vent above the table.

As with the first article, the last few lines led to the next story, providing the background that Towns had also been accused of violating a woman named Shannon McDougal nine years earlier in Columbus when he was twenty-six. It concluded with the fact that Towns had been acquitted of that crime in less than a month.

The point the author made without stating it was clear: Towns had gotten away with it back in 1973, meaning what happened to that thirteen-year-old girl in 1982 could have been prevented had the justice system not failed.

The final clipping wasn't a story. It was a very small—less than three lines—snippet from the "Announcements" page of the same Columbus newspaper. It was dated September 2, 1973, one day after the date on Cory McDougal's birth certificate.

The birth announcement of Shannon McDougal's son, Cory, one day earlier at 12:57 p.m., was pithy and sad. The father—Nelson Towns—was awaiting trial for sexual assault and had vehemently denied the accusation, insisting the intercourse was consensual.

It seemed odd that an announcement under such circumstances exited at all, but regardless, it was the final link confirming Cory McDougal was born to a sick father, abandoned nine years later, and then became Jimmy Patino. Brad and Charlie stared at one another with more questions than answers. The Jimmy Patino they'd known all their lives was originally Cory McDougal, the son of a man who'd sexually assaulted at least two women, in 1973 and 1982.

All that was left in the envelope was a handwritten note from Emily. The cursive, blue-ink message said she'd tried to get more information about the allegation in Butler, but that the library had no records. She'd also checked for any leads regarding the current whereabouts of the boy, Cory McDougal. But again, despite her best efforts, she was unable to find anything. His name wasn't mentioned in any other documentation that she or the Columbus librarian could locate. The final sentence urged him not to spend too much time on such a sad project.

More than anything, the note made him feel guilty. Guilty for lying to Emily and making her read those articles. Guilty for looking at JoAnn Patino the way he did. Guilty for fighting with his father. For the lying, cheating, stealing, swearing, drinking, dipping, and just about everything else he'd done wrong in life.

Most of all, guilty for thinking he'd had it rough.

18

Charlie spent the rest of that day and most of the next feeling sick to his stomach. As much as he hated how small Germantown was and the fact privacy didn't exist, at least it protected him from things like that newspaper article. Sheltered, closed off, call it what you want, the thought of such awful crimes had never even crossed his mind before that day. He missed his sheltered upbringing immediately, and knew he'd never get it back.

After leaving Bartelso and vowing never to return, he and Brad rode back to Germantown without a word. The excitement, anticipation, and even the fun of playing detective was gone just as quickly as it had come. He wanted nothing to do with it now, and wished he could go back and undo his decision to go to the Patino house.

After a night of fitful sleep, he felt no better the next morning. A piece of toast and glass of juice later, he checked the atlas and encyclopedia sitting on the shelf.

Butler, Ohio appeared to be a lot like Germantown: just under 1,000 residents, mostly white, very predominantly Christian, family oriented, one main street that ran through its center, and on the Mohican River. It too was innocent and unassuming. Not the kind of place where things like that happened.

When he walked out of the house—against his mother's wishes— he vowed to let it all go for a while. Barry Ray needed them, but another day like the one in the library would be too much to handle. He wondered if they should hand over what they'd learned to Sheriff Thrower and get back to baseball and summertime. The questions rolled through his mind like skates at the rink. Would Sheriff Thrower do anything with it? If he didn't, would it all be a waste?

Would he and Brad be punished for breaking into the Patinos' house? They did break the law.

The questions were overwhelming so he decided to take a slow walk into town. Despite the heat, it felt good to stroll south down Hanover St., known as Highway 7 to most folks just passing through.

Usually in the summertime there were some pick-up basketball games at the town's park, laughing children walking the streets, and teenagers cruising the strip, but he saw none of that today. Even The Alibi, one of the most popular bars had a ghost town vibe. Typically, the 10 a.m. hour wouldn't be a deterrent. The flower shop and a few others posted a sign offering prayers for Jimmy Patino, several block parties had already been cancelled, and a nasty gloom hung over the main drag like a dark gray cloud over a baseball game. The small town still just didn't know how to handle Jimmy Patino's death.

He thought about Sarah and even considered heading over to Brad's, more to see her than him, but decided to pass. Perhaps it was good for them both to have some space.

After passing the fire department, a couple of hundred feet north of the St. Boniface Cemetery, he was ready to head back when he heard his name called. There was a sense of urgency to it, and he turned to see scrawny Shane Littleton running towards him with his arms spread.

"Charlie, I'm glad I found you!"

He wasn't sure he felt the same, but he forced a smile. "What is it?"

Shane took off his glasses and rubbed them on his plain, white shirt, replaced them atop his equally plain face, and grabbed Charlie's hand. Shane ran faster than Charlie thought he would, dragging him behind with surprising strength.

"What is it?" he asked again, more earnestly.

"You'll see," Shane answered, heading for the entrance.

Shane told Susan behind the counter they'd be right back and weren't going to skate, and she let them through. There were only a handful of skaters, mostly teenagers, with AC/DC blasting over the

84

loudspeaker during the free skate. Shane eagerly led him to a table next to the railing about twenty feet from the concession stand. The smell of a fresh hot dog reminded him he didn't bring any money, but it was encouraging that his appetite had returned.

"Okay, dude. What's up?"

Shane's excitement abandoned his face, replaced by a fearful stare that he imagined was supposed to be stoic. It wasn't. He could see the trepidation in his eyes, and suddenly he felt bad about demanding Shane speak up.

Shane swallowed hard, as if summoning courage, and whispered under the music. It was barely audible, and he pulled himself in closer.

"Do you see that guy in the blue jeans and green shirt? The one with his back to us now going around the turn?" he asked, shifting his eyes towards the rink.

There were a lot of jeans, but not too many green shirts. It didn't take long to spot the guy.

"The one with the two girls."

"Shh. Yes."

Two girls hung onto the bulging arms of Brandon Doracco, one on each side. One blonde, the other a redhead. Four years older than both at twenty-two, Doracco stood tall and puffed out his chest, highlighting the evidence that he knew his way around the weight room.

Doracco had moved from out of state a few months earlier and wasted no time dazzling the ladies. Several of Charlie's classmates were happy to throw themselves at him. Doracco's rugged good looks, older age and bad boy mystique gave him an unfair advantage over other potential suitors that drove resentment, but it made sense to Charlie that Shane didn't even know who the guy was. Shane was only twelve, and Doracco hadn't even attended high school there before moving to town.

As Doracco and the girls made the turn around the back of the rink and headed towards the tables, Shane ducked his head behind him, blocking the view of Doracco as he made the turn. Charlie looked at the girls even more than Doracco, the blonde on the left particularly worthy of his attention.

"Did you see him?" Shane asked again, once they'd passed.

"Yeah, it's Brandon Doracco. What about him?"

"That's the guy who held the knife to my throat."

19

Brad was skeptical as usual.

"Why would Doracco give two craps about Shane? He's a stud, the new guy, chicks dig him, jocks like him, and he's got a totally awesome ride. Why would he do that?"

"I don't know. But that's what Shane said. I asked if he was sure, and he kept saying yes. I believe him."

"There's a surprise. He could still be yanking your chain."

Brad sounded like his father, whom Charlie was still considering going to with all of this.

But the fact Sheriff Thrower hadn't really investigated Shane's claim, despite the fact he'd told Charlie he would, sat like a brick in his stomach. He wouldn't say as much to Brad, but overall he felt Sheriff Thrower was in over his head. He'd been sheriff for thirteen years and did it just fine when it meant cruising from gas station to gas station to get coffee and giving out an occasional speeding ticket. He, like the rest of the town, thrived on the mundane and the routine.

But this was neither.

He and Brad were under a tree at the park, the baseball field a hundred feet in front of them. Brad paced back and forth in small steps, not leaving the shade the magnificent oak provided, while Charlie sat at the base of the tree. They both had a tobacco dip in.

"You're right. Shane could be lying. But if he was, wouldn't he want to keep the story vague? You know, 'Some guy hurt me. I don't know his name or what he looked like.' He wouldn't give a lot details."

Brad nodded, and he continued.

"But Shane didn't do that, man. He gave as many specifics as he could from the start. He didn't recognize the face because Doracco just moved here and was already out of school. So of course he wouldn't recognize him. But he gave a description; it just wasn't enough of one for me to know it was Doracco. And then he pointed him out when he saw him. I don't think he'd do that if he made it up."

"Maybe Shane's not as smart as you think."

They both chuckled at the notion and even Brad dismissed it with a wave. Shane was a genius, but even an idiot would know better than to point someone out if it was all made up.

"Let's tell my dad?"

He didn't respond right away, and decided to choose his words carefully. "I was thinking...we might not want the cops to question Doracco."

"Why is that?"

"Think about it. If your dad questions him, Doracco will know Shane spilled the beans on what happened. He may even assume you know, if not both of us."

"Assuming any of it actually *did* happen. Remember, there's still no proof."

Charlie nodded his head, spit out a mouthful of brown dip juice, and continued. "Either way, it gives Doracco a heads up. He might not do what he was going to do otherwise. Maybe he starts covering his tracks. Or maybe he doesn't go places he would've gone."

"You think Doracco killed Jimmy...or, I mean, Cory?"

"I don't know. Seems like a stretch...I can't imagine anyone I know killing someone else. But now that Shane actually pointed someone out, I guess it's a possibility. But like I said, if your dad runs and questions him now, at the least it could get Shane another serious ass-kicking, at worst it could actually tip Doracco off if he did kill Jimmy. Or...Cory."

Brad let out a deep breath followed by more pacing and cursing in a nasty whisper. His best friend didn't want any part of this, never did, and never would. And here he was, bringing it to Brad again.

"Sorry man. Forget it. You've done enough. I just wanted to tell you what Shane said. Sorry for dragging you into this again." He stood up and stretched his back.

"Where are you going?" Brad asked.

"I'm going after Doracco."

"You're going to follow him?"

"Just for a while. I want to see where he goes, what he does. I'm not going to talk to him, and I don't plan on him seeing me."

Brad sighed. "Just let my dad take care of this."

He secretly wished that Brad wasn't destined to be sheriff one day, but with how similar he sounded to his dad, it wouldn't be that much of a surprise. Germantown's barber, mechanic, plumber, florist, and electrician were all children of previous owners.

"I can't tell your dad," he said. "Not right now. I don't want Doracco to know Shane snitched on him. If you want to tell him, I can't stop you. But I'm not going to...yet."

Brad took a deep breath. Much to his surprise, Charlie could tell his buddy was considering it.

"Tonight?"

"Tonight."

Another long sigh, followed by a forced grin. "Come by the house. We'll leave together."

"Will do. Thanks, man."

"I just hope we know what the hell we're doing."

They embraced in a firm hug, patting one another on the back. A gentle breeze emerged from the stillness like it wanted in on the bro hug.

"One question," Brad said in a soft voice as they separated.

"What's that?"

"What if Doracco sees us?"

"He won't."

"But what if he does?"

He closed his eyes for a moment. He hadn't considered that very real possibility.

"We run."

20

The sun was down and the clouds covered the moon. Still a summer night, Charlie started to sweat under his black T-shirt. He wore black sweatpants to go with it, and Brad did much the same with a similar shirt and a pair of black jeans. They wanted to blend into the night, to "become one" with the darkness. Charlie didn't want to take any chances, not with anything, and the long-sleeved protection was worth the extra sweat.

It was a little after eight when they spotted Doracco sitting at the car wash. He wore faded blue jeans with holes around the knees and his signature loose-fitting gray T-shirt with ripped sleeves, exposing bulging biceps and a homemade barbed wire tattoo on his left arm. "Cool" written all over him, he was talking to several junior college girls, showing off his classic wheels.

The car was a blue 1961 Oldsmobile Super 88 Starfire convertible coupe. And it never failed to draw the ladies. They touched it, rubbed it, "oohed" and "aahed" all over it, feeding Doracco's ego by flirtatiously complimenting him on how shiny it was. It was the ultimate chick magnet, and Doracco wasn't afraid to use it.

He was the quintessential "too cool for words" kind of guy. He moved into town just a few months earlier and had already dated the three hottest girls in his class. Cocky personality with the looks to back it up, he had curly hair down to his shoulders, longer than most guys, a slender girth to complement broad shoulders, and sideburns that ran the length of his face. He was tall, almost six-foot-three, but didn't play sports. Instead, he put his effort into perfecting the art of tail chasing.

Doracco wasn't much of a model citizen. He was a truant with other things on his mind, not caring much what folks of authority had to say. The first day he got into town, he got a citation for parking his moving van on the street overnight, and then mouthed off to the patrolman who issued it. A week later, he got a visit from Sheriff Thrower for busting some guy in the mouth. Evidently, the guy, who was just passing through town, had somehow challenged Doracco's alpha status at the gas station. Thus began his quick and rewarding road to social fame. The day after that fight, his popularity and mystique had grown immensely.

Doracco had a deep voice that projected well enough for them to hear it from across the street while sitting on top of Brad's ATV. Doracco chugged another beer while the ladies cheered. Charlie couldn't help but compare the sweet convertible Doracco was driving to what they had. He had no room to complain about the ATV, a Honda Foreman 400 workhorse with front wheel drive, 395cc engine and five-speed transmission that helped it move through rugged terrain, but it was no Starfire. Brad's father knew the sheriff from Centralia, who confiscated it in a case and was able to get it cheap for Brad's birthday.

"You really think Doracco did it?" Brad asked.

"Let's find out."

It was a scary thought to him that they could very well be tailing the person who killed Jimmy, beat up Mack, and threatened Shane at knifepoint. It made him again question why he was so determined to get in over his head. But then he remembered Barry Ray.

"How's Mack?" he asked to get his mind off it.

"My dad said Kurt told him he was getting better. Still won't let me visit him."

"Me neither. Why do you think that is? It feels like we should at least be able to say hi, don't you think?"

Why didn't I go after him?

"Couldn't tell you."

"Any news on Barry Ray?" he asked.

"They set a preliminary court date in Carlyle. A few weeks from now. Still says he didn't do it." A moment of silence. "Here we go," Brad said, motioning towards the car wash.

Doracco hopped into his car and waved goodbye to the girls. Inevitably, he would meet them later. The night was young, and the tiger was on the prowl. Charlie guessed he'd cruise the strip for a few hours to grow both the quantity and quality of his prospective list.

But he was wrong. Doracco pulled out of the car wash and took a hard left onto eastbound Highway 161 leading out of town. Brad started the ATV and they turned onto the same road, keeping their distance at two cars behind. The car in front of Doracco kept tapping its brakes and it was clear he was looking to pass but couldn't because of westbound traffic. It was a good thing, too. There was no way the ATV could keep up if Doracco pushed the pedal to the metal.

The bugs smacked their glasses, the wind lifted Charlie's untucked shirt up and he squeezed Brad's waist the way he wished Sarah would squeeze his. Aside from the bugs, the gusts of wind were refreshing on the sticky evening. He kept his mouth shut and breathed through his nose because bugs at fifty miles per hour never tasted good.

After two miles on the highway that led all the way to Belleville, Doracco took a right onto Turkey Run—a country road they knew well. Charlie assumed Doracco would have a few more drinks before heading back to town. They followed the convertible and quickly entered a cornfield that ran parallel to the road. Flattening the not-quite-knee-high stalks of corn with the ATV, they sped through the fields of darkness with the lights off.

Doracco's car was racing ahead, and because they'd just re-tarred the roads, they heard rapid-fire dinging as he accelerated well beyond what the ATV could muster. They'd lose him soon if he didn't slow down.

Doracco turned onto another country road at the stop sign and they followed into the adjoining cornfield. They passed through someone's yard and went around back, reentering the cornfields on the other side. The lack of moonlight made Brad's eyes focus harder because the lights remained off and the field itself was very dark. The bugs made their usual chirps as critters fled for their lives moments before the ATV rumbled through.

Doracco slowed down because the road was hilly compared to County Line and you couldn't see over the hill. They knew those fields like the back of their hand and were able to make up for reduced speed by taking shortcuts through a couple of tiny creeks, the water splashing up on their legs a small price to pay. They plowed through patches of wooded areas, riding along paths that others had made with ATVs of their own.

But it felt like Doracco was going a long way out. Charlie didn't have the slightest idea where he was headed, and these country roads were far from where most teenagers cruised around. He was well on his way to Bartelso, taking the back route, and Charlie silently prayed he wouldn't have to see the library again. There weren't any other cars on the two-lane, cornfield-lined, asphalt road.

Then Doracco came to a screeching halt at an intersection of another country road, sliding on the gravel before stopping next to a parked car on the side of the road. Brad killed the engine from about fifty feet away, concealed in the cornfields. They got off the ATV immediately and dropped to their stomachs. Then they crawled as quietly as they could to the edge of the cornfield, offering a clear view of the intersection. They were covered in mud, but nothing mattered except not being seen.

21

Charlie pulled out the binoculars and looked through them with great reluctance.

The remote location and unfamiliar car waiting there had his hands shaking, and he wasn't sure he wanted to see whatever was about to happen next. Brad had his eyes closed and was summoning the strength to open them. They didn't make a sound. They'd agreed beforehand: no words could be uttered. Their silence hung in the air as the whistling wind shouted in their ears.

The parked car was a run-of-the-mill beige Chevy Impala, far from new with brown interior and no noticeable features. He didn't know the year but he knew from the wear and tear on the bumper that it had seen its fair share of windshield time. There was no license plate and its lights were off, but they could still see Doracco walking towards it.

Then, a person slowly got out of the car. He wore a black ski mask that completely covered his face, and sported a hunter's camouflage jacket with a pair of old, filthy jeans. The dried dirt on the front of them matched the work boots that came up to his shins. As with the Impala, there were no noticeable traits. Every guy in Germantown owned a camouflage hunter's jacket, an old pair of jeans and a pair of boots like the ones he was wearing. He wasn't distinctly tall or short, nor fat or skinny. The jacket concealed his chest, so Charlie couldn't tell if he was strong like Doracco or weak like Shane.

The black mask had two small holes near the eyes and one for the mouth. He looked like a bank robber from the movies, the nemesis of the heroes he grew up watching. His heart was racing like a Clydesdale's as Doracco approached him. They met in between the two cars. Brad's breathing was so loud he jerked his arm to silence it. It wasn't possible to be too careful.

He couldn't make out any words as they spoke, nor could he recognize their voices. They could barely hear them at all, and it was clear they were speaking just above a whisper.

The mask made everything especially eerie. He felt chills run up his spine as he stared into the binoculars.

Then the man in the mask handed Doracco a paper-sized brown envelope. Doracco looked inside but didn't take out its contents, and after a very brief moment looked back at the man in the mask.

Charlie could see then that Doracco was nervous. He kept looking around, jerking his head this way and that, and through the binoculars he saw Doracco biting his lip and shifting his weight from one leg to the other. It was clear, at the very least, that Doracco was uncomfortable—either because of whom he was talking to, whatever was in the envelope, or both.

Just then, a loud, obnoxious call from a crow that couldn't have been more than five feet away howled through the quietness. They both jumped, but he forced himself to keep quiet.

Brad didn't.

His best friend let out a yelp—an uncontrollable, involuntary shriek that wasn't very loud but was still no crow. He covered Brad's mouth with his hand and prayed Doracco and the man didn't hear.

Doracco and the man turned their attention to the cornfield they were hiding in, and he could only hope it was because of the crow.

"What the hell was that?" he heard Doracco exclaim. They were the only clear words they heard the entire time.

Brad jerked his hand from his mouth and they both froze like ice sculptures. He didn't even want to wipe the sweat that had dripped from his hair into the corner of his eyes. They were statues physically, but mentally he was like a gymnast doing cartwheels.

They heard Brad scream. Oh, no. They're going to find us.

Then the man in the mask turned away to pull something from the Impala's front seat. Charlie knew immediately what it was. He swallowed hard and covered his own mouth, then scooted back into the cornfield as much as he could without drawing attention to any movement, and urged Brad to do the same by pulling him with his other hand. They kept their heads down and mouths shut. They got just a few feet back when the bright flashlight shone into the field above them.

He tried to not even breathe. They couldn't do anything more. They were going to be seen.

The light moved up and down, left and right, and all across where they lay. He waited for them to come through the fields with shotguns, find them, and kill them. They'd hunt them down like deer and then dispose of their bodies in some unimaginable way. The unexplained disappearance of two local teenagers would be on the front page of *The Germantown Sun*.

After what seemed like an eternity, the flashlight finally turned off. They didn't dare move. Not a single muscle. He heard two different cars start, one of them clearly the Starfire with a failing muffler. A few seconds later, one of them peeled out and spun the gravel and tar into the fields at a rampant pace. He could tell it was headed back in the direction of town.

The other car was still running. It sat there for a while and he couldn't hear anything else. He prayed again. Whenever he thought he was going to die, the few times it had happened, he always turned to God.

Eyes clamped shut and head forced down into the ground, he didn't even try to summon the courage to look up.

Miraculously, that car too drove away. Slower than the first, but clearly in motion and moving away from them. He put his arm on Brad's shoulder and leaned into him. They didn't try to talk about it, assuming there would be another day and time.

They were wrong.

22

After the long country ride through the darkness, bugs slapping them in the face and dust kicking up around their eyes, they finally made it back to their neighborhood. They didn't look for Doracco or anyone else on the strip. They both needed to get home, to rid their bodies of the filth and clear their minds of the fear.

They rode through the side streets and familiar roads. As they approached Plum Drive, the road leading towards Brad's house, they saw a familiar and unappealing sight. Brad killed the ATV and they stared, saying nothing. The red and blue flashing lights were coming from Brad's house. There was no sound, but the strobe-like effect of having multiple police cruisers right next to each other was unmistakable.

"Maybe your dad got some news on the case," Charlie offered as a farfetched glimmer of hope.

"They don't use their emergency lights for that," Brad whispered.

"How the hell would I know?" Brad shot him a curt look. "Maybe Douglas Patino found out we broke into his house."

He checked the binoculars and saw four police cars sitting in Brad's driveway. He didn't see Sheriff Thrower, but quite a crowd had built up around the sidewalk. Even if Brad was right, would breaking into the Patino house really result in four cruisers being sent to Brad's place?

It reminded him of Mack's house the night he was attacked. The crowd, the questions, the jabber, lights flashing, refusal of the police to talk, the mystery, and most of all the unanswered questions. He still hadn't seen Mack since after that baseball practice.

Why didn't I go after him?

It dawned on him that Brad might be worried about his parents. Sure, his dad was the sheriff, but four cops sitting in your driveway could have been unrelated to that. What if something happened to his mom or dad? *Or*, he gulped at the thought, *to Sarah*. Charlie began to realize Brad may have welcomed the reason for the cruisers to be tied back to them breaking into the Patinos' house.

"I'm sure everything is okay." He tried to calm the tension.

Without a word, Brad started the ATV and drove up slowly towards the lights and the gossipers. Charlie's dilated pupils were blinded by the harsh brightness of blue and red siren lights. Covered in mud, dirt, and sweat, appearances were no longer important. He didn't care how he smelled or what others were saying as they walked up to the house and he caught folks pointing fingers and whispering.

They walked through the front door together and saw Sheriff Thrower standing in the living room. His spirits were lifted when he saw Brad's smile, but that was destined to be short-lived.

Sheriff Thrower was on the landline phone and appeared highly agitated. He paced around the room and almost yelled into the receiver but couldn't finish his sentences. The taut cord stretched from the wall in the kitchen and the conversation was very one-sided.

"It's a mistake! Listen to—"

Then Sheriff Thrower was quiet, and turned his back to them.

"I didn't—"

More silence.

Sheriff Thrower finally turned around and said he had to go. He gently hung up the phone and beamed at them both in a sad, almost depressing manner. Charlie's eyes grew wide and he thought he saw the sheriff's lip quiver.

"Where have you two been?"

After a brief pause, Brad answered, "Riding around on the ATV."

He waited for Sheriff Thrower's reaction. The face would tell instantly whether he bought it or Brad had just made things worse. Lying was optimal if you got away with it, but it was a risky bet and Charlie wondered if it was a wise one.

"Where, in a mud puddle?"

Brad's face almost gave it away. He still had relief from seeing his father, but fear was just as present.

"No, we were just—"

Just then two uniformed police officers he'd never seen before walked through the front door. They had very matter-of-fact looks on their face, with tunnel vision towards Sheriff Thrower at first and then them. Finally, they motioned to Sheriff Thrower.

"It's time, Sheriff," one of them said.

Badges protruding from their left breast pockets and blue dress shirts visibly stiff from over-starching, they both stared intently at Brad and him with clear determination. But for what? One had short black hair spiked up with gel, police hat in his hand. The other, who did the talking, had short blonde hair and wore glasses.

"Okay," Sheriff Thrower whispered. "Just give me a minute."

What the hell did "it's time" mean?

Sheriff Thrower looked at Brad with soft, wide eyes. He spoke softly, just above a whisper.

"Brad, you're going to have to go with these officers now."

"What?"

"Brad, listen to me!"

"Yes, sir."

"I know you didn't do it. I know this is a mix-up and I'm going to get it straightened out. Do you hear me? *Do you hear me, son?*"

"Yeah, Dad, I..."

"Don't say anything. I'll meet you at the station."

"What? What did I do?" Brad panicked, his jaw wide open, shaking his head.

"Brad...listen to me, son. They found the gun that killed Jimmy Patino in your bedroom."

"How did—"

With that, the blonde-haired policemen interrupted the father-son chat and pulled Brad away. Brad's face grew redder as he screamed he didn't do it. He begged his father to help, and then Charlie. Charlie could tell Brad's wails broke the Sherrif's heart as

100

the officer handcuffed him and read the Miranda rights. They proceeded out the front door for the entire assembly to watch him get pushed into the back of the police cruiser.

Sheriff Thrower walked away from him and towards a hallway, his hands over his face. Charlie stood there, listening to Brad's screams of protest, unable to think.

23

Charlie woke up the next day after an evening full of nightmares and looked in the bathroom mirror.

The gun...the actual murder weapon...was in his room. Brad killed Jimmy Patino.

Brad's wide eyes, their years of deep friendship, and Charlie's heart begged him to refute it. He'd known Brad since before kindergarten. He thought about all the times they'd had—riding bikes in the lightning, poker, bowling, that first screwdriver drink while watching a movie, the inrush of memories was like a jolting current.

After they'd taken Brad away, Sheriff Thrower came back to the living room and asked a few questions. Where did they go on the ATV? Why were they so muddy? Stymied and horrified, he didn't tell him about following Doracco, or anything about what they'd learned at the Patino house or the library in Bartelso. Terrified that he'd join Brad in the cruiser for breaking and entering, not knowing what to do, and not being able to talk to anyone, he panicked and made up a very realistic story instead to explain the night and mud away. Did he not trust Sheriff Thrower? Did he think he was somehow involved? Why did he not, at long last, just tell the truth. The whole conversation felt wrong but he perpetuated it anyway. The only honest answers he gave were that he had no idea why the gun was there and absolutely did not think Brad did it. And, of course, Brad had never mentioned anything about it.

After the painful exercise in dishonesty, he was almost certain Sheriff Thrower saw right through him. He expected to feel cold steel on his wrists as well, but instead Sheriff Thrower told him to get home and tell his mother what'd happened. He told him to call if he thought of anything, and gave one of those looks that said he knew there was more than had been shared. Finally, he offered a long hug and told him everything would be okay.

He didn't believe him.

With one friend behind bars already, another arrested for the same crime, and the third still recovering from being assaulted, he had no one left. He felt alone and helpless, but even more terrified.

The actual Remington Model 760 pump-action rifle that was used to kill Jimmy Patino—or Cory McDougal—was found under Brad's bed behind a footlocker. The police had evidently gotten an anonymous tip about the gun, and ballistics had already matched it to the weapon that put three bullets in Jimmy Patino's chest. He didn't know when they got the warrant to search the house, but that had obviously occurred long before they got back from following Doracco.

Much to Charlie's surprise, his parents didn't scold him too much. His father had just gotten back from the Georgia trip, and aside from a few questions about whether or not he knew anything further, his folks didn't push him too much. He could tell the pain in his mother's eyes and even his dad was gentle with the questioning.

He paced around town, slowly, thinking and contemplating without much to show for it. *The Germantown Sun* was having a field day and he tried not to even look at the headlines, much less read the articles. The only helpful tidbit was that Barry Ray was expected to be released within a week but would likely be kept from the public at his family's request.

No one called him. His good friends were all gone and anyone who knew him was keeping their distance. He was alone and empty, but he somehow knew it was going to get worse before it got better.

24

"Hi, Sarah," Charlie said softly, watching her slowly put one foot in front of the other while keeping her head down. She was wearing blue jeans and a white tank top walking on Ash Drive, a side street near a construction zone where a new house was being built. She waved hello, but her body language was sluggish and her beautiful smile didn't emerge.

Her perfect brown eyes looked bloodshot and tired from what had to be repeated crying. Why hadn't he cried? Brad was his best friend, and he was there when two policemen dragged him away. What was wrong with him?

"You were there when they took Brad, right?"

"Yeah, I was there."

"Do you think he really did it? He says he didn't, so why'd they take him away?" She sounded innocent and ignorant at the same time.

"I don't know, Sarah."

"They said Jimmy Patino was killed between nine and ten. If that's true, there's no reason they should think Brad did it."

Now he listened intently, once again having underestimated her.

"He was on the other side of town, south of the park, helping one of my dad's friends move some stuff out in his barn. If he was there, there was no way he could be killing Jimmy."

Just then it hit Charlie like a lightning strike. Why he hadn't thought of it before was beyond him, but that didn't mean it didn't happen. Brad working at the farm had come up when they were playing cards before Barry Ray was arrested. Brad came to the table and slapped a fifty down on the table. Barry Ray grabbed it, demanding to know where Brad got it. And then Brad told them all that his dad asked him to help old man Larry Cates move some stuff around in his barn. He'd worked all morning and then Cates handed him the crisp bill. Brad said he tried to give it back but old man Cates insisted and told him to keep it a secret from Sheriff Thrower, who would never let Brad keep it. *Go buy a six-pack or something else you shouldn't have,* Cates had said.

A burst of enthusiasm coursed through his veins as he recalled the exchange.

"Do you know what time he started?"

"He was gone when I came down for breakfast at seven-thirty, I know that."

"When did he get back?"

"Around ten-thirty."

"Then what did he do?"

"Took a shower because he smelled like he'd been rolling around in a pigsty. Then he changed and left for Mack and Barry Ray's place to meet you for poker."

He looked for every angle where a younger sister would try to get her brother off, but nothing jumped out. Old man Cates lived pretty far from where Jimmy lived and from County Line Road, at least by bike. About twenty minutes. That was the thing about small towns—the rustic lifestyles meant big parcels of land and few neighbors. It wouldn't be possible for Brad to get there in time even with the ATV, and Sarah was right that there was no way he killed Jimmy if he was at Cates's farm when it happened.

"Did you tell your dad?"

"Yeah."

"What did—"

"I don't want to talk about it," she sighed. As hard as it was not to probe for more information, he saw the sadness in her eyes and knew it wasn't the time. She stopped walking and looked right at him, no words, but an abundance of emotion.

"Can we go in there?" she said, pointing towards the house being built. He figured she didn't want to be talking about her brother's arrest out in the open—not in Germantown, where anyone could be watching or listening. He understood that.

The house was a sprawling rancher with a three-car garage and winding sidewalk. Nobody was working on it at the time, and he had no idea why. It was warm, but no warmer than any of the other days that summer. And there was a gentle breeze, which made it better than most to be outside building a house. The foundation was laid and the house had been framed and sheathed, but there was no plumbing, electrical, insulation, or even drywall. There was a "NO TRESPASSING" sign posted, but there was no fence.

"Sure," he replied.

They made their way through what would be the garage and headed through a doorway that led into what he guessed was the kitchen, leading into the would-be dining room. The lack of appliances, carpet, decorations, furniture, and doors prevented him from being able to appreciate it as a house with its wood frames, hardwood floors, nails exposed, and piles of construction materials in every room.

"My dad told me someone called the Aviston police department and said they knew where the weapon was: underneath Brad's bed, beneath a blanket behind his footlocker. The Aviston chief called my dad and there were already other cops at the house. They'd found the gun."

Aviston was eight miles northwest and he hardly ever went there. He wasn't sure the police could obtain a search warrant based on an anonymous tip, but it seemed a moot point now. The bigger question was where did the tip come from in the first place.

"Was it your dad's gun?" he asked as they sat down on the hard floor of a room that had no window cutouts and would likely become the dining room.

"He said he'd never seen it before. The cops took it to a lab and the lab people said it was the gun that killed Jimmy Patino."

The fact ballistics had matched the bullets from Jimmy's body to the ones in the rifle's chamber found in Brad's room, had analyzed the barrel to determine it had been recently fired, resulting in the conclusion it was the murder weapon did not bode well for Brad's innocence.

"Did they get any fingerprints?"

"My dad didn't say. I don't think so," she said, pulling her long brown hair back and out of her face.

"Hey, Sarah," he said softly, "I'm sure they're going to let him go when they find out where he was all morning."

"But why did they even arrest him?"

"The gun, Sarah. It's hard to—"

"The real killer could've put it there, right? I mean, wouldn't that be what you'd want to do if you were the killer. Put the gun somewhere else, then tell the cops where it is. They arrest someone who didn't do it and you get out free."

"That doesn't change the fact they still have to arrest him based on the evidence they have. If the murder weapon was really in his room, I don't know that they could have done anything else. Alibis can clear Brad later, but do you really think they can't act on that?"

He thought of telling her about what Brad and he had been doing, what they learned, etc., but thought it might be overload. She was a mess.

"I'm sorry, Sarah."

She shrugged. "My dad isn't the lead on the Jimmy Patino case anymore."

He neglected to mention that not only did that seem inevitable, but that it was a good thing. Beyond the conflict of interest, Sheriff Thrower was in over his head from the start with Jimmy's murder case.

"The cops in Aviston?"

"I don't think so. My dad mentioned the state police."

She sighed again. She sat Indian style, arms folded on her knees and back hunched over helplessly. His legs were extended straight out and his arms behind him, supporting his weight.

"It's just not fair," she whispered, her head pointed straight down, robbing him of a glimpse of her big brown eyes and petite nose.

His father's voice echoed in his mind: *Life's not fair.*

"I'm so sorry, Sarah." He gently put his hand on her back. "Once they do the background they'll—"

She suddenly thrust herself at him with a lurch and he fell backwards onto the hard floor, but didn't feel any pain. Sarah Thrower then pressed her lips aggressively into his, her tongue pushing its way deep into his mouth.

Feeling a step behind but not complaining, he interlocked lips with his best friend's sister and gasped for air through his stuffy nose. She made a soft, low-pitched moan that made him want her more.

Then, it stopped as abruptly as it began. Sarah said she had to go and smiled before heading out the door, leaving him to soak in the moment. Finally, he got up to leave and tried to run through the scenarios in his head.

If someone planted the gun in Brad's room, it meant several things. First, the killer was not Brad or Barry Ray, and was still out there. Second, whoever it was knew Brad or at least of him, well enough to plant the weapon and frame him for murder. And third, authorities were even farther from solving the case than he'd imagined they were.

But there were things that didn't make sense, the biggest being the most obvious: *Why?*

With Barry Ray already in custody and awaiting a court date for committing the crime, why would the real murderer take the risk of planting the weapon on someone else?

The first possibility that jumped into Charlie's mind was the killer had something against Brad and there was more backstory than simply the killer not wanting to go to jail. Maybe he'd wanted to frame Brad all along and accidentally framed Barry Ray instead. Or it could be that the guy got his jollies watching the police follow the cheese through the maze and toying with people's lives at the same time. On the other hand, what if the weapon being planted in Brad's

108

room had nothing to do with the killer, but rather was done by someone Barry Ray knew trying to get him off the hook?

Trying to figure that equation out with so many variables didn't seem practical or worth the time, and he shook his head quickly trying to erase the mental whiteboard. But there was one explanation that he couldn't shake. What if the killer had been stirred? What if he'd felt the pressure coming from Brad and he following him? He commits a horrible murder of Jimmy Patino, gets the wrong person arrested for it, and thinks everything is peaches and cream. Then, all of the sudden a little pest named Shane Littleton gets in the way and says he knows Barry Ray didn't do it. He tries to fix the problem, but now he's got two other guys, both of whom know Barry Ray, to worry about, who present a bigger problem than Shane.

So he starts to chip away at that problem, too.

He thought of Doracco and the man in the Impala. He still had no idea where the man fit in, or even what role Doracco played. Other than threatening Shane, something he had no proof of other than Shane's word, Doracco hadn't done anything. It's not illegal to meet in a cornfield. But it begged the question, *what's next?*

Charlie was. Barry Ray had already been incarcerated, Brad was heading there soon, and he was the only one left who knew about Shane and Jimmy Patino's real identify. Playing detective had put him into serious trouble, and he worried that the killer couldn't frame someone else. For him, maybe the killer would need to take another approach to solve the problem.

Maybe for him, it was death.

25

Charlie spent the next day trying to do anything that could stop him from thinking about the fact he was on someone's hit list. He told himself that he was simply wrong, that this was all just a horrible misunderstanding. That everything about the past week, except for meeting up with Sarah, was a dream. He wasn't thinking clearly.

He rode his bike to the intersection of the country roads where Doracco met the mystery man. It was a long ride and he took his time, his mind searching for all the things he hoped to find only to end up empty-handed.

The same two roads and endless row of cornfields were there. No noticeable tire marks, clues or indications that the two cars were there a few nights ago, no point in looking anymore. Still, he got off the bike and looked around, hoping like a dog he'd be thrown a bone. But he didn't get one.

Then he got back on his bike and headed towards town. He hadn't been to baseball practice so many times that Skip perhaps assumed he'd quit the team, but he didn't care. He needed the distraction. Since Charlie was just a bench-warming compadre anyway, Skip didn't bat an eye at the fact he hadn't been at practice since the day Mack ran away.

Why didn't I go after him?

But Skip and the team were sure to miss Brad. Brad missed his first and only baseball game of his life because he was in jail last night. That made Charlie sad, knowing that he wasn't where he belonged. He didn't think Brad killed Jimmy, and he was relatively certain that he was where Sarah said he was. But he also believed that if he hadn't dragged Brad with him to go into the Patinos' house and to the library and to the cornfield to follow Doracco that Brad wouldn't have been arrested in the first place. The ever-growing guilt had begun to pile up in his mind.

A part of him wondered if he'd be able to handle practice without seeing Brad, and all the behind-the-back comments and staring that was sure to happen. But he also knew he needed to get away from himself. He needed carefree activities to keep his mind occupied. He knew if he did that, when he turned back to what was going on, it would be a little fresher and maybe sharper, too.

It was a near perfect day for baseball. A little humid, but everyone was used to it by then. Not a cloud in the sky, a light breeze, and not unbearably hot.

Despite the stares and the awkward looks he got from pretty much everyone on the team upon arriving, he decided he was going to use the time to exercise his body in the hopes that his mind would get a breather. He didn't speak or even look at anyone, he just got right down to business. It seemed to be doing the trick at first, but it didn't work for too long.

He was the first to hit and imagined that Doracco's face was on each of the balls coming in. He swung hard, with passion, slamming the meat of the bat—called the sweet spot—into as many baseballs as were thrown. He swung hard enough to get a full sweat going. A home run swing on every pitch, whether it was a good location or not. After the very best round of batting practice he'd ever had, he sprinted to right field to shag fly balls.

Standing alone in right field, he shagged fly balls more aggressively than he ever had before, sprinting to the spot and using two hands on every play. Skip even mentioned that he was impressed. He dove for a few out of reach, aggressively charged base hits that made their way on the ground to the outfield.

"So, they tossed your buddy into the slammer, eh?" a snickery and still bruised Jason Hand said as he walked up to him.

Charlie didn't want to deal with Jason, but knew there wasn't any avoiding it. He tried to ignore him, but that gave Jason only more incentive to try harder to illicit some reaction to avoid embarrassing himself in front of the others.

"Too bad you didn't play like this before they threw that jerk off in the slammer. You might've played a little."

That didn't bother him much. Jason was right.

"I guess the loser told you to play hard for him since he'll never play again. What a tool; the sheriff's own son in the slammer. You gotta love it."

That bothered him.

"How's your face feeling?" he asked. In addition to the plethora of acne that littered Jason's cheeks, he now had tape on the brown frame of his glasses to hold them together, and a black eye that went well with his mangled nose.

"It'll get better before your friends do. I hope Brad and that wimp Mack Olson know they had it coming."

He turned and looked at Jason, fury starting to build.

"Stop talking about my friends. Go play with yourself, Mr. Handy."

It was an easy target that should've been used more than it was with the last name of Hand.

"You think you're all tough now, Charlie, just cuz you've got friends in the slammer and another who got the crap kicked out him—"

"Not as bad as you did."

"Screw you and your friends, Jefferson."

He hadn't heard anyone use his last name in a long time. Folks in town almost always just used first names; but while it actually took him aback, it didn't stop him from continuing the conversation.

"You're the handy one. Screw you."

"Why don't *you* go play with yourself. You're the one who doesn't have any friends left."

He squeezed his quadriceps and clenched his fists, even the one in the baseball glove.

"I told you to stop talking about my friends."

"You mean the criminals and the limp noodle?"

He dropped his glove and charged Jason like a mad bull. Jason didn't expect it, and when he saw him coming he froze like a deer in headlights. He plowed into his chest and knocked him flat on his back, much the same way Brad had done, and started ripping him apart. His own rage surprised him. He took all the aggression he had towards Doracco, *The Germantown Sun*, his father, and the whole crummy week and channeled it into direct blows on Jason Hand's face.

He aimed for and hit the bruises that were left there by Brad. To Charlie, those bruises were nothing but targets. Giant ducks on the pond.

Jason cried immediately even though Charlie didn't do a third of the damage to him that Brad had done when it was all over. Skip yanked him off rather quickly and it felt like it was over in the blink of an eye.

"Unbelievable, Charlie!" Skip exclaimed.

Twice in one day. That felt strange.

"I thought I told all of you no more fighting on my field!" Skip screamed.

Jason got up and looked at him, blood still flowing from his nose, and gently touched his bruises before quickly pulling away because of obvious pain.

"Want to talk about my friends some more?" he asked him, ignoring Skip's yelling.

"Get out of here! You're done! Get off my field, and don't come back!" yelled Skip, as if it was entirely Charlie's fault. But he didn't care, nothing as trivial as baseball or fights mattered any more. Nothing that used to mean everything meant anything: cards, beer, girls, baseball, riding bikes, all of it seemed unimportant. He walked away without a word.

In the background he heard Skip chastising him, talking about how the day he *finally* showed some passion on the field, he *had* to turn it into a fight. He ridiculed Jason as well for *poking the damn bear.*

He climbed on his bike without so much as a goodbye from anyone on the field. They all stared, watching him ride away. The silence was almost serene. Kicked off his first organized team, he headed home slowly. The exercise was over; now it was back to thinking. And when he got home, there was another unfortunate surprise waiting.

26

"Charlie, come in," said a hoarse voice.

He looked up, surprised as well as scared, to see Sheriff Thrower. He sat at the kitchen table next to his mother, a cup of coffee in his hand. He wore the same uniform he'd worn every day since becoming sheriff. Charlie thought of several things in that moment: Brad being in custody for murder, the baseball games he'd miss for the rest of the summer because of it, the crime the sheriff was supposed to solve but was now no longer connected to, and how all of that fit together. He also thought about Sheriff Thrower's daughter, Sarah, and wondered if the sheriff knew how Charlie felt about her. Something inside said he didn't want to find out.

His father, evidently in between runs to Georgia and Huntsville, leaned up against the cabinets in the kitchen. He wore his favorite camouflage deer hunting hat and a long-sleeved shirt tucked into a pair of work pants—his road driving outfit. He must've just gotten back, or maybe was called back. Charlie hoped it wasn't the latter.

"What happened?" asked Sheriff Thrower, pointing to his shirt. Unbeknownst to him, some of Jason Hand's blood had stained his shirt.

"I got into a fight at practice," he replied. There was little sense in lying.

"Did you get into that fight for the same reason Brad got into one?" yet another voice spoke out. This time it was Kurt Olson, sitting in the living room connected to the kitchen. Charlie turned to his right and saw him sitting on the couch, his left leg over his right knee, staring straight at him. He folded his rough hands into each other and rested them on his stomach.

When Charlie saw Kurt's face, without its famous smile, he thought of Mack and the same question.

Why didn't I go after him?

Kurt rose and walked towards the kitchen, joining the rest of them. Apparently, it was a party that Charlie was a part of but didn't know about, like a sad surprise party. He looked at his parents, Sheriff Thrower, and Kurt as though waiting for the shoe to drop. Kurt extended his arm for a handshake.

"How are you, son?"

"I'm...I'm okay. How's Mack?"

"He'll be okay, too. But he's still recovering. I told him you've been by to see him, and he sends his regards. I hope you understand why I can't let anyone disturb him."

He nodded, even though he didn't.

"He should be back to normal in a couple of months. I know that seems like a long time, but when you're my age six weeks isn't that long."

"Charlie, why don't you sit down?" his mother asked in a sweet voice, really the only kind she had. He did as instructed, at the table with her and Sheriff Thrower. His father remained leaning against the kitchen cabinets, cigarette in hand. Kurt walked around to the fourth and final seat at the table and sat down, but only after his father declined.

That was his father: on the outside looking in.

"Son, I asked you a few weeks ago to stay out of the Jimmy Patino investigation," Sheriff Thrower began. "You told me you would. You told me you'd leave the police work to the police, and I believed you. Why didn't you?"

Confronted so directly, he didn't know what to say. How did he know? *What* did he know? Should he come clean with everything? The Patino residence, the information he and Brad learned there, the library articles, the night in the cornfield, Shane identifying Doracco...Was it finally time to sing like a canary?

"What do you mean?"

Sheriff Thrower didn't answer. Instead, his dad—in a calm yet frightening voice—put things in perspective.

116

"Don't play games, Charlie. He asks the questions, you answer them."

He nodded, prompting the sheriff to continue.

"Charlie, my son was arrested yesterday for a crime I'm certain he didn't commit. And it made me realize that Barry Ray is just as innocent. If he'd killed Jimmy Patino, the gun couldn't have possibly wound up at my house. Barry Ray shouldn't have spent one day behind bars."

Charlie nodded, waiting for the part where this came back to him.

"Being a servant of the law, I believe, even when it's my own son, that justice prevails. The system works; the innocent will be released, the guilty found as such. But that can only happen when the investigation is not hindered or tampered with."

He was pretty sure the entire room heard the gulp that involuntarily slipped out, and it was little use trying to hide his trepidation.

"Charlie, I know you have the best of intentions. I know that *if* you were to be involved with an investigation and were trying to figure things out even though I asked you to stay away, that *if* you were doing that, you'd be doing it for good reason. And Kurt knows it too. We both know that if you were snooping around, trying to solve the case, you'd only be doing it because you believe our sons are innocent and you want to help."

"And we thank you for that sentiment, Charlie," interjected Kurt.

"But at the same time," continued Sheriff Thrower, "when you do that, you're interfering with the investigation that will allow justice to prevail. So while you're trying to help, you're actually making things worse for our sons. That is, of course, *if* you were doing anything."

It felt clear that Sheriff Thrower didn't know everything. If he did, there's no way the conversation would be happening the way it was. If he knew that Charlie was talking to a trespasser, a lying high school student, or a spy, and that he had just made out with his daughter, the Sheriff wouldn't have sounded so nice. Charlie didn't know where the conversation was going, but he knew it could be worse.

"Charlie," a soft-spoken Kurt said as he leaned towards him. "My son has been locked up for almost a month now, arrested by a dear friend of mine whom I respect very much. My other son is in bed, still recovering from an attack that he suffered through no fault of his own. I feel rotten. I feel cheated this summer, and that life hasn't been very fair. But I too believe in justice, and I'd like to join Sheriff Thrower in asking you to keep away from all of this."

"It's also not your place," his father hissed.

"Do you understand what we're saying, Charlie?" The sheriff's eyes were warm and inviting, but something felt forced. It was as if he was trying to make himself look amiable, and it didn't seem natural at all. But what else could he say?

"Yes, I understand."

"I'm glad, Charlie. I really am," Kurt said.

"And so am I, as is your father," began the sheriff. This was where the hammer was dropped.

"But I also know you and I have had this conversation before, and I thought we came to the same conclusion then. And I have reason to believe you haven't exactly been living up to what we agreed to."

He tried to remain calm but felt like he was being interrogated. The only things missing were the overbearing bright white light and the unidirectional perspective glass. What did the Sheriff know and how? Did Brad tell him something before the gun was planted? Had he been spying on them while they were spying on Doracco? Did he know who the man in the mask out in the country was? His mind asked all the questions but didn't produce any answers.

"There's also some concern on our part, Charlie," Kurt said. It was the bad cop—good cop—caring cop routine. And Kurt was the one who cared.

"If we're right, the killer is still out there. And if we know you're looking into things, the killer may know as well. And we don't want anything to happen to you or anyone else. We've already seen one young man murdered, another beaten, and two arrested this

118

summer. The sheriff isn't on the case anymore because of this, and the killer is still out there. I don't want anything to happen to you. None of us do. But *if* you interfere with the investigation again, you could get hurt. And the state police won't be so understanding."

It was on the tip of his tongue to tell them about Doracco, to rid himself of whatever he knew and try to get back to normal life, but he remained silent.

"That being the case," Sheriff Thrower continued, "we've decided that between your parents and me, we'll be keeping a very close eye on you."

Charlie didn't respond, other than to look at each other person in the room. His mother had tears in her eyes.

"You parents will watch you at night, and we'll keep a close lookout for you during the day."

"You are not to leave this house unless you ask your mother," snarled his father. "I'll speak with your baseball coach and inform him you will no longer be able to participate." He decided not to let him know that such a call was unnecessary. "No exceptions, son."

Charlie sat there, paralyzed, determined not to show emotion. Everyone looked back, until his mom broke the silence.

"It's the best thing, sweetie. Just until this all blows over.

"Charlie," Sheriff Thrower continued, "don't make me arrest you for interfering with a police investigation. It's not my case anymore, and we need to let the state police do their job."

27

He sat there like a prisoner in his own home, holding an unopened *Sports Illustrated* while staring at the deluge coming down outside. It was Monday morning around ten, and he was sitting alone, sitting on the large windowsill of his bedroom. His view was obscured by a big oak tree that he'd watched grow over the past eighteen years, its leaves concealing the streets of Germantown. So much felt hidden these days, not the least of which was the answer to who killed Jimmy Patino.

He'd sat in church the day before listening to the Lutheran pastor give a sermon about doing the right thing in hard times. Pastor Bob pulled scripture from the books of Galatians, Job, and Daniel in a way that felt like a direct message from God. *Let us not become weary in doing good.* Feeling like the Apostles may have when they were wrongfully imprisoned, he just hoped it worked out better for him than it did for John the Baptist.

Unable to talk to Shane Littleton, questions about where Doracco was the day Jimmy got killed, the mysterious man in the mask, Jimmy Patino's real identity, or why two of his good friends were still in police custody for the same crime that neither likely committed remained unanswered. They were like splinters in his mind, like an itch he couldn't scratch. The ringing phone startled him, causing Charlie to jump and bang his elbow on the window frame. He shook his arm and muttered under his breath, then clenched his teeth and inhaled sharply as he picked up the phone

"Hello?"

"Hello, is Charlie Jefferson there?"

He didn't recognize the voice.

"This is Charlie."

"Charlie, hi there. This is Mrs. Hunter!" The voice's enthusiasm made him feel bad that he'd had no idea who it was. His silence must've tipped her off.

"Come to think of it, I don't think I ever introduced myself. You may remember me as Emily. I'm the Bartelso librarian you met a few weeks ago at the Reference Desk."

"Oh, hello, Mrs. Hunter," he replied, picturing her thick glasses, gray hair in a ponytail, and the warmth of a grandmother's smile in a younger-looking woman.

"I'm sorry to disturb you at home, but I got your number from the forms you filled out and remembered your project was due this summer."

Was there more information about Jimmy Patino? Thrill surged through his veins. He turned around to make sure no one was there even though he was certain he was alone, then hunched down beside the bed, the phone's cord stretching from the nightstand beside it.

"It's no bother at all, ma'am."

"Okay, good. Do you remember the second article I gave you, referencing Nelson Towns?"

He reluctantly pulled the paper copy articles out of his top desk drawer.

The second article was dated September 4, 1982, and described the horrible crime Nelson Towns had committed in Butler, and then referenced a similar allegation in Columbus nine years earlier resulting in a child that had recently been abandoned.

"Yes, I have it with me here."

"As I told you I would, I kept looking for more information about the unfortunate allegation against Mr. Towns from Butler in 1981. The one that ..."

"Yes ma'am, I know what you're talking about."

"I wasn't able to find much, but I did learn the name of the boyfriend the minor was dating at the time. I don't know if that will help your project, but it's something."

"Anything you have would be very helpful. I appreciate it very much."

Emily offered an appreciative "mm-hmm," indicating she was glad to help. It made him feel a little guilty again, lying to the only person who was actually trying to help him.

"The boyfriend's name was Michael Thrower. He was seventeen at the time."

His heart at first skipped a beat, then raced terribly fast.

"Excuse me, ma'am. But did you say Thrower? T-H-R-O-W-E-R?" He spelled it out.

"Yes, that's right. Michael Thrower. T-H-R-O-W-E-R. He attended the same school as the minor. I'm sorry that's all I could find."

His mind wouldn't let him think of what to say. After a few moments of silence, he forced out some words.

"Thank you very much, ma'am. I really appreciate it."

"There's one last thing. One year to the day of the alleged incident in Butler, Nelson Towns died in a single car crash outside rural Pennsylvania. His vehicle swerved off Highway 62 near Tionesta in the middle of the night and was discovered the next morning in the Allegheny River. The blood screen from the autopsy report revealed significant levels of multiple illegal substances in his system at the time of the crash as well as a blood alcohol level of .21, more than double the legal limit even at the time, when it was higher than it is now. No one else was injured, and the official cause of death was drowning. Charlie, perhaps I shouldn't say this, but it sure feels like justice found Mr. Towns in the end."

The fact it happened exactly one year later felt super coincidental to him, almost *too* coincidental, but he couldn't deny that he agreed with Emily's sentiment.

"Charlie, is everything...okay?"

"Yes, sorry. I was just thinking. Thank you again."

"You're welcome. If I find anything else, I'll let you know."

28

Less than a half hour later he was on his bike, pedaling through the rain on his eighteen-speed with only one thing on his mind: *Michael Thrower.* The boyfriend of the minor assaulted by Jimmy Patino's biological father. He didn't know anyone by that name or if there was a connection to Brad's family, but he knew he had to find out.

When his mother got home from the store, Charlie asked her if he could go to the bowling alley to try to have some fun. She hesitated, studied his face like she was trying to decipher ancient hieroglyphics, and calmly replied, "I'm trusting you, Charlie. Don't make me regret it."

He felt bad about it, but Joe always said desperate times call for desperate measures. Plus, he was in fact going to the bowling alley. Given the rain, Sarah would most likely be there too.

As he pedaled faster into the rain, the pellets of water bounced off his face like bugs on a hot summer night, creating a painful sensation up and down his cheeks. He wore sunglasses to protect his eyes despite the sun being buried beneath a blanket of gray clouds.

He felt lucky Sheriff Thrower didn't charge him with something piddly just to make him wear an ankle monitor. He figured it was because Sheriff Thrower was trying to keep his involvement with the case on the DL from the state police, and obtaining an ankle monitor and the surveillance manpower that came with it prevented him from doing so, but Charlie was thankful nonetheless.

As he pedaled through a stiff wind that had abruptly emerged out of nowhere, his windbreaker completely soaked and face dripping wet, he couldn't stop thinking about Michael Thrower. Who was he and what was his connection to the Thrower family Charlie knew? Was there even a connection? Was it just a coincidence? How many

Throwers could there be in the world? Likely more than he realized. Did Sheriff Thrower have any family in Butler, OH?

He arrived at the bowling alley and tried not to look down the stairs towards the dark Legion Hall where Shane and he had met. He didn't even want to see that room.

The noises of the bowling alley on a rainy summer day drowned out everything else. The sound of balls crashing into pins with a resounding pop and subsequent clatter of pins dropping and falling everywhere. The cheers and jeers that inevitably followed those sounds, much to the joy or chagrin of the bowlers watching. The roll of the ball on the alley itself, the soft humming that got louder as it got farther away, contrary to what you'd think.

Germantown's bowling alley hadn't implemented a computer for automatic scoring yet, so while a few folks kept score with a pen and paper, the vast majority simply didn't bother. Bowling and math were like oil and water.

She was in aisle four, in the far back seat, slouched up against the chair with her legs extended outward. She didn't appear to be bowling, or particularly happy to be there. There were three other girls with her—he recognized them all as classmates—and they were laughing and cheering each other on while she sat there quietly.

He approached aisle four and said her name softly. She heard and lifted herself up, pulling her legs in and sitting up to turn around. When she saw him, she revealed an ever-so-small smirk, a brief smile that was quickly replaced with a straight face.

"Hi," she said softly.

"Hey there. Can we talk for a minute?"

She got up and walked past him, motioning for him to follow her towards the doors. They pushed through the first set of double doors and stood in the tiny confines in between. It was much quieter and brighter.

"How are you?" he asked.

"Better now," she answered with a fuller smile than before. His heart pumped faster.

"Listen, can you do me a favor?"

"Is this about Jimmy Patino?"

"Well..." He paused. He didn't want to lie to her. Able to justify it for his mom, he couldn't find a fair angle with Sarah.

"Yeah."

"Charlie!" she screamed, making him thankful for the double door's insulation. "My dad told you to stay away from that. He told me to tell him if I found out you weren't! Even Kurt asked you not to get in the way! Why are you doing this?"

He wasn't surprised Sheriff Thrower asked his daughter to keep tabs on him, but he was disappointed. He didn't want to put her into a compromising situation, but Joe's words about drastic times echoed in his mind and he pushed forward. He stared straight into her beautiful brown eyes.

"I just have a question for you. I'm doing this to help the others. Barry Ray, Mack, and Brad. Don't you want to help your brother?"

He immediately regretted saying it. Sarah didn't say anything, but her wrinkled brow said it all.

"I'm sorry, Sarah. I shouldn't have—"

"What do you want to know?" she said with caution, almost in a calculated way.

"Really, I'm sorry," he said once more.

"I know. What do you want to know?" She thrust her head forward and raised her eyebrows in a gesture that said *let's get on with this.*

After a long pause, "Have you ever heard of someone named Michael Thrower?"

She squinted her eyes and tilted her head for a few seconds, then with a small shrug said, "He's my uncle."

29

"You have an uncle named Michael Thrower?"

"Yeah. I've actually never met him in person, but Dad has talked about him."

The space between the double doors suddenly felt too small, triggering a claustrophobic sensation that made him feel like he couldn't breathe, like there was no air. He motioned for them to step outside, shielded from the rain by the small balcony cantilevered above the entryway.

"Why do you ask?" she said plainly.

He'd prepared his answer on the ride over, one that neither lied nor would make her worry.

"It may be nothing."

"What's that supposed to mean, Charlie? You want me to answer your questions but don't want to tell me why you're asking?"

"Sarah, look—"

"Tell me why you're asking about him."

It would've been easier for him on multiple fronts to just spill his guts. He hadn't talked to anyone about Jimmy Patino's real identity except Brad, and he was now in jail awaiting formal charges. Sarah was getting angrier by the second not knowing what was going on, and he could address both issues at the same time by coming clean. And yet he felt the natural urge to protect her, by letting her remain ignorant of the ugliness of the situation. He realized then how much he was starting to care for Sarah Thrower.

"Listen to me," he whispered. "I need you to hear me and believe me." He got even closer to her and could smell a faint hint of her perfume, his face inches from hers. "I can't talk about it right now, for your sake. I don't want you to be involved, but I need to know whatever you know about Michael Thrower. Trust me, Sarah, I'll tell you everything if I ever get the chance. But now is not the right time."

She frowned again and shook her head. After a long pause, their faces and lips close to one another, she nodded.

"There's not much to tell. Like I said, I never met him."

"Anything you know could help."

"He's my uncle, four years younger than my dad. All my parents have told me is that he's kind of messed up. Into drugs and stuff like that. A long time ago he tried to hurt himself and almost died."

"When did they tell you about him?"

"When I was real little. They just mentioned to Brad and me about an uncle we had that we should pray for."

"You've never seen him?"

"No."

"And why did they want you to pray for him?"

"Because of the drugs and how messed up he is. He's in some sort of mental hospital now. I think he's on medication for schizophrenia."

"Do you know which hospital?"

She shot him a sideways glance. "*No.*"

"Does your dad see ever him?"

"I don't think so. I think they had a fight."

"What makes you say that?"

"Look, Charlie," she said, looking him straight in the eye. "Dad never talks about Uncle Michael. I've only heard his name a few times in my life, and I haven't heard it for a long time until today. It was like Dad didn't want anything to do with him. Mom either. For all I know, he's not even real."

He nodded slowly. "Do you know how long he's been in a mental hospital?"

"No. Because I haven't even met him, I guess I...didn't think about it."

He could tell from the way she held her breath and wrinkled her nose that Sarah wanted to ask why he wanted to know. The rain had lessened to a gentle drizzle, and it'd grown quiet enough outside the bowling alley for him to hear the water dripping from a nearby gutter. The slow and steady plinking had an eerie feeling about it that made the hair on his arms stand up. He cleared his throat twice to try to shake it off.

"Is there anything else you can tell me? Have you ever seen a picture, or did he ever write you a letter?"

Sarah blew the wisps of hair off her forehead to clear her line of sight and looked up towards the overcast sky, like she was searching for something. Almost like she was trying to pull anything she could out of her memory bank, but it just wasn't there. He sighed when she quietly shook her head.

"There really isn't. Sorry, Charlie."

"That's okay, Sarah. I really appreciate your trust."

She smiled. "Do you think Brad will be okay?"

It was a question that begged to be answered favorably. She was looking for support, for a glimmer of hope that all would be well and she'd get her brother back.

"I think he will. The state police just have to clear some stuff up, but when they do, I think he'll be back on the baseball field."

She gave a slight nod then embraced him, grasping his back and pulling herself into him. Her head buried in his chest, he closed his eyes and savored the floral aroma of her silky hair. He imagined that if beauty had a smell, this was it. She unclasped her hands and pulled back just enough to make eye contact, her hands now gripping his upper arms.

"I won't tell my dad anything. And I'll try to learn a little more from my mom. But you have to promise me something," she said with wide eyes.

"What's that?"

"Be careful, Charlie. Just be careful."

"I will."

She released his arms and her eyes welled up. "I don't want to lose you too."

He stood all alone, speechless, for a few moments after Sarah slipped back inside the bowling alley. Then he walked to his bike, the raindrops hitting his head and running down the side of his cheeks. Still smelling the scent of beauty, in his mind he realized just how much he didn't want to lose her either.

30

The next morning, Charlie woke up and sat on the back patio in athletic shorts and an old white T-shirt with the phrase "No Hope With Dope" emblazoned across the front that he'd gotten at an anti-drug rally at school a few years ago and was so comfortable it'd become his favorite. Clutching his baseball glove, a glass of orange juice on the table next to him, he was trying to make heads or tails of everything he'd learned. At just before eight, the temperature was still a relatively pleasant 75 degrees and the humidity was a mere fraction of what it would be come afternoon.

He repeated the series of events one more time in a soft whisper in an attempt to keep it all straight. Fifteen years ago, a man named Nelson Towns assaulted a thirteen-year-old girl, who was at the time dating a shy seventeen-year-old named Michael Thrower, Sheriff Thrower's brother. After the crime, Towns was arrested and his son was adopted by Douglas and JoAnn Patino, who changed his name to Jimmy Patino. There was no indication of what happened to his biological mother. The Patinos just happened to live in the same small, Southern Illinois town that Sheriff Thrower did, some 500 miles away from where the crime occurred. Almost twenty years later, Jimmy Patino is shot to death with a pump-action Remington Model 760 rifle, and Sheriff Thrower himself is heading up the investigation...until his own son becomes a primary suspect when the murder weapon is found in his room.

The whole thing reeked of conspiracy, but there was no proof it was anything but a gigantic coincidence. How could he learn if there was more? He contemplated the possibilities, by thinking through where each of the players in the story was now.

Brad was behind bars for committing a crime he now thought Sheriff Thrower could have actually committed; poor Barry Ray had been behind bars for almost the entire summer.

What if everything was connected, and the story about Jimmy Patino's father was the glue? What if Sheriff Thrower had something to do with the murder as some sort of revenge for what happened years ago to his brother's girlfriend? But the more he considered it, the more he realized the idea was outrageous, and as porous as the baseball glove he was holding.

As convenient as it would be to have a central point of connection that made the entire puzzle come together, it just wasn't that simple. Michael Thrower, the sheriff's brother, was in a metal institution, and he was the one who might have a motive. Sheriff Thrower had two children and a nice life. Why would he do something like that? And why now? The other point was that Nelson Towns was the one who committed the terrible crime back in 1982, not his son.

And why did the Patinos adopt Cory McDougal, the son of such an awful man? They could've had another child—Scotty was six years older than Jimmy, so they already knew they could have kids. And people certainly have many valid reasons for adoption, but why Cory McDougal? Even more confusing, why conceal it from the rest of the community? Was it to protect Cory/Jimmy from the backstory in a small town? It seemed particularly contrary to character for Douglas Patino to hide anything that would make him look good politically. The fact that he would take a young person in and give him a chance was good PR.

Then there was Doracco. How did he fit in? The guy wasn't from here, and he didn't seem to have any connection whatsoever. And, Charlie reminded himself, before he got the call from Mrs. Hunter at the library, he was convinced that it was Doracco who had killed Jimmy Patino. Should backstory from fifteen years ago really change that? He reminded himself of what Shane Littleton had told him about Doracco, and the fact Shane had identified him in the first place.

And what about the man with the Impala? What did he and Doracco talk about? Did he pay Doracco to kill Jimmy Patino? What was in the envelope? Who was the man? There were endless questions around that, and suddenly he was nauseated.

Shane could be lying for all he knew. It didn't seem likely, but maybe he wasn't threatened by Doracco. Maybe he was just trying to protect himself against the bully Doracco the way his brother failed to protect himself against the bully Jimmy Patino. Maybe he didn't want to lose his lunch money or get beaten up, so he took a proactive approach.

And yet, of all the unknowns, the one most mystifying to him was Brad. The gun was in his room...how did that happen? If he was really working at old man Cates's place, why wasn't he released yet? Brad had been so unwilling to dig deeper into Jimmy's true background, Doracco, and the man in the Impala. Charlie suddenly found himself wondering why. Barry Ray was as much Brad's friend as he was Charlie's, so why wasn't Brad just as eager to find out what really happened? Was it because he really did have something to do with the murder?

The never-ending stream of questions flooded his mind like a river after the dam burst, washing away its basic foundation. It penetrated his home and had stripped him of so many things he'd previously taken for granted. Alone on the resulting floating island and surrounded by the dangerous waters that put him there, he promised God he'd never take them for granted again if he could find solid land.

Flustered, he took some deep breaths and got up from the bed to head outside to breathe the free air, deciding he was going to mow the lawn. It was the one chore he actually enjoyed, and he hoped the smell of fresh cut grass and the hum of the Toro engine would drown out all the clutter.

On the doorstep was *The Germantown Sun*, and its now typical front-page update on the Jimmy Patino murder investigation. The articles continued to offer absolutely no substance whatsoever as to how the case was progressing, yet people gobbled it up because it was the biggest news in the history of Germantown.

In a few small towns nearby, there were some ongoing protests that provided the meat of today's generic update. Folks held up signs saying they shouldn't let their children be corrupted by this summer, how it was wrong that Sheriff Thrower wasn't allowed to lead the investigation, and even a poster asking if the case would've been handled differently had Jimmy Patino been a minority. Race clearly had nothing to do with it, but the platform's iron was hot and folks wanted to strike.

The protests did seem interesting at first—Free Speech in action—but they quickly lost their allure. People in Germantown don't protest, and neither do people in any surrounding towns. This wasn't Pennsylvania Avenue or Berkeley; it was the center of the Midwest breadbasket, where tradition and conservatism prevailed.

He walked towards the garage and the lawnmower's temporary reprieve, and noticed his bike resting up against the side door despite not putting it there. He noticed that there was something taped to the seat. Immediately, he knew something was wrong. He looked around and didn't see anyone; the neighbors next to them were old and a fence separated the garage from the yard, and there wasn't anyone out in the open.

It was a brown envelope, like the one that he saw the masked man give Doracco. On the front, under the clear tape that held it to the bike's seat, was "BRAD" written in a black marker. Just then he heard his mother say goodbye on her way out to the store from a few feet away, and he separated himself from the bike and blocked the view of the seat.

After he forced out a response, his mother walked through the open garage door and started the car. He waited with equal parts exhilaration, fear, and impatience. It felt like waiting for the last bell on the last day of the school year, with a good dose of fear injected.

The regular, mundane brown envelope one could buy in packs of fifty at any discount store sat atop his bike, silently waiting. He felt almost certain it was not good, and considered throwing it away...for about two seconds.

He carefully pulled open the scotch-tape-sealed cover and peeked inside, seeing only one piece of paper. It had crisp edges and felt heavier than normal notebook paper. But when he read it, he no longer cared what kind of paper it was.

I know you're secretly investigating the Patino murder. You think you're so smart. But you'd better stop. If you don't, you'll regret it, and so will she. You mention this to anyone, you won't see tomorrow, and neither will she. Back off, smart guy. I'll be watching.

31

Paralyzed, Charlie stood by the garage door for a few minutes before stepping inside and shutting the door behind him. He leaned back against the windshield wall, resting his spinning head and taking a long, slow breath. He blew it out slowly to the count of ten and closed his eyes. Finally, his knees stopped shaking and he felt like he could walk, so he decided to mow the lawn to see how good the Toro engine really was at drowning out any other noise. Pushing it slowly one line after another in the relatively pristine lawn, he tried to piece together where to go from here.

The note implied that whoever wrote it knew about his visits to the Bartelso library, as well as perhaps about the night he and Brad had followed Doracco on the bike.

He imagined Doracco's face—that smug expression, the way he walked and talked when near the ladies. He wanted to wipe the grin right off Doracco's face and make it so he could never talk again, and to bust his kneecaps and paralyze him from the waist down so he'd never walk again either. He pushed the mower harder and faster as he fantasized about backing Doracco into a corner, sweat starting to drip from his face onto his now green-rimmed gym shoes. He'd forgotten to change into his grass-cutting shoes and his new Nikes had paid the price.

The assumption behind his rage was that Doracco wrote the note, but it didn't have to be and he knew it. Sheriff Thrower knew he'd been investigating behind his back and even admitted to him that it didn't make him happy. Or maybe it could have been someone else altogether.

But whoever it was, he knew where Charlie lived and obviously felt comfortable enough to be seen near his house. In reality, it didn't take much to know where he lived. Not only was there a phonebook listing all of the nearly 1,000 residents in Germantown, but most people knew where everyone else lived as a general rule.

He thought about asking his neighbors if they'd seen anyone around the house, but decided against it. The Sevels wouldn't do any good and based on the lack of cars in the driveway, it didn't look like anyone was home. Both the Sevels and the Clevelands, their other neighbors, used their garages to store crap instead of cars. He never understood it, but he didn't understand a lot of things.

When he reached the halfway point in the lawn, he noticed the lines were far from straight and thought to himself that there would be no trim. He thought back to yesterday, and the ride he took through the rain. Did he see anyone? Did anyone look suspicious in the bowling alley? Did he ride past anyone who appeared to be looking at him? The last time he went by his bike was yesterday, when he'd tossed it down on the lawn and went inside. Between then and now, someone had dropped off the note.

He couldn't remember anyone or anything that looked too suspicious. It was like most things in life. When you're actively looking for something, it jumps out at you. When you're not, you could walk right by it and not even notice it was there. He cursed out loud—his voice muffled by the Toro—for not being more careful. Even Shane had been more careful, leading them both down to the dark and desolate American Legion to have their discussion. It was just another example of Charlie being in over his head.

The "she" in the note was most likely Sarah, which made him even more upset. How could he just ride his bike casually over to the bowling alley and talk to her in plain sight? How could he expose both of them and not think anything of it? This was all his fault.

He finished the lawn and was covered in sweat, the summer heat already in full force despite it being just shy of midday. He walked the mower back to the garage and passed his bike and the trash can with the remnants of the brown envelope inside.

He knew what he had to do now, what was most important: keep Sarah safe. He could try to figure out who wrote the note and what it meant for him, but that was secondary. He wondered again if she'd been threatened directly. She didn't seem alarmed yesterday, though it was possible that whoever left the note contacted her after their meeting at the bowling alley. But his gut told him no; that she hadn't been contacted. And while that gut was partly responsible for getting him into this mess, it was clear that he had no other viable option.

He ran inside and packed a bag, stuffing it with sandwiches his mom had made for supper that night and a bunch of non-perishables. He added a few sets of clothes, but didn't really know what he'd need. Randomly picking a few shirts and a couple of pairs of pants, he jammed them into the bag and headed towards the cookie jar. It was money for emergencies only, but this was just that. He emptied the jar with one smooth dump, the clinking of change momentarily filling his ears as an avalanche of coins and bills cascaded into the bag.

Then he went into the basement, to the back room with a closet that was always locked. He took the hanging key from the hook and opened the door. After he grabbed the .22 caliber handgun, a box of bullets, and the knife, he ran upstairs and out the door to hop on his bike.

32

It was exactly 1:15 according to his watch.

Sarah was walking out of the high school's gymnasium carrying a bag likely containing her clothes, pom-poms, and cheerleading shoes. Tryouts were a big deal for the girls even though most who were on the squad the year before were shoo-ins. He knew she would be there.

In Germantown, the middle and high school grades were combined into one building, seventh through twelfth grade, with one primary hallway for high school and the other for junior high. It still didn't have more than 400 students total. No air-conditioning, no science laboratories, old, musty walls coated in lead paint, vinyl floors likely full of asbestos, and a very drab aesthetic.

It didn't bother Charlie because he didn't know any better. Most didn't. Half the students in the school had parents who went to the same building. It was not uncommon for teachers to teach three generations of the same family. Superintendents and principals were required to live in the district, meaning their children went to the same school they worked at every day. Too many teachers socialized with the students like they were peers. It all added up and contributed to the small-town stereotype.

Sarah wore shorts, a pair of gym shoes, and a skin-tight T-shirt. Other girls walked beside her and waved enthusiastically as they climbed into their parents' cars. He knew she liked to walk. It was about a mile to her house and Sarah loved taking walks, even after practice. She told him once that she liked the peace and quiet of a walk by herself. Plus, he thought to himself, she's not in any rush to get back to her house.

He stood in the cornfield surrounding the backstop fence of the junior high baseball field, about five hundred feet from the gym.

Through the binoculars, he watched her make her way towards the country road that led away from the highway to the east and towards the cornfields where he was standing to the west. She'd cut through the gravel parking lot and into the grass that became the outfield for the baseball field, making a straight diagonal to meet up with the country road just behind the backstop.

In contrast to the Legion field where the high school team played in the park, the junior high field was a pit. The uneven, rocky outfield was an injury waiting to happen. It was overused, under-treated, and a real eyesore with its half-dead grass and rocks.

Her face looked sad, somber. No smile, lips pursed, eyes staring straight ahead. As he watched, she dragged her feet on the hilly and sporadically rocky green and yellow grass that was in such poor shape that other junior highs refused to play on the field for fear of injury. When she cut through the dry dirt infield and through the opening in the fence between the visitor dugout and the backstop, he returned the binoculars to the duffle bag. All the cars and other girls were gone. The parking lot five hundred feet away was empty and there was no one else at the field. It was just the two of them, and a whole lot of country.

"Sarah," he whispered. Her head sprang up and she looked to see him, standing half-concealed in the almost harvestable corn, looking back.

"Charlie?"

"In here," he replied. She followed his voice and her eyes met his. Her tan legs and adorable nose commanded attention, but he did his best to ignore them both.

"Charlie. What are you doing here?"

Initially, he envied her. She hadn't received a note from someone threatening her or her loved ones. She didn't get warned to stay away from an investigation that made less sense by the minute. She didn't lose all her friends. She could still go to cheerleading tryouts and try to have a normal summer. Then it hit him just how bad she had it, too. It wasn't her friends she lost, it was her brother. It was her father who was removed from the case, and she had a lot more stress at home than he did. She may not have received a note, but she was in the same danger that he was and didn't even know it.

33

"Sarah." He paused. "I need to talk to you."

"Charlie. I was worried about you," she said softly.

"You were worried? Why?"

"At the bowling alley. You seemed so...weird."

It was as if she'd chosen a word with such obvious awkwardness that she knew it wasn't quite right for what she wanted to say, but was the best she had to offer.

"It's a weird time. But what do you mean?"

"I don't know." She ran her hand through her long, lustrous hair. "All your questions about my uncle, it kind of freaked me out."

He breathed a sigh of relief. She hadn't been contacted. If she had, she would've either told him or revealed it with her voice or face.

"Did anything happen last night or this morning that made you worry more?"

"What are you talking about? Charlie, stop keeping things from me. Either tell me what's going on with all of this or don't mention it again. Why were you asking about my uncle? Why are you waiting for me in a cornfield? Why are you asking me if anything happened? Is something *supposed* to happen?"

"No, not at all. I just—"

"Stop." She held up her hand. "Listen to me, please. If you're not going to tell me the truth, then just stop talking. Don't lie to me."

The vast difference between telling a lie and not telling the truth could never have been more evident to him than at that exact moment. When his silence confirmed he wasn't going to tell her everything, he knew it would be robbing her of any kind of closure. That would make her even more upset with him, but her safety had to come first. He had to listen to her request and stop dragging her into things that could get her hurt.

Rather than get upset or accuse him—both would've been understandable—she walked closer to him in the cornfield. Both of them hidden by the corn that stretched over their heads, eliminating the wind as well, their soft voices grew even softer and he could smell her regular fragrance even through the sweat she'd worked up at tryouts.

She got to within a few inches of his face and whispered. "I know you're doing something you shouldn't. I know you're in danger and not telling me because you care about me." She stared at him with those large hazel eyes, the sun's reflection belying the tears that had begun to form.

"I want you to be safe too, though, okay? I don't want to lose you either."

They were the same words she'd said before running back into the bowling alley.

"I'll be okay," he responded, trying to sound easygoing and as natural as he could. But in his mind, he didn't believe it. "And I really appreciate your caring."

"I care about you, Charlie," she said to him, getting even closer. Close enough for a kiss.

"You have to promise me something."

"What?" she mouthed, putting her hands gently on his file arms, as she had at the bowling alley.

"That you won't try to find out anything about your uncle, or mention that I asked about him. Promise me you won't ask any questions. Even to your dad." As he said it, Sarah started to kiss his him. He wanted nothing more than to kiss her back, but he pulled back.

"*Promise me.*"

She looked him in the eyes before finally whispering, "I promise." Then she closed her eyes for a few seconds before saying, "I have to go work at the florist, but meet me on Thursday. I want to see you."

"I want to, Sarah. I really, really do," he hesitated. "But maybe we shouldn't."

"I know you don't want anyone else to see you," she whispered, putting her arms around his neck. "But I want you to meet me. Right here, in this spot. Same time. Right after tryouts."

Staring into her wide, moist eyes, he knew it probably wasn't a good idea. But all he could do was nod quietly.

34

The next day two stories appeared in yet another special edition of *The Germantown Sun.* The first was a minor missing person blurb about Charlie, though it didn't get much hype. A short back-page article with a small black and white picture and note to inform the authorities if anyone saw him. No additional comments or details. But it was the other story, the one he'd heard on his pocket radio and prompted him to pick up a paper from the gas station five miles from Germantown, that was the headliner.

After an extensive investigation of his whereabouts leading up to the murder of Jimmy Patino, Brad Thrower officially became the second person released from custody in a matter of months. It was what Charlie had expected to happen, but it happened more quickly than he'd anticipated. The evidence had simply concluded that "based on the timeframe of the murder and the suspect's whereabouts during that timeframe, it wasn't possible that Bradley Thrower killed Jimmy Patino."

Charlie sat in the old library, tucked into a corner, hiding from everyone and everything he'd ever known. With his head resting up against a brick wall, legs stretched out in front of him, he blew out a breath and smiled briefly thinking of Brad. Maybe this meant things really could get back to normal, that he and Brad could get back on the baseball field and just move on. He also silently hoped Brad had kept his mouth shut when Sheriff Thrower asked him what Brad and he were up to.

But a bigger part of him was relieved for different reasons. No matter how unlikely it seemed, the mere possibility that Brad was connected to Jimmy's murder had really shaken him up. Brad was his best friend, someone he thought he knew better than himself sometimes, but you never really know about someone, and that possibility had lingered in his mind like stale air on a windless farm. Now it didn't have to.

Of course, the article further explained, the murder weapon had been found in Brad's room, which left some unanswered questions. And there was still no mention of the mysterious anonymous call. He couldn't figure out why the papers had omitted the fact that *somebody* called the police and told them about the weapon, and that it might be the same *somebody* who actually committed the crime. Maybe the police could find out who that somebody was?

With no prints on the gun, there wasn't much more to go on, the article elaborated. Only that the ballistics report had confirmed with near one hundred percent certainty that it was the gun that killed Jimmy Patino. The case had been turned back over to Sheriff Thrower.

There was no mention of Barry Ray, who'd remained hidden from the community and world in general as far as Charlie knew ever since his release. It made him wonder if the investigators had any leads the papers weren't aware of, because to the outside it looked like they'd really botched it: two wrongful arrests and bupkis to show for it now. Was this really the best the police could do?

There had to be something else. But what?

He pushed his back against the brick wall and held the bag on his lap. The gun inside felt so awkward and heavy. The hard metal didn't go with the soft bread and snacks. He'd already eaten two of the sandwiches and it had only been one day since he left. He knew he had to pace himself, or he'd run out before the week was over. Then what?

Brad's release only reaffirmed his suspicion of Doracco. He really wanted to talk Brad, but knew that was impossible, especially with Sheriff Thrower back on the case. He stretched out on the matte carpet floor and put his hands behind his head, staring up at the broken ceiling tiles that stared back at him. The dilapidated old building was a few tiles shy of being condemned and probably should have been already. But in this small town, nobody

145

complained about its condition. A few people still came in to read occasionally. That was all the town officials needed to keep the old library open.

Doracco.

What was his connection? Did he somehow know Barry Ray on a more intimate level? He was new, and didn't know any of them until a few months ago, but maybe there was backstory worth digging into. The guy had a nice car, the ladies loved him, and he sported the perfect lifestyle. He had it made in the shade as far as Germantown in the late 90s was concerned. But what was his connection to all of this? And more importantly, why?

He couldn't get the image of Doracco with the man in the Impala out of his mind. Shane Littleton was either the best, most unexpected liar he'd ever seen, or there was a connection between Doracco and Jimmy Patino. He'd spent nearly all day thinking about what it could be and had come up with nothing.

As he stared at an empty bookstack, Charlie made the decision that he had to find out more about Doracco. It was almost seven o'clock in the evening, and he'd been huddled in the closed library for over twenty-four hours. He hadn't seen another person since he walked through the front door, which he did right after he left the cornfield he'd met Sarah in. In fact, he'd avoided people to the point of standing on a toilet seat during the final check by the young teenager librarian hired to lock the doors. There was no security system of course, so all he had to do was avoid being seen and he had a place for the night.

He did worry about his mother and how she might be feeling, but still he knew this was best, considering the note he'd received. He didn't even want to think about what his father would do. But even more so, he worried news of his disappearance might actually make his dad happy.

He knew he couldn't do this forever, and that food and time was running out. *Now's the time*, he reasoned with himself. He'd been backed into a corner, and this was his only way out.

He couldn't trust the police; they'd tried to keep him away and refused to look into what he'd found out. He couldn't ask his friends; they were either related to the police or completely unreachable because of incarceration or injuries. He couldn't lean on Sarah or his mom; he needed to keep them away from this for their own safety.

With one final nod and a resounding grunt he forced himself to get up. He headed towards the bathroom and was climbing out the window before he could talk himself out of it. He walked so fast he almost tripped. The gun wasn't in his duffle bag anymore. It was in his pocket, his hand clutching it tightly.

35

There was only one place Doracco would be on a hot, sticky summer night: the roller rink. A creature of habit, when not meeting mysterious men in Impalas, he'd drive around, drink some beer, visit the car wash, cruise the strip for ladies, and even stop off to say hello to a few at the gas station and park. But in Germantown, all roads led to the rink.

Charlie walked there using side streets and trying to avoid human contact. The hot summer night had caused sweat to drip steadily from his forehead. He also couldn't deny that he felt like a criminal, one who was about to escalate his crimes from misdemeanors to felonies. Until that point, even breaking into the Patino residence and running away—with a touch of theft to boot—still felt relatively innocent. What he was contemplating doing now would not only trump that real quick and in a hurry, but could also very well end his life.

He thought about the note he'd received, more specifically, "she." Assuming it was Sarah, who could really hurt her? And would what he was about to do make it even worse for her? He'd been warned to stay away for her sake, and he was pretty much doing the opposite.

And yet, sitting back waiting to see what would happen didn't feel any better. The lesser of multiple evils, at least he was trying something instead of just waiting for something to happen to Sarah or him.

Or so he told himself.

When he reached the rink he stood across the street up against one of two large trees that shot up nearly thirty feet. Hidden from the streetlight by the shadow of the trees, even the full moon didn't counter the darkness he was in, though his shirt still had a wet patch from his throat to his navel. He wiped his face with the dry, bottom side of it and stared ahead.

The binoculars dialed in on Doracco's classic muscle car in a matter of seconds, it was hard not to notice its brilliant shine and massive engine. It was parked in a handicapped space as close to the rink as possible. As he considered approaching it, Charlie once more took stock of his situation.

He had two friends previously behind bars and then released, and another recovering from an attack. He'd made out with his best friend's sister, run away from home, was warned by the police to stay away from what he was doing now, got a threatening letter to do the same, and now held a gun in his pocket. He'd already broken into someone's home and a public library, misled numerous people like Emily the librarian to get information, and lied to his mother. He knew he was desperate.

It was hard to believe just how much he missed the poker games with Brad, Mack, and Barry Ray; the beer-drinking, baseball, late night bike rides to McDonald's, bowling a few frames, and in general just having a normal summer. He realized how much he'd taken it for granted after it was gone.

He walked slowly to within ten feet of Doracco's blue 1961 Oldsmobile Super 88 Starfire convertible coupe. It did look sweet, shining with both confidence and a fresh coat of wax. The tires glistened. The windshield was pristine, the dark blue Neptune hue looked like deep ocean blue, and it was painfully obvious why it worked so well on the ladies. The white top was down and a large pair of fuzzy dice hung from the rearview mirror. The interior was impeccable too, slicked with a fresh coat of Armor All. A cloth blanket rested behind the driver's side that he guessed Doracco kept to protect the leather during backseat recreational activities.

Coming from the rink he heard the loud sounds of Don McLean's "American Pie" blasting out of the loudspeaker. The facility stood on top of a hill, up about thirty steps with a ramp that ran alongside for wheelchairs. The lights were off and he saw the

149

reflection of the large disco ball in the center of the rink through the windows lining the front wall. He didn't see anyone nearby and scanned the area for any evidence of activity. Then, trying not to think about it, he let the desperation take over, shut his eyes, and hopped over the side into the backseat. He tripped trying to go too fast and fell headfirst into the soft leather, which absorbed most of the blow, but still hurt.

He quickly scrambled to get under the blanket and position it so he could peek out from underneath it. He tucked the duffle bag under the driver's seat and out of sight, after removing one item. His mind was spinning, his heart was racing, and his hand with the gun that still felt too heavy was shaking.

36

He heard Doracco's voice—that deep tone with poor enunciation— from what seemed like quite a long distance. Doracco was talking casually, hopefully not planning on giving one of the ladies a ride in the backseat. Charlie realized that if that happened, he was screwed. He didn't have a backup plan.

Doracco said "see you later" and the voice grew closer. Not louder, *closer*. He was near the car; he was going to get in. Charlie braced himself and tried not to make a sound, inching his eyes out from under the blanket—the smallest portion of it near the bottom— and saw Doracco moseying towards the car.

Doracco's black T-shirt was tight against his skin, the jeans he wore hung loosely near the ground and tight around the waist. His strong pectorals bulged, and Charlie realized just how strong the dude was. Up close and personal was far different than seeing him through binoculars.

He pulled shut the small section of the blanket he was looking through, and hid himself from view completely, praying that Doracco didn't notice the bulge of his body under the blanket. It was a large blanket, but he it didn't seem quite big enough to hide his frame completely.

He heard the car door open and Doracco got in the driver's seat, shutting it behind him. The start of the engine followed, and he was glad because if nothing else, it gave a little cushion room in the *don't-make-a-sound* department. He was wet and sweaty and sticky under the blanket and longed to rip it off and breathe the free air. Humid as it was outside, it was a lot more pleasant than being under the blanket.

Doracco revved the engine, its 394 cubic inch V-8 proudly demonstrating impressive power, surely to the delight of the ladies within earshot. When the car shifted into reverse, he held his breath and refused to exhale. He refused to scratch any of the numerous itches that abruptly emerged all over his body.

The car moved backwards and then came to a halt, then it was driving forward, slowly for the moment. He knew what to wait for. He was anticipating the increase of velocity, the burst of acceleration, the feel of breeze that would come with speed, and the courage to do what he'd come to do.

Anxiety penetrated his skin from every angle at the same rate that sweat exited it. He only had a few minutes and he knew it. If he didn't do it soon, Doracco would stop at the car wash or somewhere else and he'd be screwed. His only chance was now, while he was still driving.

The gun suddenly felt heavier and more cumbersome in his slippery hands. He shut his eyes and took one final breath, then whipped the blanket off and in one smooth motion brought the gun up, sticking it into Doracco's back right shoulder blade.

"What the hell!" Doracco screamed. The car swerved into the other lane and he jerked the wheel back to the right.

"Shut up, Doracco. Don't think I won't pull the trigger." He tried to sound tough, like a man's man, but his voice still was at least an octave higher than Doracco's and it didn't possess near the same authority. But the .22 would do most of the talking.

"What the hell is this?" Doracco didn't appear scared of the gun or even come across as that surprised. He continued to drive but looked back at Charlie with more anger than dread.

"Just drive. Go out to the country roads and we'll talk."

"Your ass is grass, dude."

"*Drive the car!*"

"You're crazy, man. Out of your mind." Doracco wasn't yelling, and he said it almost like he was saying it to himself.

"Just drive the car. Highline Road. Head north."

Doracco didn't respond, but did as asked. Highline Road was a two-lane gravel road with tall cornfields lining both sides and intersected with Main Street a few blocks east of the roller rink.

He still kept the gun low and dug it into the back of Doracco's shoulder. He felt tight resistance and could sense Doracco's stress, but the guy was still as strong as an ox. No wonder the high school football coach at the Catholic school in Breese was wooing him.

"You're the crazy dude, the guy from the paper they said was missing. I read about you." Doracco said aloud without looking back.

"Crazy enough to do this. You took everything from me, so I can do this to you."

"What did I do to you?"

"Just drive the car."

It seemed important to him to come across as confident and capable. If Doracco smelled blood he would try to expose the wound, the alpha male approach, but as long as he believed he could actually get shot, Charlie had a chance.

But the truth was Charlie knew he didn't have it in him to hurt Doracco. Did he really have nothing to lose, or did he stand to lose everything? Was this really a last hope, or was he just trying to make it seem that way?

He pressed the barrel of the .22 into Doracco's bulging muscle even harder, wanting him to feel pain.

They stayed on the country road for a few minutes, and Doracco didn't try to do anything. He wondered for a moment what he would do if Doracco started to swerve the car or pick up the pace. He wasn't wearing a seatbelt, the car could go from zero to 60 in nine seconds, they were driving on less-than-even country roads with numerous potholes and dips, and there was nothing to hold onto except the headrest. If Doracco goosed it, he would've dropped the gun, soiled himself, and fallen out of the car all at once.

Fortunately, Doracco didn't try that. On the contrary, he drove pretty slowly. Charlie could also tell Doracco was gripping the

153

steering wheel pretty hard, his knuckles turning white, and that confirmed to Charlie that his bold approach was paying off.

Keep it up.

The breeze stopped the flow of sweat that dripped from his face and did feel good, but nothing could help his heartbeat. His shaking knees also confirmed that had he not been sitting in the car, he wouldn't be able to stand up without them buckling.

At the east-west Medina Road intersection between the outskirts of two small towns, he decided it was time. There were no cars as far as the eye could see and he knew the roads well because he and Brad used to take the ATV all around the area. It was as good a spot as he was going to get.

"Take a left here," he instructed Doracco.

Doracco mumbled something inaudibly and Charlie responded by pressing the metal gun deeper into his shoulder.

"Stop the car," he ordered him.

"Here?"

"Here."

"You want me to stop the car *here*?"

"Yes, *here.*"

They were at a quiet, unused stretch of unpaved country road halfway between intersections and surrounded on the north and south sides by cornfields. The crescent half-moon provided some illumination but there were no streetlights or headlights from opposing cars. There were also no houses for a good long stretch. The farmer who owned all the land lived on the northwest corner of the property, and it was at least a few acres away from the house. Since it was privately owned, there were no inhabitants in between.

Doracco came to a slow stop, and Charlie ordered him to give up the keys. He then leaned back slowly, still pointing the gun at Doracco. His forehead felt dirty and sweaty, despite having just wiped his brow. He was breathing heavily and tried not to show his nervousness but knew he was failing.

Doracco twisted his upper body around to turn and look at him. Charlie saw Doracco's long, curly hair up close and personal. It hung near the shoulders loosely and his face was chiseled.

Even with the gun, Charlie felt outmatched.

37

"So why you sticking a gun in my face?"

Doracco said it in a voice that was more bemused than angry. He cocked the gun and saw fear in the older guy for the first time. Doracco was fishing for answers but wouldn't cast out too far. He was afraid. Brandon Doracco was actually afraid of him.

"You're going to answer some of my questions first."

"O-okay. What do you want to know?" Doracco said nervously.

"Tell me about Shane Littleton."

Doracco stayed quiet, his furrowed brow an obvious tip-off that he was surprised to hear the name.

"I don't know nothin' about him."

Charlie moved the gun a foot to the right and pulled the trigger with all his might. A shot cried out from the barrel, the bullet going through the front windshield, and Doracco jumped when it did. He kept his eyes pointed straight at Doracco, trying to follow the gun's lead: all business. Secretly, he was proud of myself just for pulling the trigger and not hitting anyone or anything.

"What the hell, dude!" Doracco screamed, tussling in the front seat.

"I'm done being jerked around. Shane Littleton. Start talking and don't lie to me again or I'll pull the trigger for a second time. Why did you hold a knife to Shane's throat?"

"O-okay. C-can, c-can I get a smoke first?" Doracco stuttered.

He nodded and Doracco pulled out a Winston Light. Gold pack all around with red letters, except for the Surgeon General's Warning in white with black letters. After lighting it with hands visibly shaking and taking two of the biggest drags Charlie had ever seen, Doracco exhaled deeply and looked him straight in the eye.

"I don't know why, or what it was about me..."

"Get to the point."

"A couple weeks ago I went out to a bar in Silver Creek to meet this chick. We'd met at the June Jamboree carnival and hit it off and she said she wanted to hook up at the joint. It turned out to be a bust—she didn't show—but I stayed there for a few hours and got lit."

"By yourself?"

"Yeah. It actually felt great to not know anybody."

"Go on."

"When I finally got in my car to head home, there was this brown envelope on the seat. It had my name written on the front."

Brown envelope.

"I opened it up and there was a note that said if I wanted to make a quick five hundred bucks, I should drive to some place I'd never heard of the next night at nine o'clock sharp. I remember it said that because it felt so old. Who says 'sharp' anymore? There was a map, and this place was circled on it, way the hell out there. I'd never been there."

"What was it?"

"I didn't see a name, but it was off a road called Hoffstetter. Pretty far north, out of Germantown past St. Rose, almost up by Pocahontas."

Way far north. Charlie remembered being in the cornfield with Brad, staring at an intersection that he'd never really looked at before or spent much time at. Between it and the brown envelope, a not-so-friendly pattern was emerging.

"And it was out in the cornfields?"

"Turned out to be, but I'd never been there so I didn't know that then."

"Seems like a hike if you weren't sure..."

"Yeah, at first I thought someone was jerking my chain," Doracco replied, shaking his head. "I even looked around for some buddies playing a prank who were planning to pop out of a cornfield or some crap like that, but didn't see any. Thought about tossing the note, but it was five hundred bucks. That'd buy me a lot of smokes, you know? And I didn't have anything to do anyway, so I figured what the hell."

Doracco seemed to be telling the truth, but he couldn't know for sure. The freak of nature muscle man didn't appear to be searching for answers or trying to come up with details on the spot. Rather, his account came out naturally, and Charlie listened intently, looking for evidence of a lie but not finding any.

Doracco lit another Winston before continuing. "So the next day I drove out to the middle of nowhere. They'd just resurfaced the roads so I got tar all over my car. Pissed me off. The whole drive I heard *clink clink clink* and going faster only made it worse so I drove real slow. The jerk couldn't have picked some other road, could he?"

"Did you see anything along the way?"

"Nah. Pretty empty road and no lights at all. For a while I thought I might even be lost but it was pretty much a straight shot. When I finally get to the joint, it's not even open. Supposed to be a white building but it was so old it looked more piss yellow than white, and there were no lights on. But there was an old Impala in the parking lot, lights on, engine running. Real piece of crap, like an old geezer's car—"

"What color was it?"

"What's the difference??"

"Just answer the question," he lifted the .22, having almost forgotten for a moment that he was holding it.

"Cool down, dude. It was brown. Light brown."

"Anything else stick out?"

"Yeah, it had dents all over it. Looked like a real junker even before it either drove through an asteroid field or was in the biggest hailstorm in history. There were tons of small bumps all over the hood, tailgate, even the doors. I even said something about it when I got out. It didn't even have a license plate."

That was as much confirmation as Charlie would get that it was the same Impala he and Brad had watched through the binoculars.

He remained silent but could tell Doracco noticed he was paying keen attention.

"That's where this whole thing took a weird turn. At first I thought it was a bunch of BS. Someone messing with me, like I said. Then when I saw the car, I thought it might've been some dude trying to get high without a wife knowing it. I figured he wanted some drugs or something and it'd be easy money."

"Okay..."

"But there was this dude in a mask. He told me to back away from his car and was all pushy, yelling at me to get away."

"What'd you do?"

"Held my ground, dude. I ain't no pushover and if some dude wants to drag my ass an hour north the least he could do was talk to me like a man. I showed him the pot I brought with me because I figured that's what he wanted."

"But he didn't?"

That's when he saw a side of Doracco he didn't expect anyone ever had. His eyes grew as wide as golf balls and filled with moisture. He held his breath for a few seconds then exhaled with a loud, sad sigh, starting towards the front seat. When he looked back and answered, his voice was soft and felt timid and vulnerable.

"No, he didn't want drugs. He got out of the Impala and was wearing this camouflage army jacket. He wasn't that tall but he wasn't short either. Maybe six-foot-two. He wasn't jacked, but he wasn't fat either. Kind of average. He had that black ski mask on so I couldn't see his face. But I...I didn't feel real comfortable being near him."

Doracco wasn't even trying to hide his fear. And this time it wasn't coming from the .22. He could tell Doracco didn't want to talk about it, and in a completely unexpected manner, felt connected to him. They had more in common than he could've possibly guessed.

"What did he want?" he asked him calmly. He still held the gun, but he lowered it and kept his eyes fixed on Doracco's.

"He told me he'd give me five hundred bucks if I scared this kid. Said he was a wimpy seventh grader who wouldn't fight back. All I had to do was scare him and the money was mine. Problem is...I...I did it."

Big, bad Doracco had no more words. He was mad at himself for what he'd done to Shane. Nobody, not Tom Hanks and certainly not Doracco, could've faked it. He knew what he did was wrong, but couldn't undo it.

That's when he found out just how wrong he'd been all along.

38

Doracco had been Charlie's scapegoat—the reason all of this had happened and the person whom he could blame for causing it. He'd pinned it all on Doracco because of what Shane had told him. He was the ruthless monster who'd done it all—killed Jimmy, or Cory, beat up Mack, framed Brad, and threatened him as well as Shane. He was Charlie's EASY button. In that way, he *needed* Doracco to be guilty.

"The first thing he did was ask me for the note that was in my car the night before, the one that led me there."

He nodded.

"So I went to my car and brought it back to him. He took it and said I wouldn't need it anymore. I asked him why he needed a seventh-grader scared, and he said the kid needed to shut up. Told me it'd be the easiest five hundred bucks I'd ever make."

"Did he use Shane's name?"

"Hell yeah, then he told me everything there must be to know about him. Showed me a picture from the newspaper, one of those academic scholar bowl pictures, and had Shane circled with a red marker."

Doracco lit another cigarette. His fourth since they'd stopped the car.

"He said Shane had been running his mouth and needed to shut up."

"Did he mention what he was saying?"

"That he saw Barry Ray Olson during the time Jimmy Patino was murdered."

"He actually told you that?"

161

"Yeah, I was a little surprised too. I knew Barry Ray got arrested not too long ago for killing that jerk-off. But I didn't want to get nobody into more trouble, so I asked him why that mattered."

"What did he say?"

"Said it was none of my business, but that if I had to know he wanted to make sure Barry Ray paid for what he did."

"Didn't it occur to you that Shane might be telling the truth?"

"I figured if that was true Barry Ray would get out soon enough. The cops would find out, you know? But if the kid was lying, and it would've gotten Barry Ray released...that's what the guy said he cared about."

"But what about you, Brandon?" Suddenly, using Doracco's first name felt appropriate. He was still holding a gun but even Doracco knew at that point he had no intention of using it. In that moment, and, he guessed, from now on, Doracco felt more like a victim than the perpetrator.

"Well, I know I didn't want to help anyone get off scot-free for killing someone. Even if Patino was a total douche bag, I don't think people should just go around killing him and then get away with it."

"Plus you wanted the money."

At that, Doracco stopped talking briefly and after a few deep breaths answered his question in a far less aggressive tone.

"Yeah, I wanted the money."

They both sat there in silence, Doracco's last comment lingering in the air like a nasty fart in a windless room. It reeked of avarice and selfishness. And Doracco knew it.

"Did he say how he knew Barry Ray was guilty?"

"No."

"Did you ask?"

Piecrcing silence answered that question before Doracco opened his mouth. "Look. You're right. I wanted the money and didn't think it through. I screwed up."

"Then what?"

162

"The guy told me all I had to do was wait for Shane at the IGA in the next couple days and back him into the alley. He told me to use a knife to really scare the crap out of him, so I'd only have to do it once. Then he told me..."

"What?"

"That the best way to do it was to threaten him and his brother. That if I did that, the message would stick and it'd all be over."

"He didn't tell you to hurt him?"

"No. In fact he specifically told me not to hurt him. He said I'd better not harm a hair on Littleton's head. But that the more scared he was, the better it would be for both him and me."

"Did you believe that?"

"Totally. The guy obviously meant business. His voice was so stern, even angry-sounding. There's no doubt in my mind."

"Did you ask 'why me?'"

"He said it was none of my business. That all I had to decide was whether I wanted five hundred bucks or not."

"Did you recognize the voice? Ring any bells at all?"

"No," Doracco answered, pausing before continuing. "Look, man, I'm shooting you straight here. I don't know who it was or why it happened. All I know is he was dressed in camouflage with a mask, drove an Impala with no license plate and a crap load of dents, and sounded legit. You can wave the gun in my face as much as you want; it won't get you any more answers."

Much as he wanted to doubt Doracco, Charlie believed him. Doracco looked him straight in the eye and didn't flinch, smile, stutter, or pause. His theory on Doracco had been wrong. The one-size-fits-all theory was flawed, and he was back to square one.

"Did he pay you right then?"

"No. He said I had to scare the crap out of Shane Littleton and tell him to keep his mouth shut first; then he'd pay me."

"You took his word for it?"

"I didn't like it, but what was I supposed to do? It didn't really feel like a choice. I did ask him why I should trust him and he pulled

163

out a crisp Benjamin from a wad of cash. Almost like a gangster roll, but with 100s. He fanned it out and I saw at least ten $100 bills. Just pulled it right out of his pocket, like he carries that sort of dough all the time." Doracco looked back at him and paused again. Then he looked down, almost ashamed, and nodded his head. "I guess there was a part of me that was a little impressed. I'd never seen that kind of coin before."

It was a rare sight in Germantown. Charlie's father rarely had more than fifty bucks in his pocket and even rich folks like the Patinos didn't often display it.

He gave me the $100 and told me it was for the meeting."

"Then what?"

"Said once I did the job he'd contact me."

"How would he know when you did it?"

"That's what I asked. He just said he'd know."

Then what happened?"

Doracco lit cigarette number five.

"He asked me if I was in, and I said yes."

Charlie felt a gentle breeze attempt to make its way through and over the corn but get stopped like an army by the tall fields surrounding them. He dropped the .22, no longer concerned with using it as a motivator but more concerned that he might accidentally pull the trigger, something he knew he'd never intentionally do tonight.

"Was that it?" he whispered, a crack in his throat.

"He told me I'd better not tell anyone about our talk, or that he'd find out and have to do something about it. I didn't ask what he meant and honestly didn't want to know."

"Why didn't you go to the cops?"

Doracco looked past him and into the sky, clearly surprised with raised eyebrows and a tightened chin.

"The cops? Are you serious?"

"Why not?"

"What would I say to them? That some guy left a note for me and then told me to threaten Shane Littleton? I don't have the note, and I don't know who he was, can't describe him, can't prove it even happened, but that I went ahead and agreed to threaten the kid for five hundred bucks anyway? Sorry officer, I just wanted to let you know before I actually did it? Just be on the lookout for a Chevy Impala—there are only a few hundred thousand out there. I don't have a license plate for you, either.

"I'm sure the cops would take one look at my weed-smoking ass and jump to the streets to find a guy I can't describe or a car that's so common half the town drives it. And I'm sure Sheriff Thrower and Podunk Germantown's finest could protect me from him, too."

Charlie didn't know what to say, but it didn't much matter because Doracco wasn't looking for a response.

"For all I knew, the cops would assume I killed Jimmy Patino. There are all sorts of good ol' boy network favors done around here. The guys gets off the hook because his best friend's uncle is the patrolman's best friend from high school, and they still haven't gotten anywhere. Barry Ray Olson was locked up, the sheriff's son got arrested a few days later, and now both are free. You tell me that makes sense. This whole stupid town's one big incest pool."

It was all too convincing for comfort. Before confronting him, Charlie had explained everything in his own mind by making Doracco the scapegoat. But now, with every word the guy uttered making more sense than the last, he felt that comforting theory disappearing.

"Nope, I only had two choices," Doracco went on. "Do the right thing and walk away, hoping the guy would leave me alone. Or scare Littleton and take the cash."

Doracco looked down again.

"Maybe I made the wrong choice."

Doracco was making a little too much sense for him, and he knew deep down that he would've done the same thing.

39

"Did he contact you again?" Charlie asked in a soft, sympathetic voice.

Doracco didn't answer. Instead, he reached across the front seat and opened the glove compartment to pull out a plain, brown envelope that had clearly been opened and then re-sealed with a single strip of scotch tape. Doracco flipped it to him with a flick of the wrist.

"About a week after I...visited Shane...I got another note on my seat. Same type of envelope, same print, same black pen. It said I should go where we met last time the next night. Eight-thirty sharp."

Eight-thirty. That was what Brad and he had seen that night on the ATV. He recalled that it was a little past eight when they saw him at the car wash. Then they watched him for a while before heading out to the country roads. The brown envelope he held now was the one the man from the Impala handed Brandon. That's why the handoff didn't take long—it was just the payment.

Charlie realized then how lucky, or unlucky—depending on your perspective—Brad and he were that night. An entire week had passed from the time Shane told him about his attacker until he saw Doracco and pointed him out. In that time, Charlie had told Sheriff Thrower about the attack and been shot down, he and Brad had gone to the library and had five nerve-wracking days while they waited for information. A lot could have happened that didn't.

And it was just by chance that precisely when Shane noticed Doracco, Doracco was heading out to the country to get his money. Strange timing. A day or two either way and Brad and he would've missed the whole thing.

"So you met him to get your money?"

166

"Yeah. He handed it to me without a word. That was pretty much it."

He thought of asking Doracco if anything weird had happened at the meeting, but the whole thing was weird and he had seen it occur with his own eyes.

"Anything else?"

"No. He said I did a good job and deserved an extra hundred. And that I'd better keep my mouth shut."

"He gave you an extra hundred?"

"Look in the envelope."

In it Charlie saw thick wad of twenties. He pulled it out and counted thirty twenties, all as crisp as if they'd come straight from the mint. Doracco, who at this point knew he wasn't going to shoot him, was biting his lip.

"I haven't seen or heard from the dude since and hope I never do. I try to avoid the kid, Shane—I was stupid and didn't wear a mask or anything. But even more than that, I...I don't know."

Charlie knew. Doracco didn't want to have to look the seventh-grader in the eye after what he'd done. As much as he tried to portray the tough guy, bully type image, Doracco knew it was wrong and wasn't proud of himself. But he couldn't hide from what he did either.

"Can you drive me somewhere?" he asked Doracco, un-cocking the .22 and shoving it in his pocket.

"Yeah, hop in the front."

He put the envelope in his pocket and clamored into the front seat. Doracco put the top up and asked where to. Charlie asked him to head to the edge of town. It would be better for both of them not to be seen together, and he didn't want anyone to know where he was going. Even Doracco.

After ten minutes of tense silence, they reached the edge of town. It was a close walk to the library and Charlie would be able to do it without being seen.

"I'm sorry I used the gun, Brandon. I thought...I was wrong about what I thought."

"It's okay. I would've done the same thing. You gonna be okay?" Doracco asked. "You got a place? A plan?"

"Yeah," he answered, as if he had something other than an empty library with an unlocked bathroom window leading to a concrete floor and a book for a pillow.

The moon was partially exposed; a large white cloud was making its way over to say hello before eclipsing its light. He watched the interplay and wished he was someone else.

"If you need anything, you let me know," Doracco said. "I know you know how to find me now."

"Thanks."

He opened the door to get out and Doracco called, "Charlie?"

"Yeah?" he answered, turning to face him for what would be the last time.

"Tell the kid...Shane...tell him I'm sorry. Please, tell him I'm sorry."

The apology was so sincere that it caught Charlie off guard.

"I will."

As he turned to leave, Charlie realized he still had Doracco's envelope. He pulled it from his pocket and was about to toss it through the open window when Doracco put up his hand.

"Keep it. You need it more than I do and I don't want anything to do with it. You have any left when you're done doing whatever it is you're doing, give it to Shane."

As Brandon Doracco drove away, Charlie thought to himself how wrong he had been about the guy.

All the lights were off and the roads were empty as he walked. Cars weren't allowed to park overnight, teenagers were the only ones still up driving. He felt a gust of warm summer wind tousle his hair like a kind, old uncle and watched it play with the tall wildflowers next to the sidewalk. The earlier clouds had parted to reveal the half moon's light, which illuminated the desolate street before him. A verse from Sunday school came to mind: "You are a lamp unto my feet and a light unto my path." He remembered the priest saying that sometimes God shines a bright search light to reveal many things ahead, but that other times only a very small lamp with just enough illumination to reveal each next step. Charlie closed his eyes and breathed, *Show me, God.*

40

After a sleepless night on the hard ground of the Germantown public library, he realized he hadn't used that time to his advantage. Time seemed like the only thing he wasn't running out of, unlike food and money, yet he couldn't figure out how to spend it. He decided to recap again.

After listening to Doracco, it seemed that the man in the mask was the one who killed Jimmy Patino. Despite the claim that he wanted justice served, using Doracco to silence a kid with violence proved he had something to hide. The man wanted Barry Ray to stay behind bars, and the most likely reason was if Barry Ray stayed the prime suspect, then he wouldn't be. Doracco was just a pawn, a means to an end.

For some reason, as he lay on the floor of the library's tiny reading room, he couldn't get "I Saw Her Standing There" by the Beatles out of his head. He'd listened to that worn old white cassette tape countless times about fifteen years ago with his mother. The happier memories commanded some mindshare and he tried to swing back into focus.

Unable to pin a name to the elusive man in the brown Impala, he got up and stretched his legs in an attempt to focus. The library was still closed, so he got up and walked freely between the stacks as he rehashed.

It was clear the mystery man was a few things: *intelligent*, since he knew to cover his tracks and picked the right person to bribe because Doracco could scare Shane to death and would jump at the money to do so; *calculating*, since he not only told Doracco whom to warn off but how, where, and when to do it in granular detail; and *dangerous*, because just by using Doracco he was committing a crime and it seemed obvious he was doing so to cover up something even bigger.

He recalled how quiet the man was out in the country, his voice kept low and the flashlight pulled out when the crow made the noise and Brad let out a yelp.

That combination of intelligence, calculation, and danger told Charlie the man could've certainly committed Jimmy Patino's murder and planted the gun in Brad's room. No fingerprints were on the weapon and the weapon was nowhere to be seen immediately following the murder. Yet when it emerged, it happened to be in Brad's room and the cops got a call telling them where to find it. Everything the police had gotten was because someone wanted them to. It seemed like the man in the Impala was that someone.

Looking for a way it could all fit together and possibly add up to something, a name emerged in his mind. Any familiar person would require some crazy mental gymnastics, but there was one name that definitely seemed more palatable to him than others. It was the last he would've originally expected, but now felt strangely possible.

41

The thought seemed outrageous at first: *Douglas Patino.*

Jimmy was the man's son. His youngest son—biological or not. The one who still lived at home, and still needed his father. With Scotty off on his own in Chicago, why would Douglas Patino want to hurt the son he'd adopted as a child and raised? It felt preposterous to even consider the possibility.

Jimmy and Scotty did disagree on pretty much everything and Douglas seemed more aligned with Scotty. Jimmy's reputation certainly hadn't helped the family name...but neither added up to a motive. The truth was he didn't see one, but Charlie kept picturing how normal and easygoing Douglas Patino was on the golf course. It was almost as if he was relieved in a way, and that's what made him consider that Douglas had something to do with it.

Maybe Douglas didn't think Jimmy was doing well enough for someone who had as much as he did. Maybe he was fed up with Jimmy dishonoring the family with all of his run-ins with the law. Maybe Douglas didn't want it to get out that he had a criminal's son living with him and for some reason that possibility had become a real threat recently. And maybe he was just crazy, and decided after all those years of being a parent to a monster's child that he was through with it and just wanted to get rid of him. None of it explained to him why Douglas would do that, but...

On the other hand, Douglas Patino did have the money, connections, and influence to get the wrong person arrested, then have the weapon planted somewhere else. He did have the pride that would make it fun for him to watch the police continue to screw up the investigation. He did have the intelligence to pull it off, and he did know how people would react to certain situations, such as

Doracco and the money. And he did have the connections to folks who could commit the crime itself.

Even though he rarely interacted with Douglas one-on-one, Charlie always got the impression and heard from others that Douglas was a real dirty politician; a businessman with a cutthroat personality and the resources to inflict pain on others without thinking twice if it would help the bottom line.

It was the way Douglas came across, and the way he acted at the golf course with his gorgeous wife sipping tea and smiling in the lounge made Charlie think that he really could possibly be guilty. He couldn't prove it, of course, but something wasn't right. They both looked a too cheery, a too everyday-like, to be innocently mourning the death of their son at the same time.

It felt like there were enough pieces to make a puzzle, but when he lined them up he knew he was missing the ones that made the critical connections. Down to one full day's worth of food, he didn't have enough supplies to hide out much longer. He did have some money and could buy another week's worth, but the question remained: What next?

Please God, show me.

Doracco's story about what happened wasn't evidence. If Charlie told what he knew to someone trustworthy and had the five hundred bucks to support his story, it might at least pique an interest. If he spent it all on food to hide out another week in the library, he'd only look more suspicious. He was already a missing person of interest in the eyes of the locals, an article in the paper and his name on the radio, so there was risk of being spotted if he tried to gather more supplies. On top of that, he was getting cabin fever and didn't want to hide anymore. He felt restless and anxious and needed a change.

Then it hit him. He could go to Richard Beller, the District Attorney who lived a few towns over. He didn't know much about him, but Beller won more than he lost and had a reputation for being a stickler for following the rules. He'd read an article or two about him in *The Germantown Sun* about his reputation as one who

173

played by the book at all costs. Considering everything that happened, a strict rule-follower seemed just what the doctor ordered.

Plus, Beller wasn't from Germantown. He had relocated from the Indianapolis area five years earlier and despite the initial skepticism the county's townspeople had about a non-local DA, Beller had managed to win their approval and was re-elected after his first term. Most of the cases were misdemeanors and small-class violations, but the fact that he was from out of state was a good thing in Charlie's mind. It was pretty thin logic, but it did seem more likely that Beller would play it straight.

He checked the clock. Not even ten a.m. The library had just opened but there was no huge influx of customers. After the teenage girl working the desk opened the doors, nobody had walked through them. Summertime is not library time in Southern Illinois.

Part of him wanted to leave right then to go meet Mr. Beller, the other remembered the promise he made to Sarah in the cornfield. He'd meet her at one to honor his promise, and then he'd keep pedaling until he reached Mr. Beller's office. It would take two hours on the bike, but he'd get there before close of business.

42

By one o'clock, the sun was at its hottest and the humidity was in full effect. Charlie put on a new T-shirt and stuffed the old, sweat-covered one in the duffle bag that was thrown over his shoulders. He stood in the same cornfield he was in two days earlier at exactly the same time, yet it felt warmer and more mysterious today. He looked over at the two or three stalks of corn that still weren't fully upright from when he and Sarah lay in them, embraced in a kiss. He thought about that kiss and wondered what would happen now. But even with the imminent meeting with Sarah approaching, his mind was solely focused on Mr. Beller, and whether going to his office was really the best thing to do.

He watched Sarah walk out of the gym in a sort of trance, dressed in such similar attire that it felt like a case of déjà vu. She exited the gym through the same doors and made her way down the same path she'd taken two days earlier with him, cutting through the parking lot on a diagonal and heading into the outfield of the decrepit baseball field.

Her facial expression and demeanor was similar to what it was a few days ago. She wasn't smiling or saying goodbye to her friends. She didn't sport the relieved expression he expected to see because of Brad's release. Instead, she kept her head down and steered through the other cheerleaders without saying a word. It almost seemed as if she was dreading meeting him. Perhaps that was just in his head, but it made him wonder.

Maybe the article in the newspaper shook her up, and she would've preferred him telling her before he became a missing person. Perhaps she was mad at him for not being completely honest with her. Or maybe she was just scared, not sure what his sudden runaway status meant.

She walked straight towards the cornfield, knowing he would be there, with a solemn look on her face. And she knew he would be there because she made him promise, and Charlie always tried to honor his promises.

When she crossed through the arid infield dirt and the rectangular-shaped dugout, he got a look at her face up close. Her eyes were bloodshot and ringed. She rubbed her hand across her face as she looked up and slowly walked to the section of cornfield where he was.

"Hi, Sarah." He didn't know what else to say.

First, a few very long seconds of silence. Then: "You came."

"I promised I would."

She looked back at him with a void expression, almost as if looking past his face and getting lost in the cloudless blue sky behind him. Her beautiful, captivating eyes were large as saucers and filled with moisture when she uttered words he'd never forget.

"I'm sorry, Charlie..."

Trying to put the pieces together, he bit his right cheek and looked back at her curiously. Then he saw it with his right eye's peripheral vision. Faint at first, then bigger and clearer.

The sun's reflection off the car shifted as it turned left off the highway and onto the country road that ran past the cornfield they were standing in. It accelerated and continued picking up speed as it approached the baseball field. The lights atop it could not be mistaken for anything else.

Sheriff Thrower reached the small walking bridge that led to the baseball field and quickly got out of the car, gun in hand. No one else was with him, but Charlie froze in panic and didn't really comprehend Sarah's pleas.

"I'm so sorry, Charlie. He told me you were in trouble! He told me you weren't safe."

He didn't even think or have time to run through the corn. Sheriff Thrower was there in seconds, and while he kept the gun pointed down, it was still in his hand. He didn't look angry, more sad.

"Come with me, son."

It was a soft voice and didn't come across as threatening, but to Charlie it felt like the devil cometh. It didn't matter what the man said or even how he looked. He tried not to think about Shane or Doracco or Douglas Patino or Jimmy Patino's true identity, but instead all of those things flashed into his mind like a lightning storm, offering brief glances of terrifying images before clearing away for the next.

Then he saw another car approaching from the other side of the field, heading straight towards him. Driving east at a more-than-casual speed, he knew it before he even saw it. It was a brown Impala. His heart sank when he saw it had no license plate and a hood full of dents.

Douglas Patino, he thought to himself, though the driver wore a mask, just as he had the night Charlie and Brad watched him meet Doracco. It even looked like the same mask.

Suddenly he felt a hard thump on the back of his head. And then, before he could even identify the driver of the Impala, everything went black.

43

He didn't know how long he spent in darkness.

It could've been minutes, hours, or even days. But when he finally did wake up, he did so in a state of confusion, followed by equal parts terror and sadness. The first thing he noticed was the throbbing pain right in the back of his head. Not excruciating, but extremely sore and tender to the touch, as if someone had taken a rubber hammer to his skull. He gently rubbed the large bump as his blurred vision finally started to clear.

As his vision came back, his memory came with it. Sarah in the cornfield, that look on her face when she apologized. Sheriff Thrower walking towards him. The Impala and the masked man driving it.

He tried to take notice of where he was. He coughed to clear his throat and implored his eyes and spirit to come back to life. They did so slowly, resisting the light they encountered. That light came only from a desk lamp that was resting on a small table in the corner of the room about ten feet from where he lay.

He was on an old couch with the side cushions partially ripped out and the inner foam exposed. The backrest was stained with varying shades of green, yellow, and black. The cushion he was on needed a slip cover more than any he'd ever seen. Yet despite its condition, it felt like a California king bed with extra fluffy pillows compared to the library floor. It felt good to rest his head on it as long as he didn't put pressure on the bump.

The rest of the room was dark, but he could see it was empty. He forced himself to rise up and didn't hear anyone or anything, but decided to stay as quiet as possible until he knew if he was alone or not.

He smelled dampness, a dampness that seemed oddly familiar. Not moldy, but musty, like a basement or a cellar. He looked around, his eyes finally acclimated to being open. The small lamp didn't offer much light, but he could tell the hard floor was dark brown carpet with various patches of discoloration here and there. There was hardly any insulation or padding on the floor and he felt the hard concrete on the soles of his feet. And it was cold. Despite it being the middle of summer, the floor felt chilly.

The room was a little bigger than ten feet by ten feet, maybe fifteen by fifteen. The walls adjacent to the couch were drywall and either white or a light tan, and there was an old sewing machine in the corner that looked like it hadn't been used in years. On the other side of the room an ironing board was pushed up against a cinder-block wall that covered the other two sides of the perimeter, and a large rectangular folding table that could seat ten people leaned against the wall to the right. It reminded him of fried chicken night at the Legion.

Nothing hung on any of the walls, and he rotated his head slowly until he saw something encouraging. The stairs were covered in a dark brown carpet, and they led somewhere. Past the stairs, along the right side of the room, was another section of cinder-block wall. Its bottom section was recessed about two feet beneath the stairs.

To the left, opposite the couch, there was a small door with a metal knob he couldn't open behind two large pillars that stood floor to ceiling and were almost icy to the touch. The door perhaps led to a laundry room or storage area, which was pretty typical of basements. He didn't want to make too much noise until he'd had a chance to fully survey his surroundings, so he didn't try to kick the door in or force it open at the moment, but it was yet another piece of encouragement.

It would, however, be the last.

There was no life to any part of the room. The carpet was worn and the walls were stained. The table with the light was covered with a layer of filth. It smelled like mold and was musty. This was clearly an old basement...but there was something else. Something more.

He knew this smell.

He got up and pushed on the door behind the pillars again. Nothing. He paused, wiped his face and looked up. Then he slowly tiptoed up the stairs, found that door was also locked, and crouched down to look underneath it. The opening between the bottom of the door and the floor wasn't wide enough to see anything and it was dark, indicating it was either nighttime in the free world or the other side of the door was just as enclosed as this one. He slowly walked back down the stairs.

How long had he been there? It felt to him like the bugs that were surely his bunkmates were now crawling all over him, and he couldn't breathe in enough air to counter his panic. Stir crazy and claustrophobic and terrified, he made his decision. There was only one thing to do. If it tipped someone off that he was awake, so be it. He wasn't going to sit quietly in a musty grave any longer.

He charged up the stairs, pounding the walls and hammered his fist into the locked wooden door with all his might. It hurt his hand a lot more than it budged the door, and he screamed *help* so loudly that it made his throat hurt. After a few moments of yelling and banging with no response, he collapsed on the top step and tucked himself into a ball to weep.

Pushing his head between his knees, he'd never felt so alone. This felt worse than he imagined death could feel; the vigor in him was gone. This was where he was going to die, and there was nothing he could do about it. The feeling of helplessness was overwhelming, knowing something terrible was going to happen but not being able to stop it, made even worse by sensing something familiar about where he was but not knowing what. He thought of his friends: Barry Ray and Mack and Brad. But mostly, he thought of Sarah. Despite it being her fault he was here, he longed to see and hug her.

Then, the door's rusty hinges, squeaking from a lack of lubrication and use, started to move ever so slightly. Light penetrated the darkness of the stairwell like a beam straight from heaven. Feeling this could be the end of his life on Earth but welcoming that to isolation, he forced his eyes to look up as the door slowly inched open. Then he froze with shock, his jaw dropping open.

44

The mask was gone, but there was no doubt it was the man in the Impala. What Charlie couldn't fathom however, was who it was. He stood at the top of the stairs and looked down, wearing a long-sleeved black shirt with the sleeves rolled up. The man didn't have the jacket on anymore, but he could tell it was him by his pants. Old, rugged jeans that were covered with spots of dirt all up and down the front, back, and side of the cheap denim.

Charlie couldn't believe it.

The man stared back.

"How's your head?" the man finally asked. He had no response. "I hope it doesn't hurt too much. Sheriff Thrower didn't mean to hit you so hard."

He gawked at the familiar face, standing above and casually chatting about him being knocked unconscious.

"You must be hungry. I fixed you some chicken."

Was this real?

After another few moments of silence, he spoke again.

"Charlie, I can only imagine what you're thinking. I know you can't believe your eyes and you must have a million questions. And I promise you, I'll answer them all. But first, please have something to eat."

He leaned backwards, enough that he extended his arm onto the third step to make sure he didn't fall, and remained silent. No words were coming.

"I'm sorry for all of this, Charlie. I really am. And I promise, you will not be hurt. Please come up and have some supper and I'll explain everything. After that, you'll be free to do whatever you want to do. I promise," he held up his hand as if taking an oath.

Feeling the vomit starting to build up, he stared at the unmasked man from the Impala. The fierce, heartless man who'd killed Jimmy Patino and caused all the trouble for Shane. The man who'd met with Doracco and paid him money to help get Barry Ray in jail. The man who'd beaten Mack after the shooting. The man who'd chased him and was responsible for this summer from hell.

45

It was clear as day when he entered the kitchen that the familiar smell was Grandpa Joe's house. It felt strange to him that such a dreadful basement was in the same house as the living room, kitchen, and bedrooms that he'd been in so many times before and had such fond memories of until now. The house felt comfortable, and he always felt very safe and happy in it.

He sat at the dining room table Joe played solitaire at every day, the same table where he'd had countless numbers of snacks during a break from the all-important Wiffle Ball game in the double lot out back. Fresh lemonade was always a treat in the hot summer months, and Joe always seemed to have a fresh cup when he needed it the most.

Joe sat across from him after fixing a plate of food complemented by a tall glass of cold lemonade. The fried chicken was crisp, the mashed potatoes creamy and filled with butter. There was no salad, but a small stack of green beans along with the potatoes, on a separate plate of course. Joe never mixed the greens with the main course.

He stared at Joe, who now wore the same John Deere hat he'd always associated with Joe. The dirty jeans that he thought the mysterious Impala man was wearing turned out to be Joe's traditional blue-jean overalls covered up by the hunter jacket that now hung on a hook next to his front door.

Joe's black-rimmed glasses were on, and his white hair was a maelstrom of roughly four-inch long uncombed loose strands that sprawled out in all directions. Joe sat down next to him with a small glass filled a third of the way with ice and whiskey. Joe didn't make eye contact, but Charlie couldn't stop staring at him.

The grandfather clock abruptly chimed and startled him. It was the first time he'd ever been scared by those clocks or surprised by their timing, despite the fact that offset times had one chiming every few minutes.

"Are you going to eat?" Joe asked, head still down.

"So it was you?" Charlie blurted out, as if pleading for Joe to tell him it wasn't so.

"The answers will come, Charlie. But you haven't eaten for quite some time. It's nearly three in the morning."

He swung his head around to the living room and checked all three clocks to make sure his eyes weren't deceiving him. It was just past 2:45 and completely dark outside. He'd met Sarah in the cornfield around one that afternoon, which meant that for nearly fourteen hours he'd been unconscious. That explained the hunger that seemed to come back to him in a hurry, but made him wonder what all had happened in that half a day. Where was Sarah? Where was Sheriff Thrower? What was Joe going to do?

Despite a ravenous appetite, he ate slowly. His mind kept wandering and he ate one small nibble at a time thinking through everything.

Should he run? Just head straight for the front door and bolt into the darkness of Southern Illinois country? Maybe they wouldn't find him in the dark, especially if he got a good head start. He could run as fast as he could, hide in one of the fields once he'd gotten away from the house, and then make the trek to Mr. Beller's office the next day as soon as it opened.

But feeling the large bump on the back of his head compliments of Sheriff Thrower, he remembered how ineffective he'd been at running so far. Plus, Joe knew his own fields better than anyone, and could have other people to help him search. There was little chance he could remain hidden long enough to make it to Mr. Beller's office. And it was still a long way to the DA's office...how could he get there without being seen?

He didn't have any options, and found motivation to stay in Joe's promise to tell him everything. He needed answers more than safety, or at least that's how it seemed. There was so much confusion in his mind that he almost didn't want to go even if he could make it.

After a few minutes of silence as he ate warm chicken and sipped cold lemonade that no longer felt refreshing, another surprise arrived when Sheriff Thrower walked through the front door.

"Is there anything else I can get you?" asked Joe once he pushed the plate aside and flip-flopped looking at Joe and Sheriff Thrower. "Would you like dessert?" He asked it in the same sweet, lovable voice of his surrogate grandfather. It was a voice Charlie could always trust and run to, the voice of a man whom he no longer felt he knew.

"No, thank you."

Manners seemed so unimportant when speaking to the men who knocked him unconscious and had presumably killed people, but old habits die hard. He'd always been very respectful with Joe. His father had beat it into him from an early age, and throughout his entire life Joe had made it so easy with his warm, infectious smile, and kind disposition.

"Okay. Why don't we head out into the breezeway?" Joe replied. With that, Sheriff Thrower pivoted around and led the way, and Joe motioned for him to follow. They walked through the kitchen with its linoleum floors and small kitchen table and he looked out the window above the kitchen sink. Darkness shielded the view of the long driveway, the double lot through the trees, and the friendly looking mailbox that said OLSON on it in red stencil letters.

It seemed so certain to him that that's how the conversation was going to be as well: dark, morbid. He would hear things he didn't *really* want to hear, things that would haunt him, and then he'd ask for more.

46

He walked through the breezeway door and sat on the tan leather couch next to Joe. It sat where it always had, under the aged chalkboard with a handwritten WELCOME sign in white chalk. Sheriff Thrower stood by the front door, his arm resting on the windowsill next to the homemade can crusher and a garbage can full of flattened Pepsi cans.

"I have to ask you something, Charlie," Joe said softly. He was on one end of the three-person couch and Joe was on the other, the middle seat in between a metaphorical chasm.

"You know about Coach's Corner, right?"

He was surprised to hear the term and didn't try to hide it. Of course he knew Sheriff Thrower's coined phrase. He thought of all his conversations with Brad and wondered where this was going. It was a term of respect, and what was uttered in the Coach's Corner was simply not repeated outside of it.

"Sure he knows it, Joe," Sheriff Thrower interrupted before he had a chance to respond. "Charlie knows all about it."

Joe looked at Sheriff Thrower, then back at him, raising an eyebrow.

"Yes, I know it."

"Good. I know you're scared. Rightly so. We haven't been super transparent with you. But as we share why, I'd ask that you ask yourself if it should be Coach's Corner or not. You can decide for yourself. We will not force you to remain silent, nor will we hurt you. But if you can suspend how you feel now and go into this conversation with an open mind, I believe you'll agree it would be better for everyone involved to consider it Coach's Corner."

Skeptical of that—of not being harmed *and* being able to share what he learned—he nodded his head.

"I'm sorry for the difficult time you've had the past few weeks, Charlie. Sheriff Thrower was following my lead, so I am to blame for how you feel now and what has happened. I know that ever since Barry Ray was taken into custody, you've had a pretty miserable summer. Hindsight's twenty-twenty, but if I could go back and play this differently I would have. I hope you can come to forgive me when it's all said and done."

He couldn't deny that Joe's words felt comforting. He tried not to let them be, and he certainly tried not to show it, but there was no denying how reassuring they felt, almost as if they could make everything else go away.

"I'm sorry too, Charlie," Sheriff Thrower said. The words were far less comforting than Joe's, considering he was leading Jimmy Patino's case, he'd threatened him if he didn't back off, and he'd given Charlie the lump on the back of his head.

Joe closed his eyes and sighed, then said, "First, Charlie, you've got to tell me what you know and to whom you've spoken."

Were the kind words and sweet voice earlier just a tactic to make him comfortable? A sneaky way for Joe to get the information he wanted out of him, and as soon as that happened, he'd get whacked in the head again? He thought of lying, dodging the question, or not answering at all. But each of the possibilities felt more dangerous than telling the truth.

He looked straight into Joe's brown eyes and told him everything. It felt surprisingly relieving as he started getting things off his chest, and he didn't hold back. He laid everything out while Joe sipped his whiskey and Sheriff Thrower stroked imaginary stubble on his chin, both remaining silent. He detailed the articles he'd found at the library with Brad, the documents in Douglas Patino's house revealing Jimmy Patino's backstory and what he knew about Jimmy's biological father, the fact that Michael Thrower was the victim's boyfriend, the conversations with Shane, the night he and Brad saw the exchange of money between Doracco and presumably Joe, and finally, the note on his bike seat, who he thought wrote it, and what he was planning to do until he got hit upside the head and everything went dark.

When he finished telling the misery of the last four weeks in a matter of five minutes, Joe and Sheriff Thrower were smiling. It wasn't exactly the reaction he expected. Smiling? After hearing about death threats, all the lies to the community, a variety of very strange "coincidences" and desperation, he would've imagined a more surprised or disappointed reaction rather than beaming smiles.

They already knew. You told them what they already knew, and now they don't need you anymore.

"Thank you, Charlie."

He looked back at Joe, shaking his head.

"What?"

"You were honest with us, son. You didn't have to be, and I can't say I would blame you if you weren't. We've not been forthcoming with you, but you decided to act like a man and tell the truth. I'm proud of you."

Proud of me, he silently challenged. He looked back suspiciously and tried to read what could've been a very clever poker face. Despite all the years of playing, he felt outmatched in this game and had absolutely no idea what to do next or how to respond. A soft breeze from the screened front door came in and elicited a shiver.

He obviously did a poor job of putting on his own poker face because Sheriff Thrower picked right up where Joe left off.

"Yes, Charlie. We knew all of that."

"Charlie," Joe continued, "we know all about your 'school project' that Emily the librarian helped you with. Breaking into Mr. Patino's house and going to the golf course to spy on him. We know you took the ATV to follow Doracco. I knew I heard a yelp from that cornfield and now I know why. Darn crows."

He was stunned.

How in the hell...?

"We also know you asked Sarah about Michael Thrower and had some interactions with her."

189

His neck whipped towards Sheriff Thrower as if on a recoil spring. Joe didn't take it any further and Sheriff Thrower remained silent, but they all knew the topic. It made Charlie feel paralyzed from the neck down.

"Charlie, we knew and still asked you because we needed to know if you'd be honest with us. Consider it a test, and you passed. And because you did, we will try our best to explain the rest," Joe said while slowly nodding.

"If you knew all along, why didn't you try to stop me?" he nearly spewed out, revealing anger in his voice.

"We tried, Charlie. You didn't listen."

"Like when?"

"We'll get to that. But before we do, you do need to know that we're not proud of what happened. I wouldn't ever wish what we had to do on my children or you, whom I've always considered family. But sometimes men have to do things in the name of the greater good. As black and white as we'd all like it to be, it's a gray world out there."

The past month he'd been chasing clues to solve the murder of Jimmy Patino. He'd never considered the possibility that the crime was just the tip of the iceberg.

47

"Charlie, justice is blind in this world. You know that, right?"

He offered no response.

"Innocence is often purchased in place of the truth, alibis can be swindled by circumstance, and we rely on a system of law and order that has proven its ineffectiveness to us time and time again. Too often the wrong people are released to the world and the innocent ones are incarcerated behind bars. The reality is, the system can be manipulated by anyone with either inside knowledge or money."

"Is that some sort of justification?" He had no interest in a lesson of right and wrong from Joe.

"What I'm trying to say, Charlie, is that what's right doesn't always happen and what's wrong often does."

"So that gives you the right to—"

"And when such situations come up, we have a choice. We can adhere to the system that has wronged us, or we can deviate from it and seek justice in our own way. It might not be legal, but you have to remember that the point is to protect the innocent and punish the guilty."

"Sounds like a justification to me."

A gust of wind rattling the screen door evoked more goosebumps. Sheriff Thrower's fidgeting by the chalkboard didn't help his nerves, but Joe's stillness made it even worse.

"Joe," he broke the silence, "I understand what you're saying, but I'd like to know what really happened to Jimmy Patino."

"Fair enough. Lesson over." Joe took a deep breath and finally got to it. "I didn't mean to involve Shane Littleton. The poor kid was in the wrong place at the wrong time, and the only thing I wanted was for him not to interfere."

"Interfere with what?"

"The truth coming out."

"What about all that talk about innocence being bought in place of truth?"

"What about it?"

"You threatened Shane to keep him quiet."

"Shane Littleton happened to see something that jeopardized my plan, so I had to prevent that information from coming out. Doracco was nothing special. He's new to town, a few years older, quite strong, and easily motivated. Neither one of them has anything to do with what happened to Cory McDougal."

Hearing Joe say that name, instead of Jimmy Patino, reinforced that to Joe, there was no Jimmy Patino. There was only Cory McDougal. He wasn't referencing the son of Douglas Patino, but rather the bastard child of Nelson Towns.

But that didn't change the fact that Joe still hadn't told him anything he didn't already know.

"Why did you want to get Barry Ray locked up? How is that right? You killed Jimmy Patino, didn't you? He is *your* innocent victim!"

"No," Joe began with a steady voice, "I did not kill Jimmy Patino. But I did have a hand in it, and that's something that I have to live with. But the end justifies the means, son."

"How is that? You've got a son and two grandkids and a country house we play Wiffle Ball at while you play your card games! Why would you have a hand in killing Jimmy Patino, an innocent victim? What did he ever do to you?"

Joe rested his head on his left hand and took a deep breath, then exhaled deeply and looked up towards the ceiling. After a moment Charlie realized what he was doing. He was summoning his own courage.

"His name was not Jimmy Patino. You told me you already knew that. His name was Cory Phillip McDougal, and he was the son of a mother who abandoned him and a father who was a monster."

"Nelson Towns."

"Yes, Nelson Towns. That man redefined what evil is. He'd been arrested seven times before he was Jimmy's age and never showed a hint of stopping his ways. He didn't care. His victims meant nothing to him. They were for his enjoyment, and he didn't care what pain he caused them. And that's where his son was headed."

"*That's* why you killed Jimmy? Because you thought he'd end up like his father?"

"Not *thought*...witnessed with my own eyes. And so did you. A few years ago a fourteen-year-old girl from Breese claimed Jimmy Patino tried to force sexual contact on her at a party. He was brought into the police station, given his phone call, and released within two hours. In all, he'd been arrested three times, but didn't spend a day incarcerated. Never even had an arraignment. Douglas Patino bought his innocence so regularly it might as well be on the shelf at Walmart."

"Why did he—"

Joe put up his hand. "One topic at a time. Let's talk about this innocent victim for a bit. Did you know he's had three similar claims against him in the past two years that never came to fruition because of a lack of physical evidence? They were kept from the public because reporters can be bought just as easily as the police. And Shaw Littleton, Shane's brother, wasn't his only victim of thievery, either."

Charlie raised an eyebrow. And silently started to regret referring to Jimmy as an "innocent victim."

"Four different elementary and middle school students came forward to tell their principals that Jimmy Patino had threatened to beat them up if they didn't give him their lunch money. Know what the principal did? Called Douglas Patino. Know what happened next? Nothing. Jimmy got detention and the principal gave the kids fifty bucks to keep it quiet."

"Charlie," Sheriff Thrower said in a calm voice, "there's no way around it. The guy had so many counts of harassment against him that they expelled him from school when he was sixteen. A few days later two members of the board and the superintendent were given large, lucrative incentives to keep him in the high school hallways. His name has come up as a person of interest in over a dozen different suspected arson, grand theft auto, and harassment claims."

"*You're the police!* Why didn't you do something?" He was so enraged to be hearing about Jimmy's wrongdoings and the total lack of responsibility in front of him.

"He did do something," Joe answered. "What you meant to ask was why didn't he do something within the limits of the law. And the answer is because the law is a part of a corrupt system that didn't work when it came to this Jimmy Patino."

Sheriff Thrower took a step towards him. "He's right, Charlie. First of all, to bring someone up on charges, you need to have a victim. It's no coincidence that the victims, or near-victims, all ended up with extra money and possessions before a case was dismissed. If someone can buy the victims themselves or their families, the law doesn't have a leg to stand on. And think about the cops in general. Evidence disappears, files get lost, witnesses' statements are claimed to be coerced after the fact. There are so many ways for money to interfere with the system of justice that it scares me. That's why I don't want Brad to follow in my footsteps."

"You're a part of that system, Mr. Thrower."

"I know...." Sheriff Thrower sighed. "But I never took money to look the other way or make evidence disappear. The biggest challenge I have to face is the mirror every day, and the person looking back doesn't know if this was the right thing to do. Doesn't it seem a shame to you that just because Douglas Patino is rich, Jimmy Patino could get away with anything? Does that *feel* right to you?"

"That doesn't give you the right to kill him. His father being a monster and him breaking some laws doesn't mean you should go all vigilante on him."

"Jimmy was headed towards escalated crimes with more victims and even scarier situations," Joe said. "Psychological reports from experts in Chicago confirmed it, along with expert reviews and trend analysis. All of the historical data and every piece of data available to us confirmed the same thing: he was turning into his worthless, pathetic father."

"And we weren't going to let that happen," interjected Sheriff Thrower.

Charlie recalled when Jimmy had pestered Denise Owens, Barry Ray's girlfriend at the time, and how Barry Ray's decision to beat him to a bloody pulp with a gym shoe seemed like an overreaction. Now, it made total sense. Barry Ray knew then what Charlie had just learned now. Still, after thinking it through, he landed on the question that it almost seemed Joe was waiting for him to ask.

"Why Jimmy Patino? Of all the sickos and pedophiles and scumbags out there, whether they got out of jail or never went in the first place, why pick him? You could've chosen someone who actually *did* commit the crime."

"You're a smart man, Charlie."

"You didn't answer my question."

"I know this may seem like some sort of vendetta against this evil crime in general, and honestly I believe that would be justified in and of itself. But the truth is, this is personal.

"We've never taken the law into our own hands before, despite wanting to and being able to justify it in our own minds. What made us do it this one time was..."

He took another long, deep breath before continuing.

"You mentioned reading about two different crimes Mr. Towns committed nine years apart, in 1973 and 1982."

"Yes."

"And that Sheriff Thrower's brother, Michael, was dating the underage victim in 1982, whose name was not released?"

"What about it?"

"In that case, the victim suffered more than any prisoner would've, and she received absolutely no justice whatsoever. It ended with Towns' exoneration after a very short trial, despite enough evidence presented to keep him locked up for the rest of his life."

"I remember. He got off scot-free."

"Yes, he did," Joe nearly whispered in a sigh.

"I still don't understand...."

Joe put his hand over his face and looked down towards the floor.

"The victim...was my daughter."

48

Charlie's heart sank and his body froze. He'd known Joe his entire life and had never heard a single word about any daughter. Sheriff Thrower remained silent and leaned up against the wall by the door. Joe took a hearty sip of whiskey and closed his eyes while swallowing it down.

"Her name was Amy. Amy Olson."

Joe's words hung in the air, motionless. He heard them, but couldn't process them. The smell of Joe's house penetrated his nose again, and his chills returned. His forehead seemed to have its own heartbeat.

"You haven't ever heard about her because...because she died. Amy was subject to pure evil in 1982 when she was only thirteen. We lived in a small town called Butler, Ohio. It was a lot like Germantown. Rural, community-focused, involved, conservative, everyone knows everyone, that kind of thing. And it was fifteen years ago, when towns were even closer than they are today.

"She'd just gotten back from picking strawberries on a Saturday afternoon when a man knocked on the door dressed like a delivery man, grabbed her from behind, duct taped her mouth shut and...Joe paused, looking up towards the sky. "Fortunately, she was able to remove the tape and alert the neighbors. The doctor said she had severe bruising and her throat would be scarred for the rest of her life."

Charlie moaned in sadness, for the first time not thinking at all about this summer, but instead focused on 1982. He watched Joe dab his eyes, clearly so distraught that he couldn't even say what happened. Charlie knew right then that Joe would never utter those words aloud because of the pain they brought.

"That night she was shaking, torn between fear and disgust. I remember she was at the front door when she collapsed at my knees. She held onto my legs tighter than I knew she had the strength to. I can still remember the pinching sensation."

Joe stopped for a moment, replaying that horrible afternoon in his mind. Charlie felt guilty because of it.

"At the time, it was just the two of us. Kurt was twenty-two and out on his own. Amy was a surprise when she was conceived, but I wasn't complaining. I loved the idea of having a baby girl. But then I lost my wife when the children were very young. Amy was only one when her mother died. Poor kid never got a woman's touch. Who knew then an even bigger nightmare was coming for the poor girl."

Another pause. Another deep breath.

"All we had was each other. After we talked, I went straight to the police station. She didn't know who her attacker was—he was an out-of-towner—but he ruined her life in less than ten minutes. I couldn't even look at him that first time."

"Son of a bitch," Sheriff Thrower uttered.

"The trial lasted a few months. You'd think that a crime like that in a small town in the eighties—or *any* town in *any* decade—would be a no-brainer for very swift and harsh justice. Case closed. Lock the scumbag up and throw away the key. Let inmates do to him what he did to others."

It was too painfully clear a "but" was coming.

"But it didn't go that way. The jury debated for three days after closing arguments and concluded that due to the lack of witnesses, the victim admitting she had her eyes closed for most of the ordeal, and the fact the neighbor only briefly saw the aggressor, the state had failed to prove Towns' guilt beyond a reasonable doubt. Because of that, he was released."

"He didn't get *anything*?"

"Not even a simple slap on the wrist. Never mind the fact Towns' fingerprints were on the switchblade. Never mind that he had a bruise on his chest from the neighbor's bat. Never mind that despite the short time window, the neighbor still identified Towns out of a lineup. DNA testing wasn't available for investigations in 1982 and people didn't have cameras on their front doors back then, but shouldn't have mattered. There was plenty of evidence, including Amy's own testimony, but none of it resulted in the justice she deserved..." Joe said in a soft whisper before pausing. "Thankful as I am to my neighbor for doing what he did, and I am eternally grateful, I wish he would've kept beating Towns with that bat. Harder and harder, until there was nothing left to hit." Joe paused yet again, wiping the corners of his eyes and taking a large sip of whiskey as if to summon courage.

"There's a saying in the justice system: It's better to let ten guilty men go free than to imprison one innocent man. I believe that. Even after what I've gone through, I can honestly say I believe that. But Nelson Towns was guilty and everyone knew it. That man deserved to die for what he did."

"Tell him what happened next," Sheriff Thrower whispered in a raspy voice before clearing his throat.

"After the trial, things got even worse for Amy. She had nightmares every night. Thirteen years old and she'd wake up screaming, yelling for me. I'd rush into her room, hold her, and she'd look like a helpless child. For hours. She'd be covered in sweat, convulsing, and howling 'no' while she squeezed my back with her fragile little arms. She kept reliving the experience, night after night after night. She was too scared to go anywhere or do anything. She couldn't eat, she couldn't see her friends. Nothing. The poor kid couldn't live. Her life was in complete disarray."

Joe took yet another deep breath.

"Kurt helped...at least as much as he could. He came home for a while and tried to cheer up his little sister, and he was the only one who ever really made her show even a hint of happiness. I was her rock, but Kurt was her sunshine. He was the only one who could brighten her spirits. Very slightly, but I thought then that with enough time maybe Kurt could bring her back to who she was."

Another troublesome "but" was coming.

"But then we got the worst news."

Charlie leaned forward and held his breath, afraid of what was coming and feeling awful about the anticipation he felt.

"Amy was pregnant." Joe paused for another large gulp of whiskey. "She was only thirteen years old when she found out she was three months along. She begged me to let her get rid of it. Abortion was out, but she implored me to help induce a miscarriage, let her roll around on her tummy, take medicine that stopped the process, whatever it took. She didn't want to give birth to that man's son."

"I wouldn't either," Charlie replied, almost involuntarily and without even being aware of what he was saying or to whom. Sheriff Thrower's bemused facial expression and pitiful eyes confirmed what a mistake that was.

"I wouldn't let her end the pregnancy," Joe said aloud to no one in particular, his eyes pointed straight towards the kitchen door.

"Legal or not, abortion was wrong. I thought about the folks out there who couldn't have children, the love that the child could receive from someone deserving of a healthy little baby. Why allow Towns' awfulness do even more damage?

"But...I guess deep down I was also afraid. Afraid of what our community and church would say. Afraid of the regret I'd have every time I looked in the mirror. Afraid of killing another human life. But in hindsight, I was wrong. I feel that regret now. Now, I feel that shame."

"It's not your fault, Joe," Sheriff Thrower said.

"All Amy wanted was to get rid of her predator's son. She wanted to relieve herself of that burden, and I should have let her. Why didn't I? She didn't want to miss school to give birth. She didn't want to face the child that came out of her. And neither did Kurt. He begged me to let her do it. All she wanted was to be free. And I didn't let her. I made her go through with it."

Charlie, in his entire life, had never seen Joe so emotional. He recalled the time when Joe witnessed his own dog get hit by a car, and being appalled that Joe didn't shed a single tear. The man was a rock, harder than Doracco or Kurt, man's man toughness. He was old school, firm, and set in his ways. But at that moment, he was an emotional wreck.

Sheriff Thrower looked at him, paused, and told the part of the story Joe couldn't.

"After she gave birth..."

The awful words weren't uttered, but they weren't necessary. Charlie knew. Amy felt she couldn't live on those terms, and made the painful decision not to.

49

"Charlie," Sheriff Thrower continued, "at the time, my brother, Michael, was seventeen. And I must say, I was a bit hesitant at first because I thought she was too young to date. But almost immediately, I saw how special their relationship was. Those two spent every waking moment together hand-in-hand. He was the perfect best friend for her. It felt like intimacy without the physical, if you know what I mean, and despite how young they were, I believe to this day he loved her and would've absolutely made her his wife.

You just can't imagine what this ordeal did to him. He had to watch his best friend and true love go through that trauma, and there wasn't a darn thing he could do about it. He saw Amy go from being one of the happiest people he knew to not being able to make it through a single day without tears."

He nodded his head, but no, he couldn't imagine.

"It was too much for Michael. I was twenty-one and tried to talk to him. I tried as much as Kurt tried with Amy to bring him into the light, but Michael wouldn't budge any further than she did. They'd talked about getting married as soon as she graduated from high school, what kind of a house they wanted, how many kids, the whole shebang. And when she...passed away... he lost it."

Now it was Sheriff Thrower's turn to pause.

"Imagine being instantly cut off from the one person you're closest to. But on top of that, first having to watch her every day, but not be able to help her. Thinking to yourself that death can't possibly be worse than this...then finding out it is."

"What...did he do?"

"He stopped caring. About anything and everything. Didn't try to get a job, drank a lot, got into drugs, refused therapy, and shut himself out from the world. He went down a self-destructive path that only led to prison and rehabilitation clinics. His perfect life and bright-as-the-sun future turned into a long rap sheet and horror story."

"He never got better, did he?" he asked, thinking of what Sarah told him.

"No. He's in a rehabilitation clinic right now, another name for a psychiatric ward. The past fifteen years he's done nothing but cause trouble and hurt himself. Know what he does? He replays the most horrible day of his life over and over and over. Doing so digs him into a deeper and deeper hole of depression. Doctors have tried everything, from hypnosis to several medications to electroconvulsive therapy, but they can't get him to stop reliving the experience.

"It's obviously not his fault, but how could I introduce my children to him when he was drunk, stoned, or both? So, Brad and Sarah haven't met him. My wife and I make the five-hour drive every month to try to talk to him at the institution, but it never does any good. He's totally fixated. All he can do is think about Amy and Nelson Towns. They even took all his pictures of her away after his second stint, where he tried to kill himself, so he wouldn't be able to stare at her and fuel the terrible engine of remorse that's firing on all cylinders in his brain. They could give that man a lobotomy and he'd still think about her. Day and night."

"Day and night," Joe repeated.

"I don't know what to do for him at this point," continued the sheriff. "I don't know how I can help. We've tried everything. After my parents died, I used all the inheritance they left me to try various psychological methods, camps, medical clinics, medicines, and anti-depressants, plus anything else I could think of to help him. I'm in heavy debt because of it, but it would be worth it tenfold if my children could play with their only uncle. If I could, for just one day, have my brother back. The brother that I knew before it all happened. The brother that loved and was going to marry Amy. I almost wish..."

203

But Sheriff Thrower couldn't finish the thought. Charlie knew what he was thinking: that it would be better if his brother were dead, and in heaven with Amy. When Sheriff Thrower put his head down and turned around to face the window, it hit Charlie hard. There was no faking this. These were two strong-willed, tough-skinned grown men who couldn't help but break down when they retold this horrible story.

"He loved her too much, Charlie. When two people love each other as much as they did, if something like that happens to one of them, it happens to both. You can't compete with love and try to separate people in it as if they aren't bound forever. Love will always win. When God calls him, Michael will join her in heaven and they'll spend eternity together free of any memory or reminder of what happened."

Joe rose and put his hand on Sheriff Thrower's shoulder, consoling him. Charlie imagined it was a scene that had played out many times over the past couple decades.

"Nelson Towns killed two people that year. One person actually stopped breathing, and the other only stopped living. At first, I tried to use Amy's pregnancy for justice. A paternity test, which they did have back then, could confirm that Nelson Towns was the father, as well as be able to identify the date of conception. I thought those two things would've gotten Towns thrown in jail for the rest of his pathetic life."

He didn't respond...the third "but" was coming too fast.

"But then the lawyers reminded me there would be no way to prove it wasn't consensual, the conception couldn't be pinpointed to the specific date of the crime, and that under Ohio law, Towns could get as little as one year for statutory. With good behavior, he would've been free in six months. The thought of putting Amy through the ordeal of testifying against and facing that scum again only to have the court give him a slap on the wrist was just too much to bear, so we decided to seek an alternative form of justice."

Charlie recalled when Emily, the Bartelso librarian, informed him that Nelson Towns had died in a single-car crash outside rural Pennsylvania. Exactly one year after the "alleged" crime in 1982. Large amounts of drugs and alcohol were found in his system. There were no other victims. The date of the accident felt like a big coincidence then. Now, it seemed an impossibility. Even so, staring at the man who orchestrated Nelson Towns's death, Emily's words rang truer to him than even before:

Justice found Mr. Towns in the end.

"Kurt and I decided it would be best to move on and try to start over," Joe continued. "He was already out on his own, and I needed a change. We agreed to never bring up Amy or any of what happened to anyone who didn't know her. We didn't want to have to talk about it."

Sheriff Thrower said, "And my parents and I decided we would keep Michael's problems as private as possible. By the time they passed away, he was in the Chicago clinic five hours away from anyone who knew him. As time went on, he grew more distant until eventually nobody talked about him anymore."

"And that's why we never mentioned Amy or Michael. It wouldn't do any good...for anyone."

After a moment, he asked the question he thought might lead to some good news. He didn't know why, but he hoped it would.

"What happened to Amy's baby? Did it get a good home?"

Joe and Sheriff Thrower stared at each other again. It wasn't just a blank look—it was as if they were telepathically asking each other something, and slight nods of their heads were answering it. He immediately regretted asking, wondering if the child had become like its father. They did what they did, right or wrong, because they saw Jimmy following in his father's footsteps.

But Jimmy, he now knew, had a half-sibling. Was it a boy? Was some other fifteen-year-old headed down the exact same path? He swallowed so hard his throat hurt. The silence hung in the air long enough for him to fear, dread, and worry about what he was going to hear. He tried to anticipate every possibility to soften the shock.

But nothing, absolutely nothing, could've prepared him for what they said.

50

"The baby Amy gave birth to was a boy. And after a year in foster homes and state care, her brother Kurt decided to adopt him."

Charlie slowly tilted his head as he connected the dots to what that meant. Joe's nodding face confirmed it.

"Yes, Charlie. It was Mack."

He looked back at Joe and waited for him to either shake his head or jump in to say that of course that wasn't the case. How could it be? But he didn't. Sheriff Thrower ever so slightly nodded his head, which made it seem all the more unbelievable.

Mack was Nelson Towns' son. Jimmy Patino's half-brother.

Not Kurt's biological child. Not Barry Ray's brother.

Memories of their childhood and any tell-signs he'd either missed or witnessed came flashing through his mind. Mack had always been quite different from Kurt and Barry Ray. He was very shy, whereas those guys were social bugs. He was always so calm and unwilling to protect himself. Physically he looked a little different, with darker hair and less prominent features, but Charlie knew lots of siblings that didn't look alike and never gave it another thought.

He thought of all the birthday parties with Kurt and Barry Ray, calling Mack "son" and "bro" as they high-fived him and gave him piggy-back rides. He thought of Mack's smiling face when he and Kurt embraced—the look that seemed only possible to come with a father-son relationship. There were times when Mack seemed odd, but he was always supported by his brother and father because he was family. Mack was loved unconditionally. Kurt cared for him the way only a father could care for his son.

It didn't add up to what Joe was saying now. It had to be a lie.

"You don't believe me, huh?" Joe asked.

"It can't be. He's Kurt's son. There's no way—"

"Don't take his word for it." He immediately stopped talking and looked over at Sheriff Thrower, suddenly forming that nagging sensation that he was about to hear or see something that wouldn't seem possible.

"What?"

"I said don't take his word for it. Take Kurt's."

Within a few seconds, Sheriff Thrower walked over to the kitchen door and into the breezeway walked Kurt Olson. He stared at Kurt as he slowly trudged down the three steps leading from the kitchen and his eyes followed him intensely, without blinking or distraction.

Kurt looked the way he always did—a large, bulging chest, modest waistline, neatly combed hair with partial balding in the back, and a pair of rugged hands that came from hard work at the factory. When Kurt shook his hand, he didn't shake back, instead he just looked into Kurt's smallish blue eyes and clean-shaven face. Kurt, wearing blue jeans and a collared shirt, looked back with apologetic eyes and a wrinkled chin.

"We didn't think you would believe us," Joe broke the silence. "So we asked Kurt to help as a backup. It's very reasonable for you to doubt all of this, but now that we're in Coach's Corner, it's time to know the truth."

"I'm sorry I didn't tell you before, Charlie," Kurt said softly. Kurt's benign voice sharply contrasted his massive frame, but that was Kurt, the definition of a gentle giant ever since he'd known the man.

"It's a hard thing to say out loud about the boy I raised as my own: Mack was the son of an evil man and a poor young girl who left this earth way too soon because of him. I never want to think of my sister in that way—and of course it wasn't her fault—but it's reality. Amy suffered a terrible ordeal, and it was too much for her to take. It would've been too much for a lot of folks. Rest in peace, sis," Kurt said, looking up to the ceiling.

Through his peripheral vision, he saw Joe take a deep breath and hold it.

"Joe and I agreed that it wouldn't be fair to Maxwell if he had to carry that story around with him all his life, especially in this small town. You know how people are here. Adults wouldn't hesitate to ask him about it, kids would torment him, goodie-goodies would look down on him and gossip about him behind his back. Even folks like priests wouldn't say anything in public, but they'd be thinking it every time he took communion. He would never get a fair shot if the town knew his story."

"And we wanted Mack to have the same opportunities everyone else did," Joe continued. "We didn't want him to be labeled. He deserved the chance to have a normal childhood, which is why I moved from Butler and kept it a secret, even from Mack."

Kurt approached him and put a hand on his shoulder. "I'm sorry, Charlie. I know how hard this is to hear. But there's no reason to look at Mack any differently. He's my son. Maybe not biologically, but he's *my son*. Nephew by blood and son by life. That's what matters, isn't it? He's been with me and Barry Ray since he was one year old, and I love them both the same. Sometimes, I wonder what would have happened if Jimmy had been given the same chance. Maybe he wouldn't have become the person he did. Maybe the apple would've fallen farther from the tree. Unfortunately, we'll never know."

In unison, Joe, Kurt, and Sheriff Thrower all grew silent waiting for his reaction. He thought about what Kurt and Joe said, and realized why Douglas and JoAnn Patino kept the name Cory McDougal out of Jimmy Patino's life. And in doing so, he couldn't help but realize that Jimmy was a victim, too. He was born to a mother who didn't want him, got abandoned at nine years old, and never felt the warm embrace of a father. Regardless of what the Patinos did afterwards, the first nine years of his life, the most impressionable, were no doubt sad and lonely.

"Did you guys kill Jimmy Patino because he was really Cory McDougal? Because of who his father was?"

"Charlie..."

"Because if what you're saying is true...then Jimmy and Mack were..."

"Brothers," Joe finished the thought.

It still seemed impossible on so many levels, and yet the three of them stared back at him in uncomfortable silence and nodded the truth back to him.

"It also means Jimmy Patino was my grandson."

"That can't be," was all he could force out.

Joe turned both his hands over to expose white palms and shrugged his shoulders. "Charlie, they were brothers, or half-brothers, in the technical sense. They had the same scumbag father and different mothers. But they couldn't be further from it in the way they lived their lives. Look at Mack and Jimmy Patino. Can you honestly tell me that you saw any resemblance whatsoever between them?"

"I'm sure you noticed how different Jimmy was from his brother, Scotty?" added Kurt. "And you know Scotty hated Jimmy. Didn't that ever strike you as odd, considering they were brothers? The truth is, Scotty found out by accident and had a tough time accepting it. Bless his heart, he never told anyone, at least as far as I know, but he learned the truth years ago and struggled with it."

He thought of all the fights between Scotty and Jimmy, of how he always assumed Scotty left Germantown in part because of Jimmy. He remembered when Brad and he walked up the staircase in the Patino home, and all the pictures on the wall. None of them showed the two boys together at a very young age, no pictures of Scotty holding his baby brother as an infant like most other multi-kid homes had. It made sense now, considering Jimmy didn't come into house until he was nine.

He remembered thinking then how they seemed like opposites, and how Scotty slugged Jimmy more than once. The fights, and the hatred that seemed to exist between them. He assumed it was tough love between brothers, but now saw the truth—they weren't brothers at all. "The truth is, Jimmy Patino was a monster who was going to

210

get even worse. We had nothing to do with that, and neither did Scotty. And Mack..."

"Mack reminds me of his mother," Joe said.

"And Jimmy reminded me of his father," Kurt replied.

Another long moment of silence. The questions started to come, and he asked the most pressing one with a cracked voice.

"How could you do it? And how'd you do it? Did you stalk him? How long did you follow him?" He asked the group, but looked straight at Joe.

Joe looked back—not with anger or aggression or hatred. Instead, Joe's face looked sincere and gentle, almost peaceful.

"I already told you Charlie, I did not kill Jimmy Patino."

51

Charlie took a long sip of lukewarm water from the bottle Joe offered him, trying to figure out what he really thought of all this and how he was supposed to feel.

He had not a clue what to think of Joe, so he started with the others. Sheriff Thrower, Mr. Law and Order, was responsible for fighting against crime, not committing it. How could he justify any of this? Did he somehow view it as protecting people? Serving justice for his brother? And Kurt, the loving, amicable man who couldn't hurt a fly in spite of his size. Had he sought revenge on Towns and his sister's death? But did that justify what he did? Did he see it as making the world a better place in the end?

Joe remained quiet until he'd given up on trying to figure it out, almost as if he'd been reading Charlie's mind the whole time and didn't want to talk over it.

"Nelson Towns should have gone to prison long before he even met Amy. You read the article about Shannon McDougal, so let's not rehash it. But understand that what happened to Amy nine years later could have been, and *should* have been, prevented. Instead he was allowed to ruin yet another young woman's life. You can judge what we've done, but in the end it feels better than doing nothing."

Charlie nodded, feeling sluggish. He didn't want to know any more. He didn't want to know anything.

"That's when you adopted Mack?"

"Correct. He wasn't even one yet. We just couldn't watch him be raised by the state. Plus, I was told that a lot of 'would be' adoptive parents wouldn't be too keen on adopting a child conceived under such circumstances, unfair as that may seem.

"We owed it to Amy. We knew it would make it harder to move on, and we knew it would be very difficult. But he was family. He deserved an opportunity and that opportunity was to be with us."

Sheriff Thrower took a seat in the off-blue broken La-Z-Boy recliner. He sighed heavily when he sat down as if exhausted and Charlie quickly turned his attention back to Joe. However, it was Kurt who spoke next.

"So I asked my wife—Jennie—if we could adopt him. Gave her the full story upfront and sought her approval. Then I asked Barry Ray how he would feel about having a younger brother. He was only five at the time, but I asked him anyway. In any event, they both answered favorably, but only one of them meant it. A few years later Jennie left. She never told me why, but I knew. She couldn't handle Mack. Knowing where he came from, it ate her up inside, like a blood-sucking virus. He doesn't know that, by the way. I saw no reason to crush his spirit."

If Kurt was telling the truth, and Charlie candidly admitted to himself that he thought that was the case, Kurt had accepted his sister's son and lost his wife because of it. It must've been horrible, yet he was still thinking of Mack, the innocent child. He could've chosen to be mad at Mack, and everyone would have understood. Perhaps even given Mack back to the state to keep Jennie. Instead, he protected Mack and kept the whole thing to himself.

"Does Mack know about his real father?"

"He does now. And so does Barry Ray. At some point I decided that if I was going to expect them to be productive citizens, I was going to have to trust them. I told them what happened and that none of it made me love them any less, that I loved them both equally. I also told them that it had to remain our family secret, for all of our sakes. And they never let me down. My sons never told a soul. I'm pretty sure you could attest to that. If they would've told anyone, it would've been you."

There was more than a hint of a father's pride. Kurt couldn't hide it—not even that night. He was right about their closed lips, and that

Charlie could confirm Mack and Barry Ray kept it a secret his whole life. He thought about all the years he'd known them. It almost seemed impossible to him that they never said anything—through all the poker games, late night sleepovers, baseball tournaments, joint vacations, fort building, long bikes rides and all the other things they did together—but they kept their mouths shut.

Sheriff Thrower broke his train of thought.

"Brad doesn't know either, Charlie."

"That's right," added Kurt. "You are the first person outside of us three, my former wife, and my two sons who knows. You might feel betrayed in a sort of way they never told you, but it was at my direction and for everyone's good."

"Oddly enough," Joe continued, "that made it impossible to truly forgive what happened to Amy and Michael. Seeing Mack reminds us what Amy went through and what Michael is still going through. Such a beautiful baby boy he was, and yet every time we looked at him, we thought about the ugly way he came to be and his ugly earthly father." Joe paused for a moment and dragged his hand across his forehead.

"We couldn't let it go, Charlie. We could forgive if forgiveness was asked. But we couldn't forget. I know it wasn't right. But the apple doesn't fall far from the tree unless it gets nurturing. Cory McDougal was only a child, but he would grow up eventually. We knew that Mack wouldn't become his biological father because we knew he'd be taken care of, loved, and cared for in a way that he wouldn't have to."

"But you didn't know about Cory McDougal."

"No," he sighed. "We didn't."

"S0 you followed him?"

" We learned about Towns' other son during Amy's trial, or lack thereof. After Shannon McDougal abandoned him in the park, we used some connections Sheriff Thrower had at the state adoption agency to find out what happened to Cory."

"What were you planning to do? If you were going to kill him, why didn't you just do it back then? Why wait until he was grown up?"

"I already told you, Charlie," Joe responded. "We never planned to or wanted to hurt him. We never wanted any of this to happen. But we felt we had to watch him. We had to be there, because if Cory turned into what Nelson Towns was, we couldn't let what happened to our families happen to anyone else. So we decided to watch him. See if he got the nourishment he needed to become his own apple. See if he turned into something in this world other than what his father was. And we prayed every day for that boy. Every single day."

"You mean to tell me you all picked up and moved...moved your homes and families and lives to Germantown...so you could follow Jimmy? You uprooted your entire lives to follow a nine-year-old?"

Kurt put his hand up and he quieted down.

"Our lives were already uprooted, Charlie. One could argue, ruined. We did what we did because we didn't want anyone else's to be ruined as well. If something happened fifteen years later and we found out about it, and we knew we could've prevented it but chose not to, the guilt would feel worse than the pain we felt from Amy and Michael."

"So yes, we picked up and moved. First, Joe. Then a few months later, Sheriff Thrower moved with his children—Brad and Sarah—but didn't tell them why. He didn't tell his wife either. He just told them he got an opportunity at the sheriff's department and it was too good to pass up."

As much as Charlie disagreed with it, and knew that wasn't how it worked in his own home, it wasn't outlandish to think Mrs. Thrower didn't know the real reason her family was moving. It was common for a housewife to go along, and Mrs. Thrower always went with the flow when it came to Brad's father's work.

"About a year after that," Kurt continued, "our family moved. Me, Jennie, Barry Ray, and Mack. Jennie left six months after we got

215

into town and went back to Ohio. I don't begrudge her. It wasn't fair—it wasn't right to put her through that. But my sister was dead and I knew the man who caused it had a son who could do the same thing down the road. I had to do something."

"Did the Patinos recognize you when you moved? I would think that might be...weird. Did they catch on to what you were...doing?"

"Not at all. To this day I don't think they know who we are relative to Jimmy, and they didn't want to know. We also stayed pretty under the radar and didn't have e-mail accounts or the Internet back then. Amy's trial wasn't open to the public because she was a minor, and remember that Jimmy was only ten at the time we moved. I was very surprised by it, but the Patinos never saw Kurt or me or Sheriff Thrower before we moved."

"Surprised? You just got done explaining why it makes sense for them to have not known you. Why are you surprised they didn't see you?"

Joe smiled and slightly nodded his head, looking down towards the ground. "You *are* sharp, Charlie. Tell you what...we'll get to that," he said while looking up at Kurt.

He waited a brief moment. "So you just planned on killing Jimmy one day?"

" *You're not listening*, Charlie," Kurt uttered in frustration before turning around to stare at the kitchen door entry from the breezeway. Sheriff Thrower leaned in towards Charley and spoke softly.

"We gave Jimmy every opportunity, always looking to give him the benefit of the doubt. When he got into trouble with the law, we let it go every time and prayed he would turn it around. When he was accused of sexual harassment, we tried not to be biased. We rationalized that teenage boys have hormones, and sometimes those hormones get the better of them. We didn't do anything rash, even as the various accusations started to pile up. But..."

Kurt cleared his throat. "But when the girl from Breese made the accusation she did, we couldn't accept it anymore. We didn't see any evidence he was going to be any different from Towns. It wasn't a question of if, but when. And we couldn't just sit there and wait for it to happen again."

"What about Mr. and Mrs. Patino? What about their pain? Didn't you make them feel just as bad as you felt when you lost Amy and Michael?"

They looked at each other for a long pause until, finally, Joe nodded his head, eyes closed. Charlie could tell it wasn't a nod of agreement. It was a nod that it was time to shock him even more.

52

"Let's be clear," Kurt said with a deep, stern undertone. "What we did was wrong. Nobody here is claiming otherwise. It's not right to take the law into your own hands, and it's certainly not right to premeditate a possible murder for fifteen years. We're all going to have to answer to God when our time comes. But that has nothing to do with Douglas Patino."

"He was Jimmy's father for fifteen years. He loved him. You don't think what you did, or planned, or whatever it was, wronged him?"

"I forget what you said...did he *look* heartbroken on the golf course that day?" Joe asked.

Charlie recalled that watching Douglas on the golf course *had* made it hard not to wonder something, but then he reminded himself again of what he'd told himself: *people grieve in different ways.*

"Just because he didn't look as sad as I expected, doesn't mean—."

"Do you think he treated Scotty and Jimmy the same?"

"No, but he was—"

Joe put up his hand.

"Charlie, the only reason Douglas Patino adopted Cory McDougal is because he and Nelson Towns worked together. And it was to his advantage to keep things quiet and Towns in his dirty pocket."

"What?" he almost yelled, throwing his hands in the air.

"You know—just like everyone else in Germantown—that Douglas Patino is a crooked businessman who operates mostly out of St. Louis and East St. Louis but has an empire that stretches well beyond. He's well-connected to gangs, drugs, prostitution, and pretty much everything else you can think of that's against the law. But also like everyone else, you have no proof or evidence. Correct?"

It was unusual for people to be so direct when talking about Douglas Patino, but he tried not to show his surprise. "It's not my job to get evidence," he answered, looking over at Sheriff Thrower, who leaned back in the recliner with a stoic, almost dazed look on his face.

"The reason he's been able to stay under the radar for so long is a combination of intelligence, extreme wealth, and employing the right kind of people in certain key positions. In some cases, people like Nelson Towns."

"Towns worked for him?"

"In a matter of speaking, yes. Years ago, before Douglas Patino was the hot shot he is now, he was trying to build market share in several different illegal businesses. The newspaper didn't mention him much, other than call out his awful crime, but Towns was pretty connected and helped Douglas with small time robberies, marijuana and meth, prostitution, gambling, that the whole lot. Nelson Towns was Douglas' main contact in Columbus, his Luca Brasi from *The Godfather.* Catch my drift?"

"He would intimidate the competition, scare it into submission. He'd get Patino's name to the top of a bidding list without actually saying it, and helped quadruple Douglas's territory. That's how Douglas made his first batch of cash. After that, he legitimized some of his operations to filter the cash and got quite proficient at hiding it. But in the beginning, his inexperience made him very volatile. *That* was when the authorities could've gotten him, but Nelson Towns gave him cover. Who knows, maybe it was some sense of crooked gangster loyalty to Towns that led to Patino adopting his son in the first place.

"The point, Charlie," Joe went on, "is that after Towns got arrested for what he did to my daughter, he was on trial to be judged by a jury of his peers. Want to guess who juror number ten was a close friend of?"

219

He looked at Joe with unbelieving eyes.

"An old classmate of Douglas Patino at Beatty Park Elementary School. We can't prove what happened in that jury deliberation room, but there's no doubt in my mind that Douglas Patino indirectly got Nelson Towns acquitted."

"Because of one juror?"

"He also had enough money and connections that all it would've taken is the right envelope with the right amount inside and the right promise for more favorable jurors. Unfortunately, it wasn't until after Towns was acquitted that we did our homework on the jury and learned of the partnership between him and Towns."

"Our guess is that the two of them made an arrangement. For his part, Towns agreed to keep his mouth shut about all of Douglas' operations. In turn, Douglas arranged for Towns to have a cakewalk of a trial and keep an eye on his first son, who was in the papers after Shannon McDougal abandoned him."

"Would he really adopt Cory McDougal out of loyalty to Towns?"

"Towns was a liability and Douglas knew it. If Towns got into trouble again it could raise enough flags to put even Douglas Patino's connections under the microscope."

"And what about Towns? Would he really care about what happened to Cory? He sure didn't seem the type or take any interest the first nine years."

"You're forgetting that Douglas got him exonerated for a crime that should have put him behind bars. That was his real interest. Plus, despite the fact that he's a sick, evil and twisted man who's going to burn in hell for eternity," Joe lowered his eyes, "every man still wants what's best for his children."

"Look," Kurt continued, "it's possible Douglas adopted him out of the kindness of his heart and Towns remained silent about their business relationship for the same reason. But the evidence suggests otherwise. We didn't bet on it then and you shouldn't now. These are men who made their fortunes hurting other people and taking advantage of the system."

The rabbit hole just kept going, deeper into an abyss of lies and deception. He wondered how far from rock bottom they were at this point.

"We're not sure who Douglas contacted to arrange the adoption, but it went through. Nobody questioned the fact that the boy he adopted was the son of a man he helped acquit a year before because no one knew the role Douglas played in Towns' acquittal. Nobody looked into all his business and found the child's father to be a key associate."

"Why didn't you say anything?"

"Because it wouldn't do any good," Kurt answered.

"What's that mean?"

"If we brought it to the authorities at that time, Douglas would've found out, bribed the right people, and made it simply go away. It wouldn't have changed the fact that Towns was a free man."

"But then he'd know we were on to him," added Joe.

"And it was more important to keep an eye on the boy."

"You could argue it was wrong, Charlie. But we tried to let the system work once and Towns got a slap on the wrist while Douglas kept growing his empire. We weren't going to let that happen again."

Charlie tried to hide the fact that he understood their decision by continuing to talk.

"So, you're just going to let Douglas Patino keep getting away with everything? You're not even going to arrest him, Sheriff Thrower? I know he's got money and maybe it wouldn't do any good. But just sitting here isn't doing any good either. You killed Jimmy Patino but decided Douglas should just get away with it?"

"That's a great question. And the truth is that we do have enough evidence to win in court. *With a fair trial.* But the crooked one that Douglas would have, and the amount of legal firepower at his disposal, would make mincemeat out of our case. Richard Beller is a competent DA, but he wouldn't stand a chance."

"So that's it?"

"Not entirely, Charlie. But we'll get to that. For now, I think it's time we tell him. Kurt, what do you think?"

"Yes, I think so."

"Sheriff Thrower?"

"Seems about that time."

Anxiety and fear make for an interesting and regrettable combination to Charlie. Part of him wanted to keep going down that rabbit hole, the other wanted to crawl under a rock and never come out.

Kurt got up and walked back into the house through the kitchen without a word. He had no idea what that meant, but Joe and Sheriff Thrower looked towards the door and he followed suit as the very long seconds passed.

Finally, Kurt came back and Charlie's mouth fell open. Standing to Kurt's right, at the top of the stairs in a pair of jean shorts and a T-shirt, was Mack.

53

They just stared at each other for about thirty seconds, eyes wide, Charlie's mind running in a thousand different directions at once. Mack's light brown hair was still on the shorter side, his blue eyes and pale skin going together just as they always had. Mack's baby face shone in the light mounted on the wall to his left, right above the three steps leading down to where Charlie stood. Mack didn't smile, but wasn't frowning either. Instead he wore an empty expression. It wasn't stoic—that description didn't do it justice. It was *empty*, void of emotion and substance.

Neither of them would be the first to speak. It felt like a staring contest and the first to open his mouth, lost.

"Charlie, you've been honest with us tonight. We've tried to do the same," Joe said. "But clearly, we've not been totally forthcoming the past few weeks."

He thought about the question that haunted him for days after that baseball practice, when Mack ran home after getting upset by Jason Hand, immediately before Mack was assaulted and they'd been separated ever since. The question that drove regret and anger in his mind and heart:

Why didn't I go after him?

"Charlie, I'm sorry we made you worry so much. Mack was never attacked."

He did his best to harness the anger he felt in his chin, his teeth pressing up against each other in a vicious grind.

"But he looked so...?"

Even as he began to say it knew, he realized he never actually *saw* Mack after the supposed attack. Every time he went to go see him, someone, usually Kurt or Sheriff Thrower, told him that Mack

223

needed to rest and recover; that they appreciated his thoughts and his stopping by, but that Mack couldn't take visitors.

"But the newspaper said it was confirmed he got attacked."

"It didn't take more than a quick glimpse of Mack with a bandage on his head, fake cast on his arm and some red makeup on his cheeks to start that engine. Reporters don't really need the details once they have the sizzle because the sizzle is what sells papers. The steak just gets in the way.

"All we had to do was figure a way to let one of them 'sneak past' Sheriff Thrower and get a passing glance at a poor young man who was moaning. The fake blood and bruise-colored eyes, along with shadow splotches all over his body were the icing. No pictures, no interviews, not enough time to get a closer look. That's all it took. *The Germantown Sun* handled the rest."

"And it would make sense that the victim's father, also the town sheriff, wouldn't want the community to find out. So when the reporter thought he'd stumbled onto the big surprise, the rest was history," Kurt added.

"Sheriff Thrower controlled the police, conducted the interviews of Mack's potential attackers, and Kurt turned away family and friends who wanted to see Mack. Mack stayed strong and hung on all summer," Joe said. Kurt nodded affectionally at Mack, like only a father could.

"Hung on?" Charlie said.

"It wasn't without sacrifice, son. Mack gave up his summer for the cause," answered Kurt. "And he'll never get it back. But hopefully he'll be back in action before too long. The papers are already running stories that he'll be okay and looks great, that there's not any broken bones or visible bruising."

He stared at Mack with confusion and anger, and Mack was now smiling. It was pride. Mack was actually proud of what he'd done.

"Charlie, you have to understand—"

" Why would you do that, Mack? Why would you make me think you were beaten to a bloody pulp?"

He was yelling so loud his throat throbbed. He could feel his blood pressure skyrocketing and expected either Joe, Kurt, or Sheriff Thrower to answer for him, but instead it was Mack who replied.

"We had to, Charlie."

"Why!" he screamed as more of a punctuated yell than a question, pouring out equal parts rage and disbelief.

Then Kurt whispered, "Because Barry Ray didn't kill Jimmy Patino."

That's when it finally hit him, like a bolt of lightning.

It was Mack who killed Jimmy.

54

Mack Olson—shy, squeamish, always to himself, faded fifteen-year-old shadow of his older brother Barry Ray.

Murderer.

"You? You killed Jimmy?" The guy he'd played poker with for years, who drank beer from the same small cooler and played on the same summer baseball team. The lanky brother of Barry Ray, who couldn't ever defend himself.

Murderer.

"Yes, Charlie. I did it. I killed Jimmy Patino. I killed my half-brother."

Mack's own flesh and blood. He killed him. Charlie wondered if they were all going to kill him next. It felt like there was no limit to what these people he'd known all his life could do.

Joe leaned towards him and put a hand on his shoulder. It felt weird—void of the loving and caring and teddy bear sensation he remembered—and replaced with something quite rigid, scary, and unwelcome.

"Let me try to explain, Charlie. You already know why we felt so compelled to do what we did. You may not agree with it, but you know. I'm sure you've got questions, not the least of which is why Barry Ray spent some time behind bars for Mack's crime.

"Kurt, Sheriff Thrower, and I discussed the situation about six months ago and the evidence was clear: Jimmy Patino was turning into Nelson Towns, and there was nothing we could do about it. We'd tried to give him the benefit of the doubt, but nature is too powerful and with parents who took him because of a business arrangement, he'd stay on that course and was headed for evil things."

"And you told Mack and Barry Ray?" he asked skeptically.

226

"Yes, after debating it for some time, we ultimately decided they had a right to know," Joe answered, now looking at Mack. "We were planning to do something we believed was the right thing to do, but it could still get us into trouble. And if it did, we wouldn't get the chance to explain everything to them afterwards. Then they'd always wonder why, and inevitably feel a resentment towards us we that couldn't bear. I hope we made the right decision as opposed to the selfish one..."

Mack put his hand on Joe's shoulder and nodded, forcing Charlie to wince. After a pause, Joe continued. "But we didn't choose for them, and we didn't force anything. We gave them the option of staying out of it altogether. I know it may seem like we pressured them, but Mack and Barry Ray both wanted to help."

"He's right, Charlie," Mack replied. "Barry Ray and I talked about it. I was Jimmy's half-brother. And he was going to keep hurting other people. I learned what happened to my mom...and I...didn't want that to happen to anyone else."

"Two wrongs make a right, is that it?"

"As a matter of fact," Kurt ignored his question, "Mack wanted to be the one to kill Jimmy Patino."

He snapped his neck back at Mack. Murderer.

"Because he's a minor and could get off easier if you got caught?"

"I'd be lying if I said that wasn't part of the reason."

"And you let it happen."

Kurt lowered his voice. "Talk like that after you've been the victim of a that crime or related to one who has. You can judge Mack's decision when it's your own mother who was deflowered by a monster and then...lost her life. When it's your own mother you never got to meet because of something that never should have happened. Until then, you need to know Mack wanted the honors. We're not asking for your approval, Charlie. We're telling you how it happened out of respect."

The words weren't said out of anger. Kurt didn't yell or shout or point his finger, but instead said them matter-of-factly. He said them

227

as though he'd thought over the same questions in his head that Charlie had just asked. As though he'd finally rationalized it in his own head as well.

"We decided, and Barry Ray agreed, that he was the best initial suspect. He'd have to spend some time in the local jail and give up part of his summer, much like Mack, and we'd solidify his alibi and story enough to give Sheriff Thrower time to properly remove him as a suspect. It made sense to keep Mack under the radar from the get-go, but we also didn't want someone else, some innocent person, getting punished for the crime either. Barry Ray was within our control, and the best option."

"Why Barry Ray?"

"Jimmy Patino helped answer that for us."

"Huh?"

"The reason Sheriff Thrower gave for arresting Barry Ray was the motive that existed. Towards the end of the school year, Jimmy made a pass at Barry Ray's girlfriend, Denise Owens. After she refused, he grabbed her. We decided that was our opening."

He remembered thinking about the motive Barry Ray and no one else seemed to have. It was, in fact, the perfect angle.

"You mean Barry Ray threatening Jimmy was all a part of the plan? To set this up?"

"When Barry Ray beat him up in public outside a track meet, on school grounds, in front of a crowd, we knew he'd get in some trouble, but nothing too serious. It was important to create a motive the public would buy, and it worked. Nobody doubted his arrest or looked for any other guilty party. But remember, Charlie, no one *prompted* Jimmy Patino to grab an innocent young woman, nor to become the man who fathered him. We all would have preferred not to need to do any of this..."

The whole fight was staged. Charlie's jaw hung open as he replayed the entire Sonny Corleone style fight in the school park. It was all a premeditated cover-up that was designed to land Barry Ray in jail months down the road. Even the words Barry Ray uttered flashed in his mind: *I won't waste time busting your face, I'll just pump your sorry ass full of lead.* It felt too outlandish to be real, and everyone just assumed it was the emotion taking control, yet it was all an act. A carefully planned act and script.

And that wasn't the only ruse.

He remembered Kurt crying the night Barry Ray was arrested; and how solemn he was the day Mack was "beaten up." Kurt acted hurt, torn apart, and alone. He'd thanked Charlie and asked him to pray for Mack before telling him visitors weren't welcome. All because they couldn't risk him finding out the whole thing was a sham.

Joe acted appalled and utterly surprised when he learned of Jimmy Patino's death. And his reaction to his grandson's arrest for the crime was so seemingly genuine that when they talked to Sheriff Thrower for the first time, Charlie worried he might faint.

That was also when Sheriff Thrower brought up the motive Barry Ray had. Joe acted surprised, as though he didn't know how to respond to such unexpected news. He pictured Joe that day he and Brad rode the ATV to his house to tell him about Barry Ray. The look on his face. The sad, confused look that turned out to be a masterful act of deception.

Even Sheriff Thrower, a man of the law, had urged him to back away and let his office do its job. The look of dread on Sheriff Thrower's face when he barged into the garage and broke up the card game to take Barry Ray away was so sincere. The remorse in his eyes. The fear. And yet, the entire investigation, the cover-up of Mack's attack, and everything in between, was a lie.

Barry Ray looked stonewalled as he was put into handcuffs. Not saying a word and going along with it, paying the price for the overall plan.

And finally, Mack himself. Acting like he was the poor little brother of someone behind bars for such a heinous crime; not saying a word at baseball practice; pretending to be helpless, as if it was a situation he could do nothing about. Watching Barry Ray get

229

arrested and pretending to be sorry, knowing all the while that he pulled the trigger on that Remington Model 760 rifle.

Charlie thought back to that game of five-card draw, before the summer turned upside down. He could still remember Barry Ray's exact words, clear as day. It seemed to him even then that Barry Ray might've been talking about something else when, right before Sheriff Thrower knocked on the door to arrest him, he said to Mack: *Almost time. You ready for this, bro?*

Now, it sat in Charlie's stomach like a brick.

"We certainly didn't get Jimmy to lurch out at Denise Owens. We had a Plan B to drive the motive, but when he did, he made it easy."

Still shellshocked, he looked at Mack. "Where did you go after...you..."

Joe replied, "After Mack did his part, he and I transported the body out to Highline Road, dumped it, and hustled him back to his house."

*Did his part...*It was hard to hear from Joe, whom he'd looked up to his entire life, and who asked Brad and him to pray for Barry Ray.

"A few hours later the body was found, exactly on schedule. By that time, he and I were in position and all set. When Barry Ray was arrested, his alibi was Mack. The two of them were supposed to be together and Mack could speak for his whereabouts. But then came our only mistake."

"Shane..."

"That's right, Charlie. Pretty sharp," Kurt answered.

Joe continued, "Shane Littleton saw Barry Ray during the time the murder occurred. Blind luck, really. There's no way we could've predicted that some junior high kid would be out in that exact field looking for bugs at that exact time. We told Barry Ray to drive to an isolated country road, away from anyone who might see him. We didn't want him at the house because then witnesses might be able to pin him there. We thought we had a foolproof plan, but that kid and his bug collection threw us for a loop."

Now it all to fit together to Charlie. Shane told him that the only person he told about seeing Barry Ray was Mack. Shane told *Mack*, of all people. It made sense—Mack being Barry Ray's brother—but because he did, Mack could tell Joe and that revealed the problem. Barry Ray was Mack's alibi, just as much as Mack was his. Shane's witnessing Barry Ray but not Mack was a threat to the overall plan because Mack would no longer have the alibi. Charlie had assumed the intimidation of Shane was about Barry Ray, but it was actually to protect Mack.

"That's why you faked Mack's attack, isn't it?

Joe looked at Kurt, and Kurt just smiled back. Sherif Thrower didn't show much expression.

"Like I keep saying, sharp as a tack. Of course, Mack's assault served multiple purposes. First, it removed him as a potential suspect in case it was in anyone's mind. Who would think the poor, nearly-beaten-to-death brother could be the one to rid the world of that scum? But it also removed the opportunity for people to question Barry Ray's alibi. Nobody could interview both of them—or should I say be expected to interview both of them—to verify each other's story. That meant all the state police, to whom we knew the case would be transferred, had on Barry Ray was motive. Motive fueled by an anger that any decent man would have after the Denise Owens incident. That alone wouldn't be enough."

He looked at Mack, who wasn't beaming with pride but also didn't appear to be ashamed. There was no evil glare, no trace of a stone-cold killer look whatsoever in Mack's face, and there never would be. And yet...that's what he was.

55

Charlie stood up and paced the length of the breezeway between the front and back doors, forming tiny circle motions with both arms as he tried to digest the litany of lies. Mack had joined Joe on the couch, Kurt remained at the top of the stairs, and Sheriff Thrower hadn't so much as budged from the old blue recliner. "What about Brad? Was he in on this as well?"

"Brad didn't know anything."

He studied Joe's face, as if that could somehow determine if he was being lied to.

"Even the gun being under his bed?"

"It was always a part of the plan, but Brad didn't know about it and that was critical."

"Why?"

"Once Barry Ray was arrested, time was of the essence because we sure didn't want him convicted. With only a motive that likely wouldn't have happened, but the murder weapon turning up somewhere else would ensure it. We needed Brad's reaction to the gun being found in his room to be genuine surprise and disbelief, so we kept him in the dark."

"You took a big risk. Brad could've gone to prison when the state police took over the investigation."

Sheriff Thrower leaned forward in the recliner and rested his elbows on the armrest, eyeing him. "You don't have to tell me about the risk we took, Charlie. But we took great care to execute a well laid plan, and as I'm sure you've heard on the news, Brad has already been released. Larry Cates confirmed that Brad was earning some summer cash working for him on the other end of town the morning of the murder, with three other part-time workers confirming it as well."

He flashed back to what Sarah had told him. She'd said that her dad had arranged for Brad to work for old man Cates that morning. It was a pre-arranged alibi for his son, knowing Brad would eventually be a suspect.

"But what if the state police didn't believe the alibi? What if they said that's the same thing Barry Ray had? What if—"

"I know how the law works. I might not be the sharpest knife in the drawer, but I understand police procedure, be it state or otherwise. With three different people validating Brad's whereabouts during the time of the murder, there was no way my son was staying behind bars. It didn't hurt that his father was the sheriff, either. Cops do take care of their own.

"The only thing the gun did was refute the notion that Barry Ray pulled the trigger. And by the time that happened, Mack was so far removed from being a suspect that we thought we were about home free."

He shook his head, unable to believe they took such a risk.

"Charlie, do you really think I'd risk sending Brad to jail without knowing exactly what was going to happen?" Sheriff Thrower pointedly asked. "Not a chance. He and Sarah don't know anything about this, and they proved it when the state police interviewed them. And they're not ever going to know anything, either."

Sheriff Thrower and Charlie locked eyes for a few awkward seconds until Joe chimed in again. "Now that Brad has been cleared as a suspect and released, the state police have passed the investigation back to Sheriff Thrower because there's no conflict of interest. But we're forgetting who the real hero here is." Everyone waited for him to finish. "Barry Ray knew the risks and took them like a man anyway. We all owe him one."

Time stood still, and it seemed to Charlie that everyone was paying quiet respect to Barry Ray in his own way. Bowed heads, smiles, and subtle nods. "But you'll still have to find the killer," he finally broke the silence.

"Of course I'll continue the investigation per due process, but unsolved cases happen all the time. News will eventually down and be replaced by something else, and the last thing country folks want is the wrong young man locked up for a murder of someone everyone knows was worthless in the first place. They'll forget about it and get back to their nice, little town quicker than you can imagine, because that's exactly what they want to do deep down anyway. After all, it could be their son arrested next time."

"The loose ends are just about all tied up," Kurt said. "Brandon Doracco is done with it already—he won't mention a word to anyone. Shane Littleton will let it go after a few months of peace and quiet and maybe a reassuring chat from you..."

He didn't respond, and Kurt continued.

"School and football season will start soon, and the papers will be flooded with fall sports and honor rolls. Communities will have their block parties, teenagers will drive around back country roads, and people will stop simply talking about it. When something doesn't affect them personally, they disassociate from it over time."

"The truth, Charlie," Joe nearly whispered, taking another sip of whiskey, "is that we planned for everything except Shane Littleton...and you."

He turned his attention towards Joe and saw with his peripheral vision that the others were nodding their heads.

"You showed some amazing intelligence and courage, didn't stop searching for the truth even when threatened, put together more of the story than anyone else, and threatened the whole darn plan by learning about Towns and following Doracco. I was impressed.

"We owe you an apology. We never meant to hurt you, and I am so sorry to put you through what we did. You simply proved too smart and persistent for your own good. It's clear you're going to be something special in this world, son."

Coming from the mastermind of what would almost certainly remain an unsolved murder, he wasn't quite sure how to take the compliment. Deep down, it did feel good. This was Grandpa Joe, a man he'd admired and looked up to for years. And it was the first time he remembered getting complimented by an older man in a long time.

"I'm sorry too," Sheriff Thrower added. "You probably have a pretty low opinion of me right now, and I couldn't blame you."

"Charlie," Kurt piled on, "I wanted to thank you. You stuck up for my son when he needed it the most and didn't stop fighting for him. Even at your own peril, you were the best friend to Barry Ray he could ever have, and I'll never forget it."

Kurt walked over and gave him a large bear hug. He didn't quite know how to respond. To the hug or anything else.

56

"What about Douglas Patino?"

After a series of hugs, pat on the backs and a momentary reprieve from the awkwardness that surrounded a murderous conspiracy perpetrated by three men he'd come to look up to and a mastermind he outright admired, the question that remained was a round peg in a square hole that still needed to be hammered home.

"I can't count the number of crimes he's committed with four hands, but we don't have any proof that would stand up in court," Joe answered. "What we do have is enough circumstantial evidence to shatter his credibility as a respectable businessman and make him some enemies he won't enjoy having."

"What do you mean?"

"Douglas Patino thrives under the radar and rakes in the cash. He doesn't care about fame and would prefer to be anonymous. Being mayor and on town boards is all about protecting his image, and he goes to great lengths to formally distance himself from his real cash-cow businesses. They're illegal, immoral, hypocritical, and downright nasty. He'd do a lot of things to keep those revenue streams disconnected from himself."

"You spoke with him already, didn't you?" he asked.

"I made an arrangement with him based on some circumstantial evidence that he wants to remain buried. A little business proposition to solve our problem that he willingly agreed to."

"What?"

"He provided some assistance I couldn't have otherwise received. For example, the Chevy Impala you saw me driving was from his company's junkyard. It's unregistered and, as far as authorities are concerned, simply doesn't exist. Some of the breaks we're about to get in the papers we can thank him for as well."

"So did he know—"

"He was not a part of the plan. But with enough evidence to convince a jury that years ago he bought an acquittal and evidence connecting Nelson Towns to his own businesses, Mr. Patino was willing to listen. As I said, he never really cared for Jimmy, that's the real shame of all of this. Jimmy was the first victim. Conceived from scum and raised by it, he didn't have a fair shot. I wish that hadn't been the case."

"What else did Mr. Patino agree to?"

"In addition to providing each of us with a large, cash token of appreciation for our understanding that none of his past needs to be dragged up now, he'll be very cooperative in helping Barry Ray, Mack, and Brad with some long term financial planning. It starts with college and goes well beyond that, with pocketbooks and doors opening all over the place."

Blackmail and bribery in exchange for silence. Douglas Patino was buying his innocence from Joe, and it didn't feel right to him at all that he could personally benefit from it.

"Money isn't everything, but it's good to know none of us or our families will ever have to worry about it."

Sheriff Thrower must've read his mind. "We're not trying to get rich here. We've been wronged, we want to prevent that from happening again, and we need to be made whole. This is a punishment for Patino and unfortunately the best we can hope to get. It isn't enough, but it's something."

Charlie sighed and fell back into the couch, resting his head against its soft backrest. He closed his eyes and then looked at the four of them with bitter yet realistic lenses: Joe, mastermind of a murderous cover-up; Sheriff Thrower, crooked lawman who wrongfully imprisoned his own son; Kurt, a father who let one son go to jail and supported the other for killing. Mack, the murderer; everyone, justice seekers until they themselves could be bought.

Regardless, the chapter was over. The past explained, the present lived, the future forecasted. As he sat in the breezeway, the sunrise coming in about an hour, there was only one question left.

"What happens now?"

Joe looked right back at him, saying, "It's up to you, Charlie. I told you already, we won't try to stop you if you want to turn us in to Richard Beller, the Illinois State Police, or anyone else. What we've done is wrong, and no doubt there's a price to pay for that. You can either hand us over to have us pay for it now, or you can keep this conversation in Coach's Corner. But one way or the other, we all know we will pay it one way or another."

"It's your decision," Kurt replied. "We'll support you no matter what, and it may very well be the right thing for you to turn us in. No matter what you choose, I'll always love and respect you."

With Sheriff Thrower nodding and Mack remaining quiet, he didn't feel the pressure he thought he might. It didn't feel like the weight of the world, more like he was worn out and exhausted, as if he'd reached the end of a long race only to find there was yet another lap. He sipped a cold Pepsi from Joe's fridge and thought of everything from his understanding of right and wrong, the impact his decision could have on not just the three men but also their families, including Brad and Sarah, what he thought he could live with the easiest, what the potential risks to either option were, and about a hundred other things. He stared at the glass bottle, the old-fashioned kind that somehow seemed to taste better, and knew he didn't want to make any decision at all. Not right now, anyway. Joe took a sip of his own cold bottle and looked him in the eye.

"So, what do you want to do, Charlie?"

Epilogue

Why didn't I go after him?

The question replayed in his mind without apology. He stared at the black upright headstone, thinking all about the Jimmy Patino murder conspiracy and everything that happened that in the summer of 1997, unable to stop asking himself why he never went after Mack Olson that day at baseball practice. Despite it feeling like the difference between paradise and purgatory, he couldn't stop asking. It'd been twelve years, and it still felt like yesterday.

It also felt so unfair. Mack could've turned out just like Jimmy had he not been raised in a loving home. The differences between the half-brothers were so great, yet so subtle. Why did Jimmy get abandoned and Mack loved? Neither had any influence over what happened at their birth, yet their paths from it were so different. Why? What drove the reasons that ultimately dictated which brother was on either end of that Remington rifle? It felt so arbitrary and random and unjust to him. A man of strong faith, even his life verse—*a man reaps what he sows*—offered little comfort.

The stiff midnight January breeze in Germantown offered a stark contrast to the heat he'd felt months ago in Wrigleyville. It was biting, cold enough that his hands were shaking. And yet, he stood motionless over the headstone without a coat, concealed in the darkness, lost in a sad stroll down memory lane. It was only the unexpected sound of her beautiful, angelic voice that jettisoned him out of it.

"Charlie? Is that you?"

He looked up as she approached. She now had long blonde hair, tied back in a ponytail hanging to the side of glistening diamond studs. She'd aged well, and despite the cold wore a light blue skirt, tall brown boots, and a modest but tight-fitting white blouse that

239

teased her lovely figure beneath. Her large, inviting brown eyes met his and when they did, he thought warmly of that cornfield behind the school's ballfield. A smile crossed his face.

"I thought you might be here," Sarah whispered, looking down at her brother's headstone. "How have you been?"

He couldn't deny the excitement he felt when she put her hand on his shoulder. Even after all these years, Sarah still had a place in his heart. He hadn't spoken to her in all that time, but he knew she was single, had never married, and lived in St. Louis about forty miles from the clutches of Germantown.

"I've been okay. It's been a long time."

"We missed you at the service," she said, inching closer.

"I missed you," he whispered.

She returned the smile. "Do you ever wonder about...things?"

"Wonder?" he answered, playing dumb but knowing exactly what she meant.

"You know...us?"

He thought of the betrayal he'd felt that day, and of her reaction to hearing the truth. But now, over a decade later, both seemed so insignificant. What did he expect her to do? She'd been told by people who loved her all her life that turning him in was what was best for him, and that he wasn't safe. She honestly thought she was helping him.

And then, after Joe, Kurt, and Sheriff Thrower filled him in on the truth about Jimmy's murder in Joe's breezeway, he'd tracked her down the very next day and blurted out the news without any consideration for how she would receive it. The same day her father was handed the case back to investigate, he'd laid it all out: how the whole thing was pre-planned, her dad's involvement, Barry Ray's innocence, and Mack's guilt. No warning and no evidence, just terrifying and shocking words. He didn't know why he was telling her everything at the time, maybe just so he wasn't the only person who had to bear the burden of knowing, but he knew even then that it was a tough position to put her in. What did he honestly expect her to do?

As he stared into her inviting eyes now, all of that seemed to fade. What mattered was how much he realized he'd missed her.

"I wonder about it more than I should," he finally answered her question."

"I wish you hadn't moved away—"

"My family needed a fresh start."

"You could have called," she sighed, grabbing his trembling cold hand with her soft, warm glove.

"I'm sorry, Sarah. I was really scared. You're right, I should have called."

"I forgive you," she replied, squeezing his hand.

To his knowledge, the truth about Jimmy Patino's murder hadn't gone any further than Joe's breezeway and Sarah. After his family moved, he had the perfect reason to duck his head in the sand and never look back. He'd avoided calls from Germantown, even from Brad, his best friend, whom he believed had nothing to do with the murder. He'd stayed away from social media as it grew more popular, refusing to cave in and reconnect, and fought off the urge to take the five-hour drive back countless times.

Some updates made their way to him nevertheless. He knew Mack was the town's electrician and Barry Ray its auto mechanic. Each had become apprentices after that summer and wound up with their own business ten years later. Mack, he had also learned, struggled with depression in his last few years of high school. "Nobody" knew why, but Charlie wasn't surprised when he heard Mack needed extensive counseling and struggled with alcoholism upon graduation. Actually pulling the trigger, no matter how justified it may have been or felt, carried a price tag. And there was no way around it. Joe was right: there was a price to be paid. Last he'd heard, Mack had gotten through the dark times, but it was a rough go for three of four years following that summer.

Brad went to college and worked as a math teacher and baseball coach in Lebanon thirty minutes west of Germantown; Joe and Kurt still lived in the same houses; Shane Littleton was an entomologist in Raleigh, NC. The happiest piece of news he'd learned was that Brandon Doracco was a married father of three working as a rancher in Montana. Douglas and JoAnn Patino were still in town, and Sheriff Thrower was coming up on thirty years in law enforcement and approaching retirement.

Charlie recalled the last time that a summer felt normal: the day he, Barry Ray, Mack, and Brad were playing poker and Sheriff Thrower came by to take Barry Ray away in handcuffs. The summer of deception and shock followed, but in the end Joe's words echoed in his mind and prevailed: *Sometimes men have to do things in the name of the greater good. As black and white as we'd all like it to be, it's a gray world out there.* As wrong as those words felt then and probably still were, preventing Jimmy Patino from becoming the next Nelson Towns had also perhaps been the right thing to do, even if Jimmy wasn't the only victim of that decision.

The whistling wind sent shivers down his spine. Or maybe it was something else that caused them. He looked at the smooth granite headstone, Brad's name elegantly etched in white against the glossy black background. News of the accident on Highway 50 made its way to him within a week of occurring. No drunk driving, no reckless behavior, no one to blame. Just a poor guy driving in the opposite direction swerving to miss a deer but hitting Brad head-on instead.

For some reason, he thought of Nelson Towns. Towns had also perished in a car accident, also the lone victim, also in the middle of the night. The similarities between them stopped there, but the justice it seemed was served in Towns's case was matched in magnitude only by the unfairness of what happened to Brad.

Brad's abrupt death had robbed Charlie of his chance to reach out, to apologize for running away, or say goodbye to his best friend. He'd put it off for too long and now his chance was gone forever, He knew the truth. And he carried more guilt for that than the poor

242

driver who hit Brad. He'd made the choice, and now he had to live with it.

"I miss him," Sarah said softly, staring into the distance, not directly at the headstone but rather somewhat above it.

Without another word he swung both of his arms around Sarah Thrower and pulled her close, her chest pressing into his, both of their hearts racing, her smooth cheek rubbing up against his grizzly, unshaven neck. She looked up at him and they got within inches of pressing their lips into one another's.

"The last twelve years have felt like a dream, sometimes a nightmare. It wasn't my fault, but I can't pretend I didn't make mistakes I can't undo now." He paused, watching her tear up, and then silently said goodbye to his best friend without even looking at his headstone. "No more regrets," he said, before lowering his lips into hers and not looking back.

For the first time in twelve years, he looked forward to the future.

www.ingramcontent.com/pod-product-compliance
Lightning Source LLC
Chambersburg PA
CBHW031942010726
47493CB00007B/2035